MASON BURGESS

BLOOD MOON

LEISURE BOOKS ❧ NEW YORK CITY

To
my mother, Dorothea,
and to the memory of my father,
George—
both of whom
never begrudged
me my interest.

A LEISURE BOOK

Published by

Dorchester Publishing Co., Inc.
6 East 39th Street
New York, NY 10016

Printed in the United States of America

his chair. "Now, what did you want to say to me?"

"Your invite, did you get it?"

"To Foley's party? Yeah. I don't think we're going to go, though."

"What?" Sharon seemed personally offended. "Let me tell ya, *nobody* turns down an invitation from Morris Collarman."

Travis wore a gentle, unthreatened smile. "How d'ya like that, I'm making local history."

"You'll be making work for the unemployment clerks."

"Come on, that's dramatic."

Sharon shook her head, slowly.

Travis watched her, then dismissed her concern.

"This town isn't much," Sharon said. "But Morris Collarman is a powerful man. He can do whatever he wants, and although turning down a party invitation might not seem like much, get better acquainted with Collarman and you'll find out that's like spitting in his face."

"Really?" Travis was now mildly concerned but didn't want to let on to Sharon.

"Really."

Travis had had no intention of attending the retirement dinner—nothing against Harold Foley, he was a nice enough guy. He was just thinking about Nicole. It had been months, but she still knew of his concerns for the Chamrais village. Not that he didn't trust her, but he couldn't be certain that the wrong thing wouldn't slip out to the wrong person. Especially in a party situation.

But now it looked as if he was going to have to go.

Sharon felt bad about deceiving Travis, but

in her mind it was necessary. In truth, Collarman couldn't have cared less if his invitation was rejected. He was giving this party more out of a sense of obligation than any deep need.

With Sharon, her attending was quite the opposite.

29

Morris Collarman met with Mayor Jessup in his Municipal Building office later that afternoon. MacFarlane was there as well. Conspicuous by his absence was William Trelevan.

The mayor, however, had not summoned him.

It was a last-minute meeting, one that was necessitated by Jessup's latest concern: the retirement of Harold Foley.

Foley and Ben Quarry had been assets to the mayor's committee. Together with Robbie Wade the two had been instrumental in smoothing over the rough patches that had blemished the veneer of the town during the past several years. Not that there really had been that many, but each had carried with it the potential for disaster. Even those incidents not directly related to the "dilemma"—such as the Lloyd Caribou murders—had depended on the intervention of Collarman's "three."

Unfortunately, that created a second

problem: the possibility that the knowledge possessed by these aides could just as easily work against the committee (and, as Jessup would be quick to add, ultimately the town). This had not been overlooked by the mayor. Potential concerns can always be placed on the back burner, but the moment does come when attention must be given them.

The moment *had* come.

Foley was retiring, his duty to the committee—his service to the town—complete. And he was moving to Winnipeg, away from the watchful eye of the committee. As time passed and he entered more deeply into his senior years . . . there was just no telling what could be inadvertently revealed.

It was indeed a possibility that could not be ignored.

MacFarlane was always in tune with the mayor, but Collarman suspected the tone of the meeting was to be serious when Jessup removed three bottles of imported beer from the porta-fridge at the far end of his office.

"You gentlemen realize it's important we talk," the mayor said in a typical opening. He handed over the beers.

Collarman said, "Why isn't Trelevan here?"

The mayor at first considered casually brushing away the question, but then realized that would just be postponing the thrust of this meeting. Trelevan was not there for a reason.

"This is something the three of us can handle," he said, and this was as much an admission of his failing trust in Trelevan as he could have revealed.

Collarman's gaze went to MacFarlane, but the good doctor had no telltale signs on his face.

If he had any hint of what exactly was to be discussed at this meeting, he didn't let on.

Jessup took his place behind his desk, his position of authority. He popped open his beer, then focused directly on Collarman.

He said, "We're going to have to decide what to do with Harold."

Collarman felt his stomach rise, its pressure start to swim up his throat. It was a frightening *déjà vu*. Because of his participation in the Keith Samuels "disappearance," he knew that the mayor had already made the decision as to what had to be done.

It was something not easily accepted.

"Not again," he said heavily, and he looked to MacFarlane for his support.

The doctor took no notice of Collarman's almost pleading stare, but did say on his own, "I don't see how we can get away with it twice."

"Besides," Collarman put in, "we're not talking about some . . . transient kid now. This is Harold Foley. His disappearance *will* be felt."

The mayor nodded emptily. "Stewart?"

"As I said, with Harold we're biting off more than we can chew."

Jessup's look was sympathetic. Professionally sympathetic. "I know," he said softly. "But can we be persuaded not to follow this course?"

Collarman spoke in Foley's behalf. "I think before we start planning extremes we should consider something. Harold Foley has more than cooperated with us through all our troubles. I've never once heard him—or Ben Quarry, for that matter—complain about compromising their journalistic principles. That may not make them top-grade newsmen, but it tells me at least that both can be trusted. As much now as ever."

The mayor clearly appreciated Collarman's argument, but it was not enough.

"Then let's consider this," he said. "Foley's sixty-five years old. In a clear mind, yes, I have no doubt that his activities will remain with him. But the question is, how much longer will he be able to think with clarity?"

MacFarlane had no choice but to agree. "For a man who's lived as active a life as Harold, rapid senility in retirement is certainly a possibility."

"But not an absolute," was Collarman's attempt at defense.

"Can any one of us afford to take that chance?" Jessup said, and again there was no room for argument or compromise.

Collarman was cornered. He knew it, and his frustration came through in an outburst.

"Then we just keep on killing! Isn't that right? It's been made clear that none of us can trust the other so each of us has to eventually die. It's no big deal. We've done it once. From here on in it gets easier."

The mayor spoke calmly. "Trelevan was kept from this meeting because I knew we'd have to contend with just that kind of attitude. No one's working against the other, Morris, let's stop this—paranoia. If you want it put in a nutshell, it's just that none of us has any recourse."

The truth of the matter was—and Collarman knew it—that Jessup was right.

30

Marv Nelson had spent the better part of
the summer preparing himself for the hunt. He
had approached nearly every older person in the
village in his attempt to collect as much
knowledge of the Windigo as he was able to get.
He had been surprised by the number of people
who simply refused to talk to him; their belief in
the malignancy of the spirit had been so great
they feared that by even mentioning its name
they would bring down a curse upon themselves.

It hadn't taken long for the entire reservation to become aware of what Marv was
planning to do. And while he had been suddenly
regarded with curiosity (especially by the
young), most people had wanted to avoid him.

Despite this, his last hours with his people
were not made pleasant.

A small group of drunken Chamrais men
cornered Marv and began berating him for what
they considered to be a selfish task. He would
not only be endangering his own life, they
argued, but very possibly the life of every

person on the reserve. The demon was sure to extend its revenge to the village.

Marv could provide no words of assurance. How could he? He didn't even know how he was going to battle the Windigo—that is, if he could first track it. All he was sure of was that no solution would be found waiting around the reserve. He had to find the spirit, study it, and hopefully then discover his weapon.

The confrontation with his people held the potential for violence, but Marv managed to free himself before their anger reached that point. He disappeared into the forest.

He waited about an hour before returning to his home, just in case the group decided to head him off there. He approached the shack carefully. When he peered through the bushes and saw no one around his property, he hurried inside to get his supplies.

It was necessary that he travel light. He was expecting to be gone for some time—probably into the first snowfall—and so considered himself fortunate to have sturdied himself to the rough surroundings and the unpredictability of the weather. This allowed Marv to carry with him only the most basic supplies.

The most important of which was his knife. Cleaned and polished for the occasion.

His supplies were stuffed into a moosehide sack. He then cut two holes into each upper end, through which he threaded a length of rope. The whole package he looped around his shoulders, with its bulk resting against his back.

Although he couldn't allow trepidation to travel with him, Marv remained always aware of what it was that he would be stalking. As aware as any man hunting an unknown could be. For, although he was an expert when it came to the tracking of the animals of the surrounding forest, he couldn't even begin to guess what the rules in this contest would be.

It wasn't that he had any kind of premonition; he didn't believe in such things. But he let his eyes wander around the shack before stepping out the door as if he really wasn't expecting to return to it.

31

Travis had never lied to Nicole before, but since so much time had passed since his "clobbering" and she still hadn't softened her position, telling her that he had to put in some evening work at the paper—when in truth he would be heading back to the reserve with Sharon—seemed the necessary thing to do.

Again the reporters drove out after a quick dinner at Sharon's. Again Travis sat behind the wheel absorbed in thought. About that . . . Sharon had been picking up funny vibes lately; she was wondering if there wasn't some upset in Travis's marriage. She wasn't basing that on anything Travis had said—on the contrary, it was his recent avoidance of talk about his wife that had caused her suspicions to develop. She knew that he wasn't the kind of guy to offer anything—and it wouldn't look right for her to start digging into his personal life—but Sharon was becoming consumed with curiosity.

To squeeze something out of him, she asked, "Is everything okay with you?"

Travis seemed genuinely caught by the question. He turned to her with a strange look on his face. "What? Why do you ask that?"

"Oh, I don't know," she said very innocently. Then: "I guess, when two people spend as much time together as we do, if something doesn't seem quite right with one of them, the other just starts to wonder."

Travis retained his quizzical expression. "I don't seem 'right' to you?"

"Well, I don't mean abnormal. It's just that you seem—different lately."

"That's news to me."

"I guess you'd know," Sharon said. "But you're sure there's nothing on your mind? Something that you might like to talk about?"

"I'm fine, really."

Although she could understand why it was hard for Travis to admit to anything, she was a little hurt that he wouldn't confide in her. What with the feelings they had for each other, he had to know that, whatever the problem, she would be on his side. She felt it was important that he turn to her; that would be the best way for their own romance to grow. To come out into the open. That was, after all, what they both were after.

Tonight the skies were darker, murkier, than they had been the first time both had come out to the reservation. The shift to winter was happening with a speed that a boy from the city could never have imagined. Travis was thinking just these thoughts when Sharon remarked, "We'll have snow in a week."

"You're kidding!" Travis said, amazed.

"What?"

"You just read my thoughts."

Sharon looked puzzled. "Huh?"

"The weather. What you just said about the snow."

"Oh," Sharon said casually.

"No," Travis went on, "I was thinking about an early snowfall when you said . . . Aw, forget it. It is silly."

Sharon smiled. "Oh, didn't I tell you? I'm psychic."

"Well," Travis tried to explain, "it—it just seemed a little odd, that's all."

Sharon straightened in her seat. "Maybe not."

They were pulling into the reserve now. Travis parked Old Betsy beside the bordering bushes as he had done the last time. He switched off the ignition, but before getting out of the car he decided to pursue Sharon's comment.

"Why do you say that?" he asked.

Sharon reached over and flicked on the dome light. She said, "Remember what I said before about two people working together so closely that both become attuned to what the other is feeling?"

"Yeah."

"Why can't the same thing happen with what they're thinking?" she offered.

"I don't believe in mind-reading," Travis said dismissively.

"I don't think it's mind-reading really. Not in the ESP sense."

"Okay, professor, then what is it?" Travis wasn't meaning to be as mocking as he sounded.

Sharon didn't seem to take offense. She gave her answer straightly. "It's like I said, people being in tune with each other. You get to know the person so well that little areas of sensitivity begin to rub off on you."

"Like dandruff?" Travis kidded.

Sharon was serious. Her expression let him know that.

"Okay," Travis said in a slightly less facetious tone. He took a moment, then asked: "You feel *we* know each other like that?"

"I don't know," she said with forced superficiality. "We do spend the better part of the day together."

Travis then said, "Yeah, but I spend more time with my wife and we don't have those kinds of experiences."

Sharon felt herself tightening, rapidly. She made herself relax. She then shrugged, again with put-on ease. "I don't think it necessarily *has* to happen with man and wife."

"Well, who does a married person spend more time with?" Travis argued. "That is if what you're saying holds any truth."

"*Travis, shut up!*" Sharon suddenly exploded. "*Just shut up!*"

Travis's face immediately registered shock. He certainly wasn't expecting this. Not from Sharon.

"Whoa," he said with both hands raised. "Look, we're just talking. No sweat, okay?"

Sharon looked devastated. She felt the blood quickly drain from her face; her head become frighteningly light. She thought that for the first time in her life she might actually pass out.

"Sharon?" Travis said with concern.

Her eyes went wide. They were like two marbles in the snow.

"I'm—sorry, Travis," she stammered. "I—I

really am. I . . . shouldn't have said that . . . to you. I don't know why . . . " Her chest was heaving; suddenly it was as though she couldn't catch her breath.

Travis had never seen her this way before and wasn't sure how to approach it. He was afraid she was losing control. He laid a tentative hand on her shoulder, and, when she collapsed into him, slid his other arm around her. He held her close in a compassionate embrace. He wasn't prepared for the pressure with which her fingers dug into him.

"Shhh, take it easy," he said gently. "It's no big deal. You—just got a little excited, that's all."

"No." Sharon's breaths were still coming in rises. "I had no . . . right to talk to you . . . that way . . ."

"It's nothing," Travis said, more firmly. "Really."

He heard her murmur something that sounded like a questioning echo. "Nothing?"

He felt her breathing gradually becoming normal again. She was still buried into him, but seemed to be coming in control of herself.

She then rose her head and . . . *she was smiling at him! Broadly!* Looking as though no outburst had never occurred.

Travis smiled back, but it was in no way genuine.

"You all right?" he asked cautiously.

Sharon's eyes were clear. "Hey, let's forget it, okay?" was her almost flippant response.

Travis hesitated. Then he nodded, with as little conviction as he'd put into his smile. It was scary; he'd never seen anyone switch extremes so quickly.

"You were pretty upset," he said. He *had* to say.

"Look, we're out here for a reason, Randall." She winked at him, then switched off the dome light, plunging them into darkness and leaving herself, in Travis's view, as a silhouette.

That was when Travis—and he was startled to be receptive to such a thought—had the sudden urge to slap her. With as much force as he could manage. Knock her into dreamland if possible.

His thinking this way was so unlike him that it made his stomach roll. He'd never so much as considered hitting a woman before. He didn't know why he was fighting the impulse now.

She's nuts, that's why! He really didn't doubt that she was.

They got out of the car. On the surface Sharon continued to smile, but she was unsettled. Travis couldn't be *that* naive, she thought. He had to know why she snapped at him. *He had to.*

"Travis?"

He turned to her, still not free of his thought.

Whatever Sharon had planned to say she consciously pushed away. She was thankful that a sound emanating from somewhere behind the east edge of the village allowed her a replacement comment.

"Do you hear it?" she asked.

Travis furrowed his brow and listened. He did hear it—the faint, heartbeat-like rhythm of drums. His eyes coursed in the direction of the sound. They responded to the orange haze that just rose behind the roof of one of the cabins like the final gleaming of a sunset.

"Sounds like some kind of ceremony," Sharon muttered.

They moved in closer. They didn't want to intrude on whatever the activity was, but were curious enough to get within spying distance.

In a semi-circle clearing several yards behind the cabins, some ceremonial act was being observed by the people of the village. It was a subdued, somewhat somber ritual, performed by only three Chamrais—who were in tribal attire—to the accompaniment of that slow, steady drumbeat.

"Looks like a funeral," Sharon whispered as she and Travis watched from a crouched position between two of the cabins, concealed behind heavy shrubbery.

It was cold now. Sharon tightened the sweater she was wearing around herself, resisting the urge to squeeze beside Travis.

"Would a village of drunks bother to follow such customs?" Travis mused aloud, as if he were trying to convince himself of the wrongness of the town's accusations.

Sharon shivered. "I guess it depends on the seriousness of whatever it is they're following."

Travis wasn't listening to her.

Something had changed between them tonight. It wasn't that Travis was holding a grudge or anything; he just felt that their relationship could never be the same. Or maybe it was that he didn't want it to be.

Sharon was picking up negative charges like crazy. The way a magnet does iron filings. She didn't want to choose this particular time to give in to those thoughts that kept coming to her—not trusting herself to react well enough—and so tried just to lock herself into the moment. It was difficult. Because *that* wasn't what was important. There was no way she could equate the two. And yet she must. Everything, *everything* depended on it.

She couldn't seem to warm against the night, but she was sure she was sweating. She was feeling very much the way she used to. The way she used to *such a long time ago.* She didn't want to go through those emotions again, but at the moment she just couldn't be sure of anything.

If only she could scream.

Travis had no idea of the confusion that raged within her. What he had started to do was move away from the shrubbery. He was chancing to get in a little closer. But that didn't seem likely unless he was willing to be noticed. There was no other coverage between him and the ceremony. All he would be able to try was to brace himself against the side of one of the cabins and hope the shadows would keep him from view.

He didn't fill Sharon in as to what he was doing, just left her crouching as he slipped away from the bushes and crawled, soldier-style, over to the cabin that was closest, which happened to be on his left. Sharon was almost ready to follow him, but he had moved fast and already had himself erect and pressed to the wall. He then inched cautiously to the edge.

At this time chanting began. Slow, funeral appropriate to the solemness of the ceremony. From his new vantage point Travis noticed the campfire-illuminated blank stares of the observers. Then he saw, with unimaginable disappointment, a flask being surreptitiously passed around by some of the younger Chamrais males sitting in their positions in back of the old guard. They were clearly not taking any of this ritual seriously.

Travis heard some quick shuffling coming up behind him. With his heart suddenly in his throat he spun his head around and saw Sharon rushing over next to him. She was fully erect, moving with complete carelessness.

"Damnit," he said tightly.

She had been spotted.

Almost all at once the voices quit chanting, the drums stopped beating.

They had been spotted.

"Think they'll scalp us?" Sharon tried to joke.

Travis turned his gaze from her. Then he rammed his fist as hard as he could into the side of the cabin. A bolt of lightning flashed through him.

And he passed out.

It wasn't until he came to much later that the fire above his wrist told him that he'd come only so close from turning the bones in his right hand into castanets. He was inside one of the cabins, being attended to by Sharon and an elderly Chamrais couple. He painfully raised his hand into his sight. It had been bandaged, professionally, in a cloth.

He shook his head miserably.

Sharon, who was sitting at the edge of the bed, said: "It's pretty badly bruised, but it doesn't look like you broke any bones."

The Chamrais man came over with a cup. "Drink," he offered.

Travis reached for it with his good hand. He held it, then hesitated. "Uh, what is it?" he asked.

"Alcohol."

"I—don't think so," Travis said, handing the cup back.

"It will help the pain," the man explained. "Like medicine."

Travis couldn't deny wanting to cut his hand off at the moment. But he wouldn't take even a drop of booze.

"No thanks, really," he declined, but with an appreciative smile.

The man took it away.

Now Sharon stepped in. "You know, if you're hurting—"

Travis glared at her, cutting her off. He didn't mean to be that quick, but he also didn't think there was any way he could have stopped himself. Still, he was struck with almost immediate guilt. He couldn't quite get out an apology, but his slow downward glance was meant to relate to her his regret at being so sharp.

Sharon read his "apology" and accepted it. Not that she was fooling herself by believing everything could be wrapped up in that. If she hadn't completely blown it all tonight, she knew she had caused enough damage to require extensive repair.

This whole thing with Sharon—*just her being there!*—was making Travis uncomfortable. He pulled himself into a sitting position and directed his attention to the helpful Chamrais couple.

The man was pouring the alcohol that Travis had refused back into a jug. Travis took particular note of this.

"Just out of curiosity, what kind of blend is that?" he asked. "It's not a commercial brand."

The man looked quickly at his wife. All he would say was that it was kept on hand as a medicine. That was telling Travis as much as if he were to admit that the village did have its own liquor supply.

It was something Travis had suspected all along.

Moonshine.

He felt he was already starting to make progress, but knew that from this point on he'd have to handle his investigation with exceptional care. Any wrong question or comment could bring down the axe. He decided to go in a different direction for the moment.

"Hey, look, I hope we didn't disrupt anything out there."

That was a stupid thing to say, and Travis realized it even before the last word came out. How could they have *not* upset the ceremony?

The Chamrais couple understood what Travis meant, however. Not that either was quick to respond to his apology. What these two had done was not appreciated. It was an intrusion. More than that, disrespectful.

"We were trespassing, Travis," Sharon said.

"I know," he said, looking at the couple. "And I'm sorry."

"How can you be sorry when you came here for that reason?" the man asked.

"I'm not going to lie to you," Travis said. "You don't just stumble onto this village. But spying on your—ritual wasn't right. We were just curious."

"And now you want to know what is behind the ceremony?" the man said.

Of course he did. But Travis shook his head and said, "No, that I'll respect."

The man smiled. He moved over to Travis and sat beside him on the bed. Suddenly he looked almost paternal.

"You are as we," he said. "If you were to be told, I would need your word that nothing would ever be repeated. If you give it, your word I will honor."

It was clear to Travis that the man believed he and Sharon had come out of the reserve with the sole purpose of observing their ceremony. Since they hadn't, Travis could give his word with honesty.

The man then looked at Sharon. Back to Travis, as if respecting his word on her trust as well.

Travis gave a nod.

Before the man could begin, however, there was a heavy knock at the door. His wife went to answer it.

A man looking only slightly younger than Travis's host stood outside. There was an air of importance surrounding him, and this was emphasized by the two young men who stood on either side of him. Like bodyguards. Travis deduced he was the Chamrais chief.

He began speaking to the man in a low voice in their native tongue: Algonkian. They conversed for many minutes, gazes and gestures frequently shifting over to Travis and Sharon, the latter of whom was now sitting silently at the main table with the woman, drinking some muddy coffee concoction.

After the two were finished talking,

Travis's host came over slowly to Travis.

"You must go," was all he said.

Travis glanced at the chief, standing straight and stiff between his two "sons."

"I would like to stay," he responded softly. Respectfully.

The man laid a hand upon his shoulder. "That is impossible."

Travis's curiosity had been piqued by whatever it was that the man was going to tell him before the chief arrived. But he knew that for the moment he had no choice but to leave.

However, he could still have his talk with the man—later, clandestinely. It wasn't something he could suggest now, though. Not under the vigilant eye of the chief.

Travis got up. He applied accidental pressure to his injured hand and the look of agony that crossed his face was as if he'd just had a tooth pulled. He'd actually temporarily forgotten about the condition of his hand. He was quickly reminded that it would have to be professionally attended to.

And how was he going to explain *this one* to Nicole?

As he walked to the door with Sharon in tow, Travis was momentarily intercepted by the chief, who stepped directly in front of him and said: "What you did was wrong."

"There is a lot I'd like to talk with you about," Travis still managed to say.

The chief was abrupt. "No talk." He then stepped aside, allowing Travis and Sharon to walk out, between the two "pillars" that stood at the doorway.

There was no shortage of people outside in the village clearing. They watched silently as the two reporters walked to the car. Sharon tried not to meet any of their eyes, but Travis walked by confidently. Most of their stares were not friendly—a few downright threatening—but Travis knew there was no danger, and that to show any fear wouldn't help his cause at all. He still wasn't through with the village. Not by a long shot.

Once inside the car, Sharon took a deep breath, letting it out slowly. She then lit a cigarette and said, "There's no guarantee this isn't going to get back to the *Clarion*."

"I didn't get the impression they knew we were reporters," Travis said as he turned over the ignition.

"They knew."

"You tell 'em?"

Sharon nodded. Then, in defense: "It doesn't seem to have made any difference with that couple, though. That guy in particular seemed anxious to talk to you."

Travis looked at her. "You take the wheel," he said coldly. "I don't trust tackling this road with only one hand."

Nicole was waiting.

That was all she seemed to be doing lately. Waiting. Tonight, though, there was a difference.

She'd called the *Clarion* office (out of boredom) to find out from Travis when he'd be home, only to be told by Robbie Wade that he'd left work at the usual time. She remained polite with Robbie, but after she'd hung up the phone she'd had the violent urge to rip it from the wall and toss it down the hall.

She knew where he was. Off on another

jaunt to the Chamrais reserve. That was bad enough. What made it worse was that he had lied to her.

Cora Bates had invited her to have a cup of chocolate with her at nine. Nicole declined, perhaps a little harshly, but her anger toward Travis was reaching its peak by that point. She instead hastily excused herself and went up to her room to wait.

Travis arrived home not long after.

Nicole listened carefully as he and Cora exchanged a few words. She heard Cora inquire—with concern—as to the condition of something. Immediately Nicole thought: *He's been hurt. Again.* She almost rushed out of the room, but then she reminded herself of how she really wanted to approach him tonight. She didn't want to lose all that anger she'd spent the last two hours building.

As for Travis, even if he hadn't injured his hand and had the evidence glaring for all the world to see, he couldn't escape his feeling of foreboding. By the time he had parked his car he was already reminded of his guilt for having lied to Nicole. He was feeling lousy all around. He was completely turned off to Sharon, and wished things hadn't happened to cause him to be. And even though he had made what he considered to be an important step with the Chamrais problem, a nagging in his gut told him that getting out there again on his own time would be attempting the impossible. As he thought about it, maybe what Sharon had said earlier had some truth in regard to him and Nicole. He just knew that Nicole had somehow found out where he'd really been tonight.

Yeah, this whole evening had turned out to

be one big screw-up.

Would he think of an apology? Could he? *Should he?* Even if there was something he could say, just what good would it do?

He stood before the closed door of their room. He glanced at his mummy-like hand.

And then his conscience hit him a repeat blow. *You've never lied to her before.*

He braced himself. Tried to tell himself that there was still the chance she didn't know. Taking advantage of that fleeting optimism, he went into the room.

Nicole was standing at the curtained window, her back to him. There was a prolonging of her avoidance of him that Travis could interpret instantly. Still, he had to see this through. He snapped the door shut behind him and held his position.

A knife couldn't have cut through the ensuing silence. The tension that filled the room.

Travis had never been this apprehensive with Nicole before.

He finally pulled himself together and said simply, "You know?"

For a moment there was no response from Nicole. But then, keeping her back to him, she took a breath and said heavily, "I can't believe you'd do that to me."

Travis grabbed the defensive. "You didn't leave me with a whole lot of choice, did you?"

Nicole spun around at him. She looked as though she was fighting back tears. "Was I supposed to?" she argued. "After I saw the condition you came home in last time."

Travis tried to slowly sneak his bandaged hand behind his back. Nicole's searching eyes caught it. Stayed focused on it.

"Oh God."

Travis thrust the hand out. "You wanna know?" he asked.

"What good will it do?"

"You meant it won't change things?"

"Not that you *lied* to me," Nicole said with emphasis.

"You know why I had to," Travis said in a softer tone.

"You made it sound so right," Nicole said, frustrated. "I convinced myself to stand behind you. Because you made me believe it was something you had to do."

"But?" Travis said, stepping in a little closer.

"You're my husband and you come home looking like you got the worst of it in some bar fight. How do you expect me to react?"

"That was then. That was my mistake, I told you."

"And how do you explain..." Nicole gestured at his hand.

Travis wore a faint, ironic smile. "The truth?"

"Can I believe it?"

"I slammed it into the outside wall of a cabin."

Nicole sighed.

"Intentionally," Travis added.

"Why?"

"I got angry. But for what reason isn't important, so don't ask."

Nicole looked close to defeat. "I don't know, Travis," she murmured.

"What?"

"Maybe I can forgive—understand—everything else. In comparison, suddenly it doesn't seem very important anymore."

"In comparison to my—having lied to you."
And this time it was Travis who said it.

"You really hurt me," Nicole said, her eyes
moist.

"I hurt myself more. You wanna know
guilt?" Travis hooked his thumb at himself.
"It's something I never want to do to you again.
I *promise* I'll never do again."

Nicole paused, then said, "I do know why
you did it."

Travis shrugged. "Doesn't make it any less
wrong."

Nicole was almost smiling. "Sometimes an
apology works wonders."

"I'm sorry," Travis said, and he stood at
the foot of the bed looking sincere in his regret.

Nicole now felt that she owed an apology.
Travis never would have had to lie to her if she'd
been more sympathetic to his concerns. She
realized she had been wrong trying to stop him
from doing what he felt he had to do. Of course,
she couldn't stop worrying, but maybe it was a
lot more damaging tying a rope around him.

"That's your typing hand, isn't it?"

Travis nodded. "Gonna have to type in
reverse for a while. Guess it won't be too bad so
long as I'm not assigned any long copy."

"Is it broken?"

Travis tried flexing his fingers. The pain
was still there all right. Flaring.

"Feels like it is," he said through tight lips.
"But I'm pretty sure it's just bruised. I'm not
playing around, though. Tomorrow I'm going to
have it looked at by Dr. MacFarlane."

"You do that."

Nicole then took a couple of steps forward,

slowly opened her arms. Travis, by now flooded with relief, went to her. They hugged.

Maybe this night wasn't such a total write-off.

32

Harold Foley's retirement party was just a few days away.

Not all last-minute preparations were of a festive nature.

Mayor Jessup and Dr. MacFarlane had gone out earlier that night to meet with "Big" Roy Cohen, who owned a garage just south of Batesville. Roy was a jovial giant of a man who had gotten a fair amount of respect from the town because of tireless involvement with its youth sports program.

He was also another of that select group which performed "favors" for the mayor's committee. Unlike the others, however, he wasn't interested in future rewards; he demanded and received *immediate* payment for his services. And he was paid well.

Roy had been told what was expected of him that coming Saturday, and he had agreed in his typically grinning way. Before the mayor left, he had handed Roy a fully packed envelope, which had been accepted without acknowledgment. It was no secret that the mayor didn't like dealing with the man, but he posessed two qualities that were vital to the committee's cause: he was fearless, and he could be trusted. So far. Neither Jessup nor MacFarlane was kidding himself that the day would never come when this particular asset would become a liability.

"That unctuous bastard doesn't have a lot of regard for us," Jessup remarked to the doctor when later that evening both were sitting in the mayor's office sharing a bottle of German beer.

MacFarlane smiled. "I don't think he's completely ignorant to how we feel about him either."

The mayor raised his glass in a salute. He sipped, then said: "That doesn't bother me. And he gets paid, that's really all that matters to him. Of course, he does his work. He didn't disappoint us with Trelevan's kid."

MacFarlane nodded.

"Maybe that's what it is that bothers me about the bastard," Jessup sparked. "He's cold-blooded."

"It's like looking into a mirror, isn't it?" MacFarlane said.

Jessup was quick to look at the doctor, but he didn't take offense. He might have, had he not known MacFarlane was speaking for himself as well. However, he did say, lightly: "For God's sake, Stewart, don't *you* go squeamish on me. I've got enough to handle with Trelevan and Collarman."

"Speaking of whom, have you talked with Morris lately?"

"Yesterday at breakfast. No charge," the mayor said, in anticipation of the doctor's next question.

"I wouldn't be too concerned," MacFarlane said. "He accepts that it has to be done."

"I know," Jessup agreed. "I just hope both will maintain that attitude. Not get carried away with irrationality."

Just then the phone on his desk rang. Jessup regarded it curiously. Who would know he was in his office at this hour? It was after ten. He let it ring a second time before his hand went for the receiver.

"Mayor Jessup," he answered formally.

MacFarlane watched with interest as the mayor listened to whomever it was on the other end. He had already deduced that it was either Trelevan or Collarman.

It was Collarman. And he was calling to check on the details for Saturday night. They were details that Jessup seemed hesitant to give.

"Morris—yes, it's been worked out. . . ." He glanced up at the doctor. "It'll be—an accident. . . ."

For some reason, listening to these words leave the mayor's mouth made MacFarlane—*squeamish*. He'd been included in every step of the planning, just as he'd participated wholly when Trelevan's young assistant had proven to be a risk. But he didn't really know the kid. He knew—very well—Harold Foley. Liked the man. And now, suddenly, hearing the mayor talk, he was struck with the reality of it. Harold Foley was going to die. Foley's wife was going to die. Yes, their deaths were probably necessary in a preventative sense. But, as MacFarlane now thought about it, there was still so much self-convincing involved. Self-convincing that—if this were really for the survival of Batesville—he felt shouldn't be there.

Jessup hung up the phone. He wore a pleased smile that the doctor wasn't entirely sure how to interpret.

Then the mayor said, "I don't anticipate any problem."

33

As his second complete day of tracking neared its end, Marv Nelson prepared to bed down for the night. Today he'd tracked long into the night (perhaps not wisely, since he was following a direction with which he was not familiar), but his hunt had so far turned up nothing. Tomorrow he was going to work his way to the eastern edge of Great Spirit Lake and cut a path along there.

Ground conditions had not been favorable. The fall temperatures made the earth too solid for such physical signs as footprints to easily be embedded; yet it was not late enough for the first snows to provide the ideal tracking environment.

The cold, however, had been biting. Not that Marv was bothered too much by it. Living where he did, as he did, he'd grown accustomed to the sub-zero temperatures so frequent in the north country.

He nestled in among the denseness of the trees, settling both his pack and himself onto a grassy knoll. He felt protected there: plenty of camouflage. For extra security, he'd strewn dry twigs and branches in a circle around the rise so that he would be quickly alerted if he were approached during the night.

He wrapped himself snugly in the quilted blanket that he'd brought along, and then he lay down to sleep.

He was out in no time.

There was a high overcast. Snow was possible, but it was a light rain that began to fall. Marv was in an unusually deep sleep, peacefully oblivious to the drizzle that came down on and around him. Not a stirring.

Only a short distance from where Marv lay, a large gray wolf padded silently through the brush. It too was not affected by the rain. It was on the prowl ... though not possessed of a natural hunger. The predatory look in its yellow eyes was intensified, its powerful jaws snapping viciously. The hunger on this nocturnal quest could only be satiated with one food. A food that its heightened senses directed it toward.

Marv's eyes flickered open. The rainfall had finally wakened him. It was heavier now, steady. Raising a pleasant, fresh smell from the ground. But there was no way Marv would be allowed to finish his sleep in comfort.

He pulled into a sitting position, drawing his knees up to his chest and folding the blanket more tightly around himself. It was too dark for him to start looking for a better-sheltered area. The sparse foliage of the surrounding autumn trees provided as much protection from the rain as he was going to get.

He was just going to have to sit this out.

Unknown to him, he was being watched.

The wolf had Marv in its sight; its eyes were attuned to the blackness—and while Marv's vision could barely cut five feet, the beast could watch his every move with accuracy. It patiently studied him.

Then it began to circle him.

The sound of the rain pattering the ground camouflaged the cracking branches.

As the wolf continued in its direction it gradually moved in closer. Its hunger had peaked. Saliva poured down from its thin black lips.

It began to pace more quickly.

Marv continued to sit motionlessly. A perfect target.

The beast had positioned itself behind him now. Perhaps at a distance of twelve feet. Without hesitation it broke off from its pattern and headed straight for the back of its quarry. It moved confidently, each muscle in its lithe body working in rhythm with the other.

It then paused at the rise of the knoll, bracing the rain-moistened earth with its forepaws. The upper part of its body began to tense in anticipation of its next move.

A low, nearly inaudible growl escaped its lips.

Just then Marv started to turn his head. He'd heard nothing, but *sensed* the presence behind him. His hand cautiously slipped under the moosehide pack where he'd placed his knife.

The wolf pounced!

Marv moved fast, but not fast enough. His hand had gripped the knife and he was halfway to his feet when the beast's hammer-like forepaws slammed into his back and sent him crashing face-first to the ground. His knife released from his grasp and shot out into the night.

He just had time to roll onto his back before his attacker was upon him. That was when he got his first look at it. The wolf's face was almost touching his—the stench of its hot breath swimming around him in a haze. Strands of saliva began to splay onto his face.

Marv, however, could keep his concentration on only one thing: its greedily snapping jaws. Rabid. The teeth were white, full, capable of shredding flesh and bone. Marv called upon all his strength to keep that snarling muzzle away from his throat. But he had no defense against the claws that were ripping at his arms, opening them.

He craned his neck in both directions, trying to spot just the gleam of his knife. It was his only hope. Already he was weakening; without his weapon he didn't see himself standing a chance.

The beast's massive head was lowering. That was when Marv loosed one of his hands and grabbed at the thick, wet fur at the back of its neck. He then quickly released his other hand, curled it into a fist, and, with all his might, drove it into the side of the wolf's face. Again. Once more. The beast felt each blow, was staggered by them. This gave Marv the opportunity to shoot out from under its bulk and gain the freedom to flash his gaze along the ground.

Several feet away he saw something glint in the rain.

He flung himself over in that direction, throwing his arms out for extra distance.

It *was* his knife!

His hand just closed around its handle when he screamed out in agony as the wolf's savage jaws closed on his free arm. He could feel the teeth grind against bone.

The bloody mess that was Marv quickly spun onto his side and drove the blade of the knife upward in a glistening arc. It completed its trail by sinking into the side of the beast's neck.

The wolf howled as the blood spurted. Its carotid had been severed. But Marv wasn't finished. Crazed with a vengeance he went about ripping the body open, forcing the razor-like blade down into the chest area . . . deeper into its softer mid-section. The insides came pouring out in a gory banquet.

The wolf toppled over, dead. Marv then rolled away, pulled himself up. He regarded the disembowelled carcass with numbness. Now it was twitching with death spasms: the nerves and muscles in final, pitiful defiance.

Then it lay still.

Marv considered his own injuries. They looked pretty bad; he knew there wasn't any way he'd be able to go on with the hunt. Both his arms were mangled and bloody. They'd have to be properly looked after. But for the moment all he could do was bandage them.

He wasted no time ripping off and apart his shirt and fashioning crude bandages from the cloth. He tied them fairly tightly at the shoulders, and this seemed to stop the blood flow. Still, he'd have to start back to the town right away. Halting the circulation for any length of time could result in gangrene. Possible amputation of both limbs.

Leaving his gear behind, Marv started east,

toward the highway. There it was possible he might get a ride into town. He'd never get there on foot. It had taken him two days of solid walking to make the distance he had.

. . . the body of the wolf could no longer sustain life. Neither its own nor that force which had intruded on it. One spirit had ceased to exist—

The other came free of the corpse by consuming it from within . . .

Twice Marv stumbled in the dark. He was continuing to weaken and found that the reason was that the bandage on his right arm was not stopping the bleeding. Already that strip of cloth was soaked in crimson.

But he pushed on.

A man not in his physical shape would never have made the distance he already had. He continued to call on inner resources to fight the urge just to collapse. Because he knew that if he did he'd never get up. He made himself look at the possibility of his dying as just another challenge he had to overcome. One that he *could* overcome. Convincing himself of that kept him going. He'd never given up before. With so much to lose, he certainly wasn't going to start now.

The rain still poured, not a help to his plight.

The moment came where he had to stop—just for a moment. He had to remain on his feet, though, and so leaned against a tree.

He felt as though he'd been journeying for hours . . . but he knew it had been nowhere near that long.

Still, how much further?

A bone-chilling cry filled the woods, surrounding him.

Marv froze. He recognized it immediately.

There was no way he could fight the demon now. Yet he suddenly realized that all along it had been he who was being stalked.

He felt its presence. Strongly.

"Not now, you bastard," he said through clenched teeth. Then he made himself push away from the tree, and he stumbled on toward the highway.

He could feel the presence following after.

Marv moved as quickly as he could but was unable to be free of it. It was beside him, behind him, in front . . .

And then, as if the Windigo had the ability to control the elements, the rain began to pour in a frenzy, blinding Marv. Obstructing his travel almost completely.

A violent wind whipped out of nowhere: *the breath of the Windigo?* Marv was much too weak to fight against its force. The sudden gusts tossed him to the ground, where he lay still assaulted by the lashing rain.

He screamed out against that supernatural power he felt growing ever nearer. That power which he knew wanted to penetrate his very being.

"*You're not going to beat me! Damn you, you're not!*"

Morning.

The day was autumn cool. Clear. There was no wind now. Not so much as a caressing breeze. That there had been a rainfall the night before was evident by the moistness in the earth. The dew-like freshness that scented the air.

Marv lay where he had fallen.

Blood continued to seep from his wounds.

But he had not yet been conquered by death.

Perhaps nothing more than sheer stubbornness kept him breathing.

His return to consciousness came slowly. And not without pain. Those first moments were neither a reminder of where he was nor a remembrance of what had happened to him.

He was too disoriented and weak from his blood loss to climb to his feet and so just continued to lie there. Oblivious to death or whatever else might come his way.

Yet he was only yards from the highway. Not that his knowing this would have done him much good. Keeping the breaths coming was about all the exertion he could manage.

Finally, though, a semblance of reality came back to him. His mind flashed on the image of the wolf. He remembered the presence. The forces of nature that had worked against him.

The presence . . .

What happened to it? Why hadn't it done whatever it was going to do to him last night? Possess him. Kill him. Why had it just left him?

Unless . . . unless it knew that his death would be like this. Slow.

No! That was where the bastard was wrong.

It wasn't going to end this way.

Marv lay on his back on the moist earth for many more minutes, trying to regain all the strength he could. Then, taking firm hold of the knife in his left hand, he dug the blade deeply into the trunk of the tree that was closest to him on that side and used it as a handle to pull himself to his knees. He then worked it out and re-embedded it yet higher, levering himself accordingly. Another thrust, pull, and he was on his feet. Unsteadily so, but on his feet. He was drained and had to brace himself against the trunk, patiently allowing the strength to once again replenish.

That was when he saw the brief distance he had to go to get to the highway.

His face broke in a wide grin.

He was going to make it!

The horrendous eight-foot embodiment of the Windigo reached out its hands for Marv, taking him by the neck and raising him off the ground. Marv struggled vainly, arms and legs thrashing. The creature then turned him around; their faces weren't a foot apart. Marv found that he couldn't look long into that demonic countenance—it was as if just for a moment the Windigo was considering its victim—but he took advantage of its hesitation to strike out with his knife. It cut into the creature's muscular shoulder, burying itself to the hilt. But to no effect. Marv yanked it out and prepared for one more thrust: into the Windigo's throat. Too late. The creature emitted its familiar eerie cry and then its mighty jaws with the saber teeth opened to capacity and closed on Marv's face. Marv's scream was cut short. He felt his brain explode before the front of his skull crunched off in the creature's mouth.

The Windigo then returned to the depths of the forest to consume the rest of the body.

34

Harold Foley's retirement party was a formal affair. Or at least as formal as a Batesville gathering could get. The men all wore suits while the women were decked out in whatever evening wear they could find in their closets.

All except Sharon Crane, who was wearing a jumper-style pantsuit. What was particularly odd about her choice of outfit was that around town she was never seen in anything other than conservative dresses or skirts. Given the formality of the gathering, she wasn't expected to choose this night to change her fashion.

The party didn't have quite the easy-going ambience of Robbie Wade's get-together a few months before. Perhaps it was the larger, more disparate crowd, but conversations didn't flow as openly.

Frankly, Travis was finding this party to be a bore.

He was still concerned about Nicole, though, and made sure he kept beside her the whole night.

There was just the faintest air of tension that he was sensitive to this evening. Maybe it was because of Mayor Jessup's presence; he'd heard that he was a man who didn't inspire the easiest mood of conviviality.

As for Sharon, her attitude toward Travis was reminiscent of the way she had behaved at Robbie's party. She appeared pleasant, but seemed to be purposely avoiding Travis or those groups in which he occasionally found himself.

Travis was receptive to this. There was no way he couldn't be. It was the same as with work. Ever since that "occurrence" at the Chamrais village it had been as though Sharon knew Travis wanted her to keep her distance and so had obliged—coldly so; she had only maintained contact with him on a thoroughly professional basis. At first that had been exactly what Travis wanted. But, as the week had rolled to an end, this kind of relationship started to become intolerable for him. Regardless of what had happened, Sharon had been too much of a friend.

Tonight he wasn't sure what to do. Should he talk to her, get this mess straightened out? Or was it for the best just to let things go on as they were? It wasn't an easy decision, and certainly not one that could be made without serious thought. But this irresolution wasn't making the party any less difficult to take.

The night seemed to go on and on. Travis didn't know why he was staying, prolonging the agony. A lot of drinking was going on around him, and by eleven he was sure that he and Nicole were the only sober ones left. Even the mayor looked a little high.

It was around eleven-thirty that Jessup and

Morris Collarman disappeared out back.

The mayor may have looked like he was relaxed and having a good time, but that was just a front he was working hard to maintain. As with his partners, this night he could have drunk to excess and still not have been affected by it.

Collarman, however, was just plain tight.

Once he and Jessup were away from the gathering, he raised his glass of rye to his lips, held it there, and said: "I'm looking at Harold and I know that in just a couple of hours . . ." He downed a quick mouthful.

The mayor spoke in an understanding tone. "Nothing is going to go wrong."

Collarman looked seriously at the mayor. "I know it has to be done," he said in an obvious attempt to re-convince himself.

"Just keep remembering that."

Collarman gazed out the window into the pre-winter darkness. He muttered, "I still wish this damn night would end."

By midnight the party was winding down. It probably could have carried on longer but most everyone was too drunk. Slurred goodbyes were made to the appreciative Foleys as the guests stumbled out the front door.

"That's our cue," Travis whispered to Nicole as the first throng of exiters went for their coats. As they stood in line waiting to shake Foley's hand, Travis noticed that his soon-to-be-former associate appeared more plastered than anyone else. His wife apparently was supporting him.

Alcohol-induced sentiment poured out as the guests continued to leave. Travis just shook the man's hand, expressed how much he had enjoyed working with him, and then got himself out the door as fast as he could. As he filled his lungs with a good swallow of night air, he made a vow never to put himself through anything like that again. It wasn't the exaggerated—and hardly sincere—emotion that he'd found hard to take. More than anything it was seeing those people he watched putting on their fronts each day coming on like gutter lushes. Those same people who were so quick to point fingers at the Chamrais.

Travis was just getting into Old Betsy with an equally relieved-to-be-out-of-there Nicole when he heard a familiar voice call to him. It was Sharon, who was standing looking at him on the boulevard.

He probably couldn't have given an answer if asked why he excused himself from Nicole to walk over to her.

Sharon started speaking before he even touched the boulevard. "Look, I don't think it's good that we keep this up."

"You're telling me this now?" Travis said.

"There wasn't a whole lot of chance inside."

Travis had to agree with that.

"What happened last week. Everything. I don't know what else to say except—I'm sorry." Sharon was clearly sincere, though there wasn't a note of emotion in her voice.

"What *was* all that about?" Travis wanted to know.

"Hah, if I knew that . . . I guess it was just a buildup of something, and you just happened to be there. Lousy explanation, huh? But I don't know how else to justify it. To be honest, I really don't even remember that night. Well, not much. But I do want you to know one thing,

Travis. No matter what else you might have thought—or are thinking—I'm not a loon.''

"I know," Travis said. But why did he all of a sudden feel like a hypocrite?

"Can we put it behind us?" Sharon asked meekly.

Travis found himself hesitating. *Could they?* he wondered.

"Sure," he said. Smiling.

Sharon looked relieved.

"Uh, would I be pushing it if I asked for one more favor?" she said.

Travis cocked his head.

"I'm kinda without a ride home."

Travis nodded, and the two of them walked to the car.

Maybe this was what a part of him wanted, but he couldn't say he felt a whole lot better.

In truth, it made him nervous.

Outside of the mayor, MacFarlane, Collarman and Trelevan (and their respective wives—with the exception of Jessup, who had been a life-long bachelor), the party had cleared out by twelve-thirty. While the women went about cleaning up, the men sat in the livingroom sipping coffee. No one was talking, though eyes periodically wandered over to the clock above the television set.

By a quarter to one MacFarlane's wife came out ready to leave. She was soon followed by Dorothy Trelevan.

"It has been a long day," Trelevan said with a nervous smile to the group. He got up to go into the bedroom to retrieve their coats.

MacFarlane then rose. Another glance at the clock.

"It was a fine party, Morris," the mayor

said contentedly, remaining in his seat. "I'm sure Harold and Marge appreciated it."

Collarman could only respond with a nod.

"We're all tired," Jessup said.

Just then the phone rang.

35

Harold and Marge Foley had been run off the road just a mile from their house south of town. According to the police report, their car had overturned in a ditch crushing the both of them. They were pronounced dead at the scene.

Sunday was a solemn day for most of the town. Especially for those with whom the Foleys had spent their last hours. It was something they found hard to accept. How could it not be when two people are so alive one minute and dead in the next?

Travis didn't hear the news until ten the following morning, when Cora Bates woke him to take an urgent telephone call. It was Sharon who broke it to him, and, of course, he was as stunned as everyone else. At the same time, he really wasn't that surprised. He remembered the condition Foley had been in the previous night. If it was he who had been behind the wheel, maybe the accident had been inevitable. He wasn't going to say this to Sharon, though. Poor taste, even though the thought remained with him for the rest of the day.

Monday, and the atmosphere around the *Clarion* was appropriately gloomy. Robbie Wade looked to be taking the tragedy worse than anyone—including Ben Quarry, who was Foley's closest friend, but who perhaps had become somewhat jaded by his years of reporting just such incidents.

Robbie had been at the office Sunday, to assist Quarry in putting together a fitting obituary for the front page of the next day's paper. Sharon usually handled such tasks, but this obit required something more personal.

Both Sharon and Travis were given the prepared copy to read Monday morning. Travis was admittedly surprised by the amount of background that Foley had had. No simple "hick" reporter was he (which was how Travis had thought of him). From Thunder Bay to Winnipeg to Toronto back to Winnipeg . . . finally to Batesville. It was like digging through a pail of caramel-coated popcorn only to find a cheap tin whistle at the bottom.

"The pace of the city got to be too much for him," Sharon explained later when she and Travis were at the cafe having a bite to eat. It was the first lunch they'd had together in a week.

"He probably could have gone anywhere," Travis said with quiet admiration—not to mention envy.

Sharon spoke pensively. "I guess what makes this whole thing even more of a tragedy is its happening just at the time when he could start doing what he wanted with his life. Work all those years planning for that day and then . . ."

Travis smiled wanly. "The one thing consistent about life is that nothing is ever consistent.''

"Live for the moment?''

"I'm no philosopher. It's just that's the way I've always thought it should be. It's okay to plan, just don't expect to always follow a schedule.''

"It sounds like you're speaking from personal experience,'' Sharon inferred.

"No. But I'm familiar with the story of a fella to whom that could have applied. *Should* have applied. For most of his adult life this guy hoarded nearly every cent he earned, supplying himself only with the basics. He never went out, never entertained—nothing. But did he have plans for his retirement years! Cruises, the best restaurants. The works. He thought. He never counted on being hit with cancer two years before his sixty-fifth birthday. He did have an impressive funeral, though.''

Sharon leaned back in her chair, holding her coffee in both hands. "I suppose that can apply to other elements in life as well. Like I wonder how many people follow the path they've always seen for themselves.''

Travis asked, "You?''

A faint shadow came over Sharon's face. Then she half-smiled. "Professionally, yeah, pretty much. Of course in that I've never held very high expectations.''

"What about your personal life? Or maybe I shouldn't be asking?''

Sharon looked at Travis with an expression that seemed to say it certainly did concern him. This she wanted him to know.

"That's never been on the right track,'' she answered, though there was no betraying of self-pity in her voice.

"How come?"

Suddenly, momentarily, Travis had the queasy feeling he was treading on treacherous ground.

Sharon replied, "What does a little girl dream about? Marriage. A family. I guess the family unit meant so much to me because we were never a complete one."

"Your mother?" Travis said gently.

Sharon nodded. "Yeah. It's like I told you before, my father and brothers did the best they could, but there was always that one corner torn from the picture."

"And it was something you wanted to be a part of?"

"I couldn't as a kid," Sharon said. "No way. Not even if my father had remarried. But as a wife, a mother—I could still capture a lot of that experience."

"Well, I came from that structure you're describing," Travis said in a strange tone of voice. "Mother, father, siblings. But I'll bet you still came out with more."

Sharon looked doubtful, but curious.

"There's no such thing as a complete utopia," Travis explained. "What you couldn't have and to this day crave, I had. And maybe, because I had it, those are years I often wish I could wipe from my memory. I'll bet that works in reverse as well."

"Think so?"

"Sure. For instance, tell me you didn't take your country upbringing for granted. All throughout my growing-up years I'd have given anything to escape the city: the scum, depression. I could tell you horror stories about some of the types who lived around where we did. The living dead."

Sharon pondered. "I enjoyed living on the farm. If I hadn't, I sure don't think I'd be living in Batesville now. But I guess—yeah, I never gave that part of my youth much thought."

"There you go."

Sharon broke in a smile. "You know, Travis," she said, and this time it was she who was speaking with admiration, "you make a lot of sense."

Travis was neutral to the sincerity of her compliment. "Sometimes I just think I've lived longer than I actually have," was how he answered, with a shrug.

36

By now Lloyd Caribou had become somewhat bolder about stepping out from the mill in
the exposing light of day. The need for food
necessitated this move. His diet had been forced
to undergo a radical change. He had been surviving primarily on the surrounding vegetation,
the craving for flesh flood satisfied with the
occasional rodent he was able to outmaneuver.
He was improving at this—his moves becoming
more stealthy and swift.

His appearance had gone to seed. Months
without shaving had resulted in a scraggly
beard. His washing had been minimal and so he
smelled as bad as he looked. His skin, from lack
of cleaning and sunlight, was erupting in sores.
There was virtually no color to it. His teeth were
either blackened or missing altogether. His
eyes, shadowed and squinting, were forever
shifting. Aware.

The most simple movement had become
deliberate, defensive.

In short, Lloyd Caribou had truly become

more animal than man. And he knew he had. His last remaining ounces of reason had made him see it.

He was entering the lake today, wading in until he was waist deep. The waters were still and clear and Lloyd cast his vision into them in his search for a meal. Fish streaked by before him and he moved with speed, but never quite fast enough to grab one. His craving for flesh was beginning to overwhelm him, and when he next saw the long silvery back of a fish as it swam over curiously to his leg, he splashed down beneath the surface, submerging himself completely, and reached out wildly for the grab. One of his hands made fleeting contact with its body but the wet, slippery skin allowed it to slide free with ease, and it disappeared into deeper waters.

Lloyd emerged from the lake like a primitive monster. Water splashed up and around him in a glistening explosion as he forcefully thrust himself up. An intense, predatory look darkened his features as he stood firm in the sun-speckled waters. And then he raised his fist and began to strike the lake surface, expending his frustrations. He threw his head back and emitted a primal yell, which echoed back to him. He continued driving his fist into the water, numbing it, and again he yelled—as loud as he could, ripping the sound up from the very pit of his stomach. His throat soon felt as though it might rupture from the force and persistence of his cry, but Lloyd didn't stop.

Then—out of the corner of his eye he caught a glimpse of something alighting on the rippling surface of the water. His yells ceased, though his mouth remained open in a mute continuation of his rage. He slowly turned his head in the direction of that black and white object. It was a bird—more exactly, a loon, though Lloyd could no longer attach specifics to his recognitions. And it was floating on the lake only yards from where he stood.

Lloyd didn't move carelessly. He spent the next several minutes just studying the bird. And then slowly, with almost imperceptible motion, he began to advance toward it. Not daring to breathe. It was as though he were moving with the smoothness of the current. The loon apparently was oblivious to his presence, or preceived no threat. Perhaps it too was absorbed with the search for food.

Lloyd got within three feet of it, and he paused.

Then he leaped. With deadly accuracy. Grabbing the loon by its neck and pulling it beneath the surface. The bird struggled valiantly in the two-handed grasp, but Lloyd had it. He wouldn't surrender this prize. By the time he bobbed out of the water the bird was dead, resting wet and limp in his hands. Lloyd was jubilant over his victory, and he began improvising a dance, which he continued to shore.

37

Harold and Marge Foley were buried and life in Batesville went on. There was still the customary solemness that accompanied those moments of reflection, but life is for the living, and once the shock has passed death is seldom dwelt upon.

Travis had all but forgotten his co-worker. Even the empty desk at the back corner of the office no longer evoked thought. It seemed to be the same with the other staffers, though their sorrow had, understandably, taken longer to diminish.

The passing of time was responsible for other changes as well. No longer was there that undercurrent of coolness that had been present during those initial few days of his and Sharon's reconciliation. As Sharon would look on it, it was back to the beginning for them. And she was so glad of it. Her desires hadn't dimmed, but now she knew that she had to be more careful. Previously lonely evenings at home were now filled with plans and fantasies so alive she felt herself in a near-perpetual high. This euphoria carried over into her workday life, and perhaps it was this constant "up" in her personality that led Travis to so quickly put aside the immediate past. Certainly he hadn't planned on this; it had just happened. And he accepted it.

The first snow had fallen, and thawed.

Winter was postponing its entry this year, and that became a source of concern for the province's northern regions. Late snow usually predicted a harsh winter. The snow should have been covering the ground for a month now. The accompanying cold had already set in (though occasional days of comfort could still be enjoyed), but it was as if the precipitation was just biding its time, priming for that one heavy assault that would do its damage overnight.

The people of Batesville were preparing for it.

Nicole was slowly adapting to her inactivity, although she knew the real test of her coping abilities would come with the snows. Sometimes, when she dwelled too long on those months ahead, she would become anxious. She had no way of knowing what to expect. How she'd be affected. But she couldn't help predicting the worst.

One afternoon she was opening up her concerns to Cora Bates. The old woman was immediately receptive to what she was saying, and, without explanation, took her by the hand out back to the tool shed. Inside, among other relics, was a bicycle—one that as of late had been seldom used, except by the occasional kid on the block who knew of its existence and would ask permission to ride it. Cora suggested

to Nicole that she take it for a nice, long ride.
Just get away for a while on her own. "Good for
the soul," was how she explained it.

Nicole readily and appreciatively agreed.
She knew that this would probably be her last
chance to "make an escape" before the snows
came. She couldn't resist giving Cora a hug.
This the old woman appreciated.

Nicole had no idea where she'd go—she
really didn't know the country that well—but
made sure to dress warmly. Woolen pullover
sweater, around which she zipped up a waist-
length down-filled jacket. She had on a pair of
heavy denims, which she tucked into knee-
length boots. She then put on a cap and mittens.
She probably looked pretty funny, but even
bundling herself this way gave her a lift. She felt
the same excitement a teenage girl might
getting ready for an important date.

She wheeled away from the big house on
Valgard Street early in the afternoon. As she
pedaled toward the north edge of town—avoiding the main street—she looked closely at the
clouds and thought how there was something
. . . odd about them. She couldn't put her finger
exactly on what it was (maybe it was just that
the country made her view things differently),
but there was a kind of heaviness to them that
all of a sudden brought her to the decision to not
travel too far.

Her one act of personal conquest, though,
slight as it might be, was to break free of
Batesville's boundaries. This she hadn't done
since arriving in town, and once out she felt a
joyous freedom that made her want to shout.

She began pedaling faster.

She soon found herself on a narrow pathway

of hard mud, which was bordered on either side by more trees than she had ever seen before. She had no idea what kinds they were—most had lost their leaves to the season and were now standing bare and bent at the sides of the path like autumn guards.

Suddenly, for the briefest of moments, she lost knowledge of where she was. She had become so caught up in her freedom that she had just kept going, despite her intentions not to travel any distance. How had she ended up on this route? *How was she going to find her way back off it?*

She calmed, let her head clear enough to allow rational thought. She wasn't lost. Of course not. All she had to do was follow the path out. It would take her to the road that would lead back into town. After all, she hadn't gone into that deep a fugue. She hadn't been riding *that* long.

She slowed and coasted to a stop. The path was too narrow for her to just circle the bike out. She had to hop off and re-direct it by hand.

She didn't like being there. She felt small and . . . too alone. Gazing up past the trees, she noticed that the gray cloud formations hadn't softened. If anything, from this vantage point they had gotten darker. Deeper. This heightened her discomfort all the more.

There was just something about them.

She wasted no time climbing back onto the bike and starting her ride out. She knew she'd feel a whole lot better once she saw the road opening.

She was pedaling fast, riding into a gentle breeze that brushed the forest's fragrance into her face. It was a clean smell. Almost soothing—

It happened so quickly that it hardly had time to register with her.

A figure darted out from the trees and halted abruptly right in the path of the bike.

The barely human face twisted in a grimace of surprise.

Nicole tried to swerve but lost control of the bike. It shot like a bullet into the trees at the path side and she was thrown off. Her head struck the ground first, knocking her out instantly.

The figure now standing impassively on the mud road was Lloyd Caribou. He watched the girl lay there for a long while. And then, when he was sure she wasn't going to get up, he approached her.

She was lying on her back. She had rolled several times before coming to rest and her face was smudged with dirt. There was a slight cut on her cheek.

Lloyd stood before her. Again he waited. Then he lowered to his haunches. His hand tentatively reached out and brushed away the blonde hair that had blown over her face.

It wasn't a primitive recognition; Lloyd smiled at her beauty. His responses, however, did not exceed that. Perhaps there was a flickering recollection of someone he had once known, but the memory no longer held much significance. His face set and he began to rise, all the while keeping his eyes locked on the face of the girl.

He stopped.

He would take the girl with him.

He knelt back down and gently pushed his hands under her neck and lower back. Then he lifted her, but not with the care he might have used if he'd had the strength of his former self. It was an effort for him, and an even greater strain keeping her raised in his arms. He had to drop her and she thudded onto her side. He tried again, this time pulling her to her feet and tossing her over his shoulder like so much dead weight.

Now he could manage her. He carried her into the woods.

38

Travis wasn't expecting to come home from work and not find Nicole waiting for him. He couldn't think of one time since starting his job when she wasn't there. Not that he thought she should be; it was just that she always was.

The only person who appeared to be in the boarding house was Rosa—in the kitchen preparing dinner—and she couldn't tell him where Nicole was. When Travis then expressed the thought that maybe she and Cora had gone out together some place, Rosa informed him that the old woman was upstairs napping.

Travis was puzzled, becoming mildly concerned.

When Cora finally came downstairs he asked if she knew where Nicole had gone. A flash of worry crossed Cora's face. Then, calmly, she asked the time. Travis checked his watch: five minutes after six. Another look of concern, only this one didn't fade from the old woman's face.

Travis responded to it. "Cora, where is

she?" he asked with seriousness.

"She took the bike out earlier," she said, keeping her voice even. "She may have just—"

Travis didn't want to hear conjecture. "How much earlier?" he asked. "What time?"

Cora's eyes met his; through them she tried to caution about worrying unnecessarily.

"About one," she answered.

Travis's eyes widened. "She's been gone . . . *five hours?*"

"I know it seems like a long time, but the countryside is so beautiful. There's so much to see."

Travis shook his head. "Uh uh," he said stubbornly. "You don't know Nicole. She wouldn't intentonally stay away this long."

Cora then gently took his hand. By now Rosa was standing in the doorway to the dining room, watching and listening.

"Travis," the old woman said quietly, "I could tell she wanted to get out. She's never really been too far from the house since you both came here. With winter on the way I'm sure she wanted this last chance to enjoy some time away from two old women." She smiled at Rosa, who remained dour-faced.

That sounded good and Travis wished he could believe it . . . but it didn't sit well with him. Neither, he suspected, did it with Cora.

"Nicole's a city girl," he then explained in a low voice. "She wouldn't go exploring parts around here she wasn't familiar with." His eyes darted about the room, as if trying to think of what to do. Then he blurted: "I've gotta go look for her. Do you have any idea where she went? Did she say anything?" That he was reacting with urgency was more evident in his words; he kept control in his tone, speaking with little alarm.

Cora had to admit she had no clue as to Nicole's direction. She tried to remain sensible about this, but she couldn't help being affected by Travis's concern, etched into his face. She offered to go with him while he searched for Nicole, but, though appreciative, Travis knew that an old lady tagging along would just slow him. If Nicole were in trouble, the last thing he wanted was to waste time.

He just hoped there wasn't a need to hurry.

Travis wasn't thinking too clearly as he traveled up and down the town's roads, trying to guess her route. In a way he was surprised that he was reacting with such worry: a strong part of him was sure that nothing had happened to Nicole. In all probability getting out for a ride like that *did* cause her to lose track of time.

But *five* hours?

He had no luck covering the town. He'd have to start looking outside. But he had a sick feeling that that was going to be like searching for the proverbial needle in the haystack. Which direction did she take out of Batesville? And what godforsaken route might she have followed from there?

"Nicole," he muttered, "where the hell are you?"

39

In the dark of the sawmill where Lloyd
Caribou had carried her, Nicole had not yet
regained consciousness. Lloyd had laid her at
the back of the mill, near his "hiding place," and
had spent the past few hours just sitting by her,
watching her sleep. Not once had he tried to
revive her. Perhaps to him she was dead.

She wasn't, and an eventual light stirring
brought Lloyd to this complete realization. He
jumped back, startled, when the quiet was disturbed by a moan. He kept a slight distance,
studying her more intently now. Instinct
brought him to brace himself in such a way that
he could pounce on her should the need arise. It
had been a seeming eternity since he had last
had human contact, and with all that had
passed—his virtual transformation—he was
clearly apprehensive.

It took Nicole a long while to even reach the
sub-surface of consciousness. Her coming awake
occurred in slow degrees, accompanied by
moans and tentative movements. Perhaps this

was for the best. Lloyd was readying himself; a more sudden wakening might have resulted in his assaulting her. The gradualness of her revival gave the now-outwardly-primitive side of Lloyd the chance to grow relaxed. He still wasn't venturing any closer to her, however. He hadn't unfrozen from his position.

Nicole's eyes opened. She blinked in the darkness. Lloyd's eyes had grown accustomed to the gloom—almost like a cat's. He still had to strain his vision some, but he could watch Nicole with surprising clarity.

Her first thought, and one that she considered with calm, was that she was dead. Existing now in some limbo. But when the pain from the lump on her head started to build with her complete return to consciousness, she knew that she had escaped that.

Then where was she?

Not only could she not see Lloyd, buried in the black, but there wasn't even the detection of breathing to draw her attention to him. He had learned by the sheer repetition how to keep himself from notice. Every muscle in his body seemed paralyzed. His breathing was so controlled he might have been arresting it.

Nicole remained stretched out on her back, now not daring to move. She just knew that if she tried to sit up or attempt any similar maneuver her head would crack open like a melon. But she didn't like not knowing where she was either.

"Travis?" she said feebly.

Lloyd held himself in position.

"Anyone?" she said, only a little louder.

Still Lloyd made no move to acknowledge her. There was no breaking in his hold of defense.

"Oh God," he next heard her whimper. Then a sound which he did remember, one which he found himself strangely not protected from.

Crying.

He somehow knew there was no threat of danger now, and he slowly rose from his crouch and stepped over.

Nicole felt a presence and immediately went rigid.

"Susan," Lloyd rasped.

40

Travis had searched for Nicole for three hours, finally returning to the boarding house before ten. He would have continued looking indefinitely but the blackness of the country night had proven too much of a hindrance.

All he was hoping now was that sometime during his absence Nicole had returned home.

She hadn't, though Cora had been waiting anxiously. Unfortunately, she had no news either.

"Something's happened to her, Cora," Travis said in admittance of his fear. His eyes were strained: red, glazed.

Cora instructed Rosa to pour him a brandy. Travis tried to object, weakly, but the old woman was insistent. At the moment Travis had no resistance.

"We'll notify the police," Cora suggested after she sat Travis beside her on the chesterfield.

"Forty miles away," Travis said with a shake of his head. "And she's not officially missing for twenty-four hours. Damn, by that time . . ." He stood up. "I gotta go look for her some more."

"Travis, there's nothing you can do right now," Cora argued. "It's too dark, you're tired. Tomorrow."

Rosa brought Travis his brandy. He took it, held it for a while, then put it on the antique coffee table, right on the surface, leaving a shadow ring. He didn't know what he was doing. Tired, yes, but how was he supposed to sleep? Unless he tried to do something the night would never end for him.

"Perhaps Dr. MacFarlane," Cora whispered over her shoulder to Rosa.

Travis was quick. "No. I don't need any doctor. I need to find my wife."

"Yes, but he can give you something to help you sleep," Cora tried to explain. "Then you'll be much better suited to look again tomorrow. You're not going to do either of you any good if you push yourself like this. Please."

Travis looked as though he was considering her suggestion, but in actuality he hadn't heard a word she said. All he had on his mind was the troubling image of Nicole lying injured and alone on one of those uncharted countryside roads.

Cora slowly came to the realization that she wasn't going to get anywhere with Travis as long as he was like this. She glanced over to Rosa, and as if the housekeeper had read her thought she stepped round to the coffee table, took the untouched glass of brandy, and returned with it to the kitchen. Once there she opened one of the cabinets and removed a small bottle of Cora's prescription sleeping pills. She crushed one into powder and swept it into the brandy. Not the wisest of moves, but Cora was concerned for Travis and perhaps it was better than the alternative. Travis could begin acting unreasonably. Become a danger to himself.

Travis unconsciously sipped on the brandy when it was handed back to him, so trapped in his thoughts that he didn't respond to the taste of the alcohol. He continued to just sit there, and Cora didn't initiate further conversation. She patiently waited for the pill-alcohol combination to take effect—not wanting to say anything that might first prompt him to go out again.

It didn't take long for him to begin to go under. Cora then had no difficulty persuading him up to bed.

Travis slept undisturbed straight through the night. It was late the next morning when he finally woke, feeling refreshed. His thoughts about Nicole were not immediate; habit instead made him concerned that he'd overslept for work. He had. By nearly two hours.

Cora Bates had taken it upon herself to call the *Clarion* that morning and explain the situation. She spoke to Robbie, who was as understanding as she could be. Robbie also promised to use the paper's influence to waive the RCMP's standard twenty-four-hour missing persons waiting period . . . if necessary. She believed the circumstances surrounding Nicole's disappearance would warrant immediate response.

Cora felt that this was at least a little optimistic news. And she wanted some to give to Travis this morning.

Travis threw on his clothes and hurried downstairs. He was angry, and by now confused. His thoughts were mainly on Nicole again, but on a less urgent level he also couldn't understand why Cora hadn't thought to waken him at a decent hour. And for the life of him he had no recollection, not only of how he'd gotten to bed last night, but of what had transpired after he'd come back from searching for Nicole. The whole succeeding period was like a blackout.

Cora, anticipating questions and perhaps an accusation, met Travis at the base of the stairs and presented him with her information before he had a chance to open his mouth. It wasn't really what he was hoping to hear, but it was something. A flicker of hope. She then offered breakfast, but Travis didn't want to lose any time. With just a hint of resentment in his voice he added that he'd lost enough already. He knew Cora meant well. Appreciated what she was trying to do. But this was *his* problem and he wanted no more "helpful" interference.

He was out the door without a goodbye.

First stop, the *Clarion*.

Cora had told him that Robbie would give him as much time off as he needed, but a check at the office was still necessary. There might be a lead there that could give him an idea as to Nicole's route. Those people certainly knew the region better than he did.

He'd never been in such a rush before. His co-workers' concerns reached him as soon as he stepped into the office, but good wishes were not what he could spare the time to stop and listen to at the moment. He went right in to see Robbie and nearly demanded whatever information she

233

could provide. He didn't care that she appeared engaged in some business at the moment. And neither did she seem bothered by his intrusion. She asked him to close the door and then sit down.

"The RCMP are sending some men up to scout the surrounding areas," she offered.

"North?"

"Seems the most likely direction for her to become lost." Robbie hesitated, then continued: "There's not a whole lot of manpower, though . . . and a lot of ground to cover."

Travis drew in an exhausted breath. "Come on, Robbie, you know I don't want to hear that."

"I'm not going to fill you with false hope, Travis," Robbie said in a practiced voice. "I'll keep the good thoughts, but . . . Well, for example, just look how Lloyd Caribou has managed to stay hidden."

Travis quickly responded, "But in his case it's intentional."

"We don't know what's happened to Nicole. Anything might . . ." Robbie didn't think it best she finish.

She didn't have to. Travis got her point and felt the nausea start to bubble. "Anything . . . including Lloyd Caribou," he said over a rise.

"Travis, we can't let ourselves go thinking that way either."

"Yeah," Travis said quickly, heavily. "But you also gotta be prepared, right?" He paused momentarily, looking back at Robbie with trouble-filled eyes. "Oh, Robbie, it's not possible that could be so. He's already killed a woman. Damn, Nicole probably forgot all about him—" With heat: "Because we've been neglecting him."

Robbie didn't want to lose her under-standing, but she couldn't allow herself to give proper acknowledgment to what he was saying. She spoke almost with a warning. "This is not the time to start bringing up politics."

"I think it is," Travis retorted thickly. "I think maybe it's the perfect time. Because maybe if we'd done our duty . . . kept the public aware of Caribou, Nicole wouldn't have gone riding off like that. So help me, Robbie, if that bastard's laid a hand on her this whole paper's gonna have to answer for it."

Robbie shifted in her seat, obvious in her struggle to retain her composure. "Look," she said, "we're jumping ahead to the worst possible conclusion . . . without any evidence to suggest that—"

"And maybe the most possible," Travis cut in. "I don't like thinking this way. But what else could have happened to her?"

"She could have had an accident," Robbie suggested, almost cheerfully. "A lot of these dinky side roads I wouldn't walk down, much less try to negotiate with a bike."

"Well, that is kinda what I've been thinking," Travis admitted, reluctantly. "But she's not a careless girl."

"No. But if that is the case, the police will find her."

Travis looked up. "Eventually. If she's not hurt too bad and hasn't bled to death," he said bitterly.

"When you came in here you asked me not to accentuate the negative," Robbie admonished.

Travis got the message. He nodded.

Robbie smiled gently, once more in control.

"I understand, Travis. It's just that it's not going to do you any good going off the deep end. You've got to keep a clear head through this."

Travis nodded again. Then he said: "Robbie, I just don't want to lose her."

Sharon was waiting for Travis as he left his office. She offered whatever help she could. Travis appreciated her consideration, but Robbie had already provided him with what he needed most: a map to photocopy which detailed the *Clarion*'s reporting radius. It was, she had explained, the most complete illustration of the area available, but even it was not exhaustive. There were just too many desolate dirt roads in the region.

"I can't get away now," Sharon told him. "But I know this country as well as anyone. If you want, pick me up at four and I'll guide you to some of the back routes."

"Thanks," Travis muttered. "I will." Then he left, looking lost.

Sharon watched him go. She truly felt for him. She couldn't imagine what he must be going through, but to see him looking so devastated upset her.

At the same time, she wasn't free of a strange sense of anticipation—one which she wasn't experiencing a whole lot of guilt over.

She wasn't holding out much hope for poor Nicole.

41

Lloyd had sat up with her all night. Nicole had herself convinced that she was being held captive.

Outside of his initial rasping of "Susan" there had been no other attempt at communication by him. Nicole had been just too afraid to speak.

This morning her head still hurt, and she was hungry. She didn't know where she was or what she was going to do. She worried over how Travis must be reacting to her disappearance. With the morning light she had gotten her first decent look at her captor, and she was repulsed. He was like some neanderthal. A true bushman. It hadn't yet occurred to her that he could be Lloyd Caribou.

All she knew was that she would have to be very careful. There was an unpredictability behind those squinting eyes that seemed to be always on her. She wasn't sure from one minute to the next what was going to happen to her.

As the shaft of light that streamed into the

back corner of the mill intensified, Nicole believed that it had to be sometime around noon. These past hours had been the longest of her life and she was starting to wonder how much longer she would be able to hold out. She knew that Travis must be looking for her. But how long until he'd find her? *Would he find her?* Oh God, she couldn't start thinking that way. Of course he'd find her. And soon. *He had to!*

Lloyd had kept a distance from Nicole ever since she had regained consciousness. He'd gone about doing little arcane duties throughout the morning but had never strayed too far from her. There were many times when he had felt the urge just to reach out and stroke her flesh, but each time he had resisted. Looking at Nicole he tried to remember. That single name, with the little significance it now held, kept returning to him: *Susan.* Somewhere there had to be so much more to it. But maybe he'd never find it. Never re-find it. He had become incapable of remembering.

The day progressed. Her captor still hadn't communicated with her, had made no effort to bring her food. If this kept on much longer she felt she'd starve.

And how much longer could he keep . . . *just looking at her?*

The shaft of sunlight was fading. The cold was deepening. Either starve or freeze to death. She had no way of knowing how low the temperature could drop tonight.

How was this . . . *person* surviving? Nicole couldn't help wondering. He was dressed in little more than rags but seemed unaffected by the cold. Had his living like this caused him to adapt? There was virtually no insulation from weather extremes inside this . . . wherever they were.

Soon night had fallen in its entirely. It had indeed brought with it a harsh cold. Nicole was cold, hungry, and desperately lonely and afraid. She missed Travis so much. Yet she was also angry with him.

Why hadn't he found her?

42

Nights preceding the coming of winter seem to descend upon Manitoba's northern regions unannounced. There is virtually no twilight as such, just a drop from day into night—so sudden one can almost hear the thud. From late September until the coming of spring an almost total quiet settles over Batesville streets after six at night. A form of evening hibernation becomes apparent. As the days of winter move closer and the dark falls yet earlier, homes are generally occupied by five-thirty. Most businesses recognize this and close for the night accordingly.

Travis hadn't even found a clue to Nicole's whereabouts. Driving all day, stopping, asking the same questions over and over. Nothing. The one minor bright spot of his day was when he had stopped to pick up Sharon outside the office and she had handed him a copy of that day's *Clarion*, the front page of which announced Nicole Randall's disappearance. Following her description, the article, in an almost personal tone, urged the paper's readership to provide whatever assistance it could. Travis suddenly could almost feel a respect for the *Clarion*. No, his respect went wholly to Robbie, who he knew had written it.

Sharon had been full of assurances for Travis, but by the time two hours of searching had passed, he was depressed and not receptive to much. Sharon had given him directions to some of the obscure roads, but there wasn't a lot of ground they could cover before the sudden darkness fell.

"I should have done some travel on foot," Travis muttered with disappointment as they slowly coursed what would have to be their last path for the night.

Sharon said, "Why don't you come back to my place? I think you should be with a friend tonight."

"I gotta check back at Valgard," Travis said quickly. "Maybe they've heard something."

"You can call from my place," Sharon suggested.

Travis paused, then said: "I wouldn't be much company."

"At least I'll be there for you."

They drove on further.

"Do you think we're going to find her?" Travis asked flatly.

Sharon was caught off-guard by the question; it was the first time she'd heard him admit the possibility of failure.

"You don't really think so, do you?" Travis then said in an accusing tone.

"Who's been telling you all night that she's going to be okay?" Sharon found herself replying.

"I know. But tell me, truthfully, in answer to my question. Up to now you've just been sympathetic."

"I can't give you a written guarantee if that's what you're after," Sharon said quietly as she took out a smoke.

"Yeah, that's what I want, all right," Travis admitted with an unfunny smile.

Sharon looked out the window into the sky. "At least it hasn't snowed yet. That's something."

Travis nodded. "But if it should before she's found . . . with the way everyone seems to think it's going to hit, what's she gonna do?"

There was news waiting for Travis at the boarding house. It was not, however, information that Cora wanted to pass on over the phone. Travis suddenly expected to hear what he had been fearing. Without a word to Sharon he rushed out of her apartment. She followed. He drove like a madman those few blocks to Valgard, squealing around corners and not bothering to stop at intersections. Sharon braced herself the whole of the ride.

She had a feeling that Travis didn't even know she was with him.

His total concern for Nicole was understandable . . . she supposed. But still so unnecessary. If only he'd smarten up and see that.

Travis screeched to a stop in his parking stall at the back of Valgard. Then, with a series of quick moves, he slammed the car into "park," flicked off the ignition, popped off the headlights, and scrambled out the door. Sharon knew he wasn't going to ask her to follow and so hastened out after of her own volition.

Travis burst inside the house. He called out for Cora.

Rosa met him in the kitchen. "Miss Bates is in the den."

Travis nodded his thanks and hurried to the den via the hallway. Cora was seated in her usual spot—in the heavy upholstered armchair by the Old World globe. She had an untouched cup of tea sitting next to her on the hexagonal end table. Maybe it was because Travis was expecting to hear bad news that the old woman looked strained and slightly lacking in color.

"Cora, what is it?" he asked urgently as he held his place in the doorway.

Cora looked across to him. Her face was grave. That alone told Travis what he didn't want to know; the old woman rarely appeared solemn.

"Sit down, Travis," she said.

Her voice wasn't exactly heavy with doom. Travis was sharp. "Don't make me wait."

Sharon came over and stood beside him. Travis was briefly startled by her presence here. Sharon had been right.

But she didn't care. She reached across and took his hand. No resistance.

"The police called with some news on Nicole," Cora said. "Now it's neither bad nor good."

"Well?" Travis said impatiently.

"They found the bike earlier tonight."

"Nicole?"

"No, just the bike."

"Where?"

"A few miles from town. On a dirt path."

When Cora offered nothing further Travis began to grow excited. "Well, was there any clue as to what happened to her?"

Cora slowly shook her head. "That's all I was told, Travis."

"No—blood, nothing?"

"Not that the officer I spoke with mentioned. He did say he'd like to talk with you, though."

"I'd like to talk to him," Travis mumbled. He then took a breath and said: "Well, at least if they found the bike they can narrow the search area. I just wish I knew what happened to her." To Sharon, tentatively: "You—don't think they'd be holding anything back, do you?"

Sharon hunched her shoulders. "Not if it was something they felt you should know."

"Yeah, that's right." Travis wasn't aware that he was perspiring.

Cora said, "I told Officer Bryant that you would be calling him as soon as you got in. The number's by the phone."

Travis quickly went to the hallway telephone and dialed the number that was jotted down on the notepad. He asked to speak to Officer Bryant, and waited impatiently while he was put through to him.

They talked for no more than five minutes. Travis received basically the same information as Cora. All Bryant would add was that it looked as though Nicole had had a riding accident. He further explained that her bike wasn't found buried deep in the woods as it surely would have been if her disappearance was related to an assault or abduction. Instead it was located just off the path, lying in clear view outside a line of trees. Officer Bryant offered to accompany him the following morning if he wanted to take a look at the site. Travis readily agreed. He then thanked the officer for his help and obvious concern.

But when he hung up the phone he was feeling even worse than before.

Why wasn't she with the bike?

PART IV

The Search

43

With the death of Harold Foley a detectable chill had accompanied further dealings that the mayor had had with his partners. Jessup had boldly anticipated no difficulty—and in the planning and execution of the "accident" there really had been none. But with the aftermath (at least with his circle) he couldn't count on the smooth running of affairs that he had hoped for.

Even Dr. MacFarlane, the one person on whom Jessup believed he could depend (regardless of the severity of the situation), had not maintained his potential. He would still meet with the mayor when summoned, but he no longer initiated such visits. Before that Saturday the mayor could expect at least one social call each week.

With Trelevan and Collarman, their changes in attitude followed the same general pattern. Any discussions with the mayor were made as brief as possible by them (and again not initiated by either), and were deliberately restricted to the issue at hand.

Alone, Jessup would ponder on his apparently deteriorating relationship with these men and wonder, in extreme moments, if this was not a prelude to a complete breakdown of trust. Perhaps conscience was a stronger force than he had ever realized. Stronger even than self-preservation. His concerns with Mac-Farlane he would not yet allow to reach that crucial stage. But with either of his other two associates ... there was rapidly developing a complete lack of assurance.

They simply were not proving themselves to be the strong men he had "needed" them to be. A major error in judgment? At such a late stage?

He was therefore understandably surprised when early one morning his receptionist buzzed to announce that Morris Collarman was requesting to see him. Jessup told her to send him in.

Collarman came inside the office and closed the door behind him. His face was set in utmost seriousness; there were no preceding amenities on his part. The mayor as well offered none, though he gestured for his visitor to take a seat.

Collarman spoke to the point. "Robbie just finished telling me that Travis Randall was speaking to her yesterday about his wife."

Jessup thought for a moment, then said; "Oh yes, she's missing or something, isn't she?"

That kind of callous attitude was what Collarman had come to expect from the mayor. But he nodded and went on.

"It's possible that Caribou might be involved." He waited for Jessup's reaction.

The mayor's eyebrows arched above his frown. He hadn't heard *that* name mentioned in a long while. He had hoped not to hear it ever again.

"No *proof* of any connection?" he said softly, in a less official tone.

"Not that I've heard. And there'd better not be either."

"Yes, agreed."

Collarman's eyes snapped over to him. "No, not just for the reason you think." He explained: "Robbie tells me that Randall threatened to make a little fuss if a connection turns up."

"What the hell for?"

"Our lack of coverage. Sweeping this whole Caribou mess under the rug."

Jessup waved Collarman's concerns aside. "The Indian's just desperate, looking for some way to vent his frustrations. There's no way he can tie the two together."

"Regardless, he's threatening."

The mayor sat back in his chair. "Well, you're his employer. Do something."

Collarman said nothing for a moment, then: "There is something I've been thinking of. And it's something that just might work to our benefit as well."

Jessup's eyes reflected his interest.

"Let's get him to work for us," Collarman proposed. "Explain the whole situation to him."

When the mayor saw no crack in his associate's expression, his own face broke in an uneasy smile.

"My God, Morris, you're serious."

"I am serious," Collarman said calmly. "Look, for one thing he could act as a liaison between us and the Chamrais when troubles start up. He speaks their language. We've never had that before."

"An invaluable asset, eh?" Jessup was rubbing his chin. "And you think he'd be willing to do that for us—as well as provide us with a 'specialized' reporting service—after he finds out we're liars and murderers?"

Collarman stood firm. "Well, of course we don't tell him . . . everything. But it's better than going the other route again. Or don't you think so?"

The mayor's expression hardened.

Collarman spoke less harshly. "You yourself have made it clear we're not the bad guys. If we explain to him why we've had to do certain things, he'll understand."

The mayor said, "I'm not convinced, Morris. We can't afford to expand this any further than we already have."

"Can we at least call the others in on this?"

Then Jessup smiled. "I have to be honest with you. I'm surprised you're feeling so strongly. It's not like you to initiate a solution."

"I have to. I don't want another life on my conscience."

"Instead you're willing to take a risk that won't just affect you, but the committee . . . and eventually the whole town."

"Like I said, if we tell him why, I can't see him not willing to help us."

"You really don't want more blood on your hands, do you? Be truthful, Morris, you're not that interested in having the kid work for us. It's just easier for you to deal with than the alternative. Now that he's threatening to make noise."

"That's exactly what I said. I'm not afraid or embarrassed to admit it. But the benefits are still there. I think we'd be wrong not to try to arrange something."

The mayor gave it a minute—all the time he kept his penetrating stare on Collarman. He then said: "All right. I suppose I can at least call a meeting. After all, we do have to help each other through this."

44

Travis and Officer Byrant arrived on foot at the spot where the bike had been found. The morning skies were overcast and there was a telling chill in the air. Travis was immediately receptive to the gloominess of the area; he felt somewhat moribund. He found it hard to understand how Nicole could have let herself travel down such a forbidding path. It was like a roadway to a cemetery, and Nicole was not the bravest girl.

Although the immediate area had been examined, Travis wanted to do some rechecking. Officer Bryant stepped back and let him. He knew he wouldn't find anything, but he understood it was something Travis felt he had to do. Travis Randall was not the first person he'd guided on a missing-persons case.

After about fifteen minutes Travis walked over to the young officer. Bryant noticed how his eyes continued to wander about the path.

Travis shook his head.

Bryant offered him a cigarette, which he

refused. The young officer then said, "You wanna know what I think? Your wife became disoriented after the fall and went off on foot to get help."

Travis could accept that. It explained why she hadn't climbed back onto the bike.

"You said it wasn't damaged?"

"Just some scraped paint," Bryant said. "Course that could have been from before. Old bike. Probably was. Anyway, that makes no difference one way or the other."

Travis nodded weakly. He again let his eyes trail the area.

Bryant dragged on his cigarette, said: "She's out here somewhere. Problem is, and I gotta tell you, we don't have the men needed to give these woods a quick yet thorough search. I think we'll find her ... but snows'll be here soon. Probably by the weekend." He looked up at the clouds. "Sooner. Listen, if you want my advice, don't depend entirely on us. Get a party of your own going."

This suggestion prompted Travis to call to mind someone he hadn't thought about for a long while: Marv Nelson. He was the only tracker he knew of. He remembered how when he had met him that night he had just come back from searching for Lloyd Caribou. He remembered how he had claimed to have a real knowledge of these woods. Travis didn't know who else he could recruit into a search team, but if he could persuade Marv Nelson to help, that might be as valuable as if he gathered a half-dozen men.

Cigarette smoke curled out through Bryant's nostrils as he finished on an apologetic note. "Wish I wasn't painting such a dark picture for you, fella. Thing is, I've lived through the winters up here. Just know, though, that the department's going to do everything it can."

"Appreciate it," Travis said softly.

Once Travis was dropped back in town he got himself ready to take another drive out to the Chamrais reserve. This trip took on a whole new importance for him: he wasn't even thinking about his concerns for the village.

He had a feeling that he was remembered by the people. As soon as he stepped from the Pontiac he was greeted with those same fixed, icy stares that he and Sharon had gotten after they barged in on the ceremony that night. No one spoke or tried to stop him, though, and he quickly made his way through the village center to the bushes that would lead him to Marv Nelson's shack.

It began to snow. Lightly. But it made Travis again realize how close he was cutting it. He hoped Marv wouldn't let him down.

When he got to the shack he rapped on the door. Waited. Knocked again. He had half-expected not to find Marv home, but that didn't lessen his disappointment. He remained standing in the cold, not sure what to do next.

And then he thought about that Chamrais couple.

Maybe they knew where Marv had gone.

They were probably the only ones in the village who could help him now. Who *would* help him.

He started back.

From a virtual drizzle the snow had begun to fall in more defined form. Still not heavy enough to cause alarm—but if it kept up, it wouldn't take long.

Travis remembered the cabin, and once he reached the clearing hurried to it. He knocked on the door, this time with a little more urgency.

It was the woman who answered and, judging by the neutral expression on her face, Travis couldn't be sure if she remembered him.

But she must have; she stepped aside to let him enter.

It was warm in the cabin. A fire was burning inside the stove.

"Your husband?" Travis asked once she closed the door.

The woman didn't answer. Instead she gestured for him to go stand by the stove. Travis did, warming quickly. But what he most wanted was for her to tell him where he could find her husband. He didn't want to become impatient.

The door opened and, with relief, Travis saw the man enter. He looked at Travis but recognition wasn't immediate. When he did finally remember, the man smiled—with the warmth one would extend to a long-absent family member.

Travis went to shake his hand, but he was waved down as if such formal greetings were not necessary between them.

Travis understood, took no offense. He said, "It's good to see you again, my friend."

The man went to pour himself a drink. Travis cringed inwardly but said nothing. He refused the offer to join him.

"I had hoped to see you again," the man said as he led Travis over to the ratty old couch that was pushed against the long wall.

Circumstances demanded that Travis come immediately to the point.

"I need your help," he said. "Do you know

Marv Nelson?''

The man looked across to his wife with an expression that for an instant seemed almost fearful. He took a swallow from his cup, grimaced.

"Yes," he then said. "I know him."

Travis went on. "I have to know where he is. Can you tell me? He may be the only person who can help me." He felt he owed an explanation. "My wife is missing. Has been for two days now. She's out in the woods somewhere, but that's a lot of ground to cover. I need someone who is experienced and knows the territory well enough to find her before the snows come. That's not much time, I know, but I believe Marv Nelson is the man I'm looking for."

There was a hesitation. Then the man said: "Marv Nelson has been gone a long while. He won't be coming back."

"I—don't understand," Travis said, and he found it hard to keep control in his voice.

Now the man thought there was something he should explain. "Do you remember when you were here that night?" he asked. "The ceremony you witnessed—"

"No!" the old woman shouted harshly, startling Travis.

The man turned to her with disapproval etched into his leathery face. "He gave me his word. I trust him."

There was no further objection.

Seconds of uncomfortable silence, then the man carried on. "The ceremony is an ancient one. There are many variations of it, yet each has a similar purpose. What you saw was done by us because of the man you are now seeking, Marv Nelson. Because of what he had set out to do.

All dances are performed to appease the Great Spirit. That night we were also asking Him not to hold the village responsible for the actions of one man . . . and to protect us from possible consequences."

"Consequences resulting from—*what?*"

"Marv Nelson's foolish attempt to track down and destroy an unkillable spirit. *The Weetigo.*"

Travis placed no importance on the name. The man understood and said, "I can't fault you for your ignorance. Where you come from tradition is no longer recognized or respected. But to the Chamrais people—there is no spirit more powerful than the Weetigo. It is a demon."

Travis couldn't afford the time to listen to Charmais myths. He spoke more impatiently than he had intended.

"I know it's important to you to hold onto your customs and traditions, but my concern is a little more urgent."

The man fell silent.

Travis felt immediate regret. "I didn't mean to offend, I'm sorry," he said as he began to rise from the couch. "Just understand that locating my wife is all I have on my mind right now." He took a breath. "And now that it looks like my getting help from Marv Nelson is out . . . I'm not sure what to do."

The man said nothing in response—offered neither understanding nor suggestion. He continued just to sit on the couch, straight-faced. Travis didn't have any doubt that he had insulted him. At the moment, though, as with anything else, it couldn't be a concern to him.

He thought he had better go. He said hurried goodbyes, which were not returned, and left the cabin.

It was snowing even heavier now. A thin, clean blanket of white already lay over the ground. Normally a pretty sight, but it brought a rise to Travis's stomach.

What was he going to do now?

45

Dr. MacFarlane and William Trelevan listened with interest to Collarman's proposal. Such a problem and such a solution were unexpected by them. Neither really had considered Travis Randall a potential concern.

After Collarman finished offering his proposition there was a quiet in the mayor's office. Jessup quickly glanced at the other two men, curious for their responses.

It was MacFarlane who spoke first, slowly, with consideration. "I suppose Morris is correct . . . about there being advantages."

Before Jessup offered his piece he looked to Trelevan and asked for his opinion. The mortician sat there with that perpetual, troubled frown on his face, apparently reluctant to commit to anything. Jessup pressed. Finally Trelevan said, "The problem will be getting him to agree."

"Exactly," the mayor snapped. "That's my concern. We can't make Randall a proposition until we've first laid everything out. Then, if he decides he wants no part, we really have something to contend with."

Trelevan nodded.

"It could be like pouring gasoline on a spark," Jessup added. "Who's even sure there's going to be a problem? The way I see it, the kid's just upset. In truth, gentlemen, I'm not overly worried."

"A threat is a threat," MacFarlane said calmly.

There was a pause.

"Yes, it is," Jessup said strangely.

It was no mystery to MacFarlane why the mayor had said that. He'd surely just been waiting for the opportunity. *The reminder.* The doctor regretted providing it.

The two exchanged a glance, but nothing was said.

Collarman spoke. "If he should turn down our offer—which I'm doubting very much—we'll just have to find a way to convince him."

"Money?" Trelevan suggested.

"That's one consideration," Collarman said. "Of course, I'd be offering him more than just money."

MacFarlane then said: "This seems to me a matter of choosing the lesser of two evils. We're guaranteed nothing either way, certainly, but if we can persuade the boy to come in with us—and yes, that really shouldn't be too difficult—that gives us the opportunity to have some watch and control over him. It does put us at a long-term risk, however."

"There is no easy way through this," Trelevan added.

"I still say we make him an offer," Collarman said firmly.

The mayor focused on MacFarlane. "Stewart, what is your definite position?"

"I say we go for it," he said. "At least there's an immediacy."

Next, the mayor's gaze went to Trelevan.

A nod, then the mortician added: "And for Stewart's reason. It means we'll sleep at night."

"Yes, persuasive argument, Stewart," Jessup said. "Personally, I'm still not convinced. But—majority rules, doesn't it? Okay, Morris, arrange to bring the kid in. We'll see what happens."

46

Officer Bryant had the windshield wipers going as he drove his cruiser through the snow up the narrow path that would lead him to within a mile and a half of the old sawmill.

He had a hunch that he wanted to play.

He could only drive in so far before the path became impassable by car. The rest of the distance he'd have to make on foot.

If Nicole Randall had found it, the mill would be the most likely place she'd be. He hoped she was there. It would be her only chance at survival.

Bryant tried to radio in his position but the harshness of the weather filled his two-way with static. He finally gave up and just climbed out of the car. Snow swirled around him in a near-blinding haze. He could see this easily developing into that storm he and everyone else had been expecting. He tightened his overcoat around himself and started off in the direction of the lake.

* * *

Nicole could hear the wind whipping outside. It made the old boards of the building sound as though they were about to be torn loose from their foundation. She knew that a storm was building, bringing with it the arrival of winter, and she felt herself rapidly losing optimism. There was no hope for her attempting an escape now; not knowing where she was, she'd certainly become lost in the snow. She really had no choice now but to wait for someone to find her. *Hope* someone would.

As if Lloyd Caribou had had a sixth sense about the weather, earlier that morning, while Nicole was still asleep, he had gone out to search for food. He'd come back mainly with vegetation, although he'd managed to catch a rat for himself. He laid the pile beside Nicole—as if he wanted to surprise her when she woke up. Her reaction was predictably neutral. She had no idea what that mixture of grass and roots was for. The last thing she would have guessed was that it was for her consumption.

Lloyd's first move toward communication had come when he tried to persuade her to eat. He pantomined the action—Nicole had understood, but she really hadn't yet reached the point where mud-laden grass looked appealing to her. What this seemingly thoughtful gesture of his did do for her, however, was lessen her fear of him.

Lloyd had gone off into a shadowed corner to enjoy his "feast." Nicole had begun to pace, from boredom and in an effort to keep warm. She heard obscene chewing and slurping sounds coming from Lloyd's corner but thought it best to keep her curiosity in check.

He wasn't gone long, and when he re-

entered her sight he was working on his last
mouthful, oblivious to the blood that dribbled
from the corners of his lips. Nicole caught a
glimpse, but quickly looked away.

Lloyd then froze, as if suddenly stricken
with paralysis. Even his chewing ceased. Nicole
looked back at him, tentatively, and watched as
his eyes veered slowly to the front entranceway.

"What is it?" she found herself saying in a
whisper.

Of course, Lloyd didn't answer. But his
squinting eyes darted over to her, took her in
with what she regarded as suspicion. She felt
herself beginning to tense.

In her mounting panic she began to shake
her head, and she mouthed: "No . . ."

Lloyd was on her, clamping his hand around
her mouth so quickly that she didn't have the
time to release a squeal. He started dragging her
over to the corner of the mill . . . to his "hiding
place."

Nicole tried to fight him off, but his
strength was augmented by his sudden desperation and her struggles were received as little
more than an annoyance.

Once close to the wall, Lloyd threw her free
with force and she crashed off the boards and
fell to the floor unconscious. Lloyd then went to
work lifting the loose floor planks. He laid her in
the hole, quickly re-covered it.

He then drew himself deep into the
protection of the shadows.

Officer Bryant burst into the mill—a silhouette standing against a background of
striking white.

Even before he was completely inside he
called out Nicole's name.

The wind blasted about him, causing him to sway in the doorway. He was exhausted from his walk and had to practically push himself all the way in. The storm was reaching its peak faster than he had anticipated. He was starting to wonder if it would be wise for him to attempt a return to the cruiser. Maybe a stay of the night here at the mill?

Lloyd listened carefully as the "intruder" carried out his search. Not being in the safety of his "hiding place" made him afraid.

Bryant had brought along a flashlight, which he shone into the dark corners. Lloyd could watch the trace of its beam, and he continued to tighten into his nook.

Bryant climbed upstairs and checked between the rows of surplus lumber. Then he descended the ladder and moved deeper into the mill.

"Hello!" he called again. "Nicole!"

Lloyd shot his gaze over to the floor planks. He watched them for a movement. There was none. *Yet.* Bryant walked to within feet of those boards.

He was clearly in Lloyd's sight. If he flashed his beam even casually in his direction he'd spot him. Lloyd was aware of the threat but wouldn't—couldn't—move.

The beam flashed in the opposite direction. Bryant held it steady as if he had picked up something. Then he started to slowly swing the beam across—directly toward Lloyd's corner. Lloyd saw it coming. He trembled, unsure of what to do.

Only inches from him—

Bryant let the flashlight drop to his side. He let out a sigh. There was no point in going on any further: Nicole Randall wasn't here. He thought how sad it was; she probably had never known how close she was to shelter.

He decided to attempt that walk back to his car after all. He didn't want to wake up the next day and find himself snowbound. The way the storm was continuing that was a definite possibility.

He went to the door, readying himself both physically and psychologically for that long walk back.

Lloyd heard the door blow open and then slam shut. He still held his position for a couple of minutes more, listening to the silence in the mill and the unsettling sound of the wind outside. Then he went over to the floorboards and pulled them up. Nicole was moaning, just starting to come to. He looped his arms under hers, pulled her up, and dragged her over to the wall, where he laid her on her back.

He replaced the planks.

Bryant pushed himself to move with some rapidity through the blowing snow. His vision was affected by the gusts of whiteness but he was sure of his direction. He was more concerned about the energy he was using up challenging the course of the wind.

There was a distinct sound to the wind—a lonely, prolonged whistle that was meant either to guide or taunt the young officer. Bryant thought, briefly, how continued exposure to that whistling could soon drive a lost man to desperation, and he tried to block himself from it.

The snow blanketing the ground would soon develop into deep drifts, but, for the moment,

Bryant's passage remained quite clear. If he had had that to contend with along with the wind he couldn't see himself making it. He was battling a force which had been building for this entry for weeks.

The high-pitched whistling kept at him, affecting him despite his blocking efforts and the knowledge that his cruiser was parked only a short distance away.

Perhaps it was because of his growing sensitivity to the wind that he was able to detect that foreign sound which insinuated itself into the domain of nature. The long, piercing cry blended in with practiced ease with the wind. But Bryant knew it didn't belong. It traveled with a long-established kinship, but that was only an illusion.

Bryant had grown up around these parts and was familiar with many of the legends of the north country. He was now remembering listening to the Charmais Indians as a boy . . . as they warned against becoming a lost traveler in the woods lest chancing to fall victim to the influences of *the Windigo*. The boogeyman that haunted every Chamrais child's dreams. As well as the dreams of many of the adults. He remembered the spirit's control of the elements, the deceptions it would use to lead one into its trap, the demonic powers it would then take hold of one with—the consuming of spirit and, eventually, body.

Bryant thought of how long it had been since he'd last given a moment to the legend. Remembering it, he now knew why.

He had reached the car.

And not a minute too soon, he thought. It had gotten as cold as he could ever remember it getting. Once inside, he started the ignition and then turned on the heat full force. He waited for the car to warm sufficiently before trying to again make radio contact with his detachment. Still heavy static. "Sonofabitch," he grumbled under his breath as he eased the car into reverse and looked back over his shoulder to guide himself out.

There was a flash of movement. One which Bryant caught so briefly that he could make out neither form nor direction.

His foot lifted from the accelerator.

It was as if the wind then rose in a crescendo, but it was not the wind. It was the sudden heightening of *that* sound!

Bryant's awareness had only a second to lock with it—

Before his door was ripped from its hinges as though caught in the vortex of a tornado-like power. The cold and snow blasted in, momentarily blinding the young RCMP. Maybe he was lucky for that—his mind never would have accepted what it was that had started to pull him free of the cruiser.

There was the somewhat hazy knowledge of his being in the grasp of something inescapable . . . the sensation of being lifted upward, ever higher until he could no longer be certain of the distance separating him from the ground.

Then a flash: a quick, blurred glimpse into the face of what had to be the devil himself.

Oblivion.

47

The storm had come and passed.

Two days of solid work were required to dig Batesville out of its memory. For Travis Randall it was a memory that would stay with him for the rest of his life. With the blizzard had come the realization that Nicole would not be found. Not alive. It was a realization that the pragmatist in him had to accept. But that didn't mean it had to come easily.

Travis never outwardly admitted his acceptance, but he didn't have to to gauge the feelings of others in the town. Those to whom he was the closest—while never coming right out and telling him of their certainty—reacted to him as though they were offering condolences. There was no bitterness, no animosity on Travis's part. He accepted their gestures for what they were meant to be.

Most of his time in these ensuing days was spent trying to build himself back up to work.

48

Morris Collarman had waited for just this time before summoning Travis to a meeting with the mayor's committee. In a pattern of thought worthy of Calvin Jessup, he believed that the boy might be in a more receptive frame at this emotionally fragile time.

The first meeting was set up: Friday, 2:00 P.M. Travis didn't show. A call to both the *Clarion* office and the boarding house produced nothing. Travis hadn't been seen at either that day.

Jessup said to Collarman: "The kid's starting to remind me of someone else with his irresponsibility." Then his gaze shifted to Trelevan, whose mind spotlighted on Keith Samuels.

Collarman as well had picked up on the mayor's not-intended-to-be-subtle allusion.

Trelevan responded quickly. "The kid's wife is dead. He's not thinking straight."

Jessup came back with the predictable: "Exactly."

"We can't classify the two together," Collarman said, defensively.

"We also can't gamble," was the mayor's retort.

Collarman broke. "You sonofabitch," he wheezed. "You had it in mind all along. You were just humoring us."

Trelevan shot the mayor a meekly challenging stare, which Jessup merely ignored. MacFarlane remained straight-faced: he never relied on such obvious tactics.

Jessup said to the group: "Wasn't our primary reason for going along with Morris's proposal *immediacy?*"

"Yes, yes," Collarman said, now feeling cornered. "But this business with his wife . . . maybe I was wrong to push it so close."

"He has our sympathy," the mayor said coldly. "But we have a consideration as well. One that extends a bit further than his."

"I suggest a week," MacFarlane said.

"And for us until then?"

"I'll keep an eye on him," Collarman said.

"Hell of a job you're doing so far," the mayor had to say.

"I'll handle it."

It wasn't quite a week. Five days. The following Wednesday. 9:00 A.M. There were no apologies, no explanations for his previous absence from the meeting. Nothing. Travis just presented himself at the mayor's office to listen to whatever it was they felt it so important they say to him.

Jessup, MacFarlane, Collarman, and Trelevan were all seated. For the first few moments following their cordial welcome and rather deliberate expressions of appreciation at his showing (there was no voicing of sympathy) an awkward silence hovered over the gathering. Regardless of whose suggestion this was, it was assumed that the mayor would speak first.

It was Jessup who began, and there was no beating around the bush. Very simply, but with a heaviness of tone that didn't belie his feelings, he said: "The committee would like you to work for us."

The committee. It was as if the mayor was excluding himself from this offer.

The confusion registered in Travis's expression was hard to interpret.

"I already have a job," he replied carefully. He glanced across to Collarman.

The publisher took over the reins. "Yes, and that wouldn't change, Travis," he said, speaking as though infused with a sudden burst of enthusiasm. "You see, the work we have in mind for you with our committee is . . . basically information oriented."

"An extension of what I'm doing?"

"Exactly," Collarman beamed.

"Well, what—would I be expected to do?" Travis asked with cautious interest.

The mayor jumped in, wanting no hesitation that might lead to suspicion of intent. "Act as a liaison, Travis. The committee and its duties are often in need of one."

Travis's eyes scanned each of the men in the office. All had practiced fronts.

"What we need, Travis," Collarman continued, "is, I suppose you could call it, a *filter*. More often than not, the wrong information seeps out. I shouldn't say 'wrong' exactly . . . it's just that prematurity results in misinterpretation. I'm sure you understand. The business of our committee is, at times, very complex."

"Why me?" Travis asked. "Why not someone more familiar with the politics of the town?"

Again Collarman answered. "In truth, Travis, you really are the only one we could consider. Ben Quarry is too close to retirement. Sharon Crane . . . well, she is an adequate reporter, but . . ."

Travis sat in silence. He wasn't buying any of this. Not for a minute. His being approached by this "committee" was for a reason far different from what they were handing him. He wasn't receiving their offer because of any great reporting ability. No, they wanted him for something else altogether. His curiosity had been piqued, however, and he was going to hear them out.

"You still really haven't told me anything," he said.

Collarman put on an embarrassed smile. "No, that's right, we haven't." His eyes fixed on his partners, then back on Travis. "Son," he said in a measured tone, "how familiar are you with the Chamrais Indians?"

Travis played ignorant. "Hardly at all," he answered with a shrug.

A pause, then Collarman said, "From what I understand, you are aware of the drinking that goes on at the reserve."

"Well, of course Lloyd Caribou," Travis said, maintaining a distance.

"Yes, I suppose that's the most flagrant effect you'd know of. But believe me when I say that never should have happened."

Travis's questioning eyes remained locked on his employer, who explained: "The Chamrais are given access to alcohol. But amounts are limited and their actions kept in check."

Travis felt the rush of an old indignation. "How are they getting this liquor?" he asked, almost as a demand. "Why?"

Collarman's voice was level. "A privately run distillery just outside of town provides it. It exists just for that purpose. The *why* . . . that's the reason we're making you this proposal."

"This still is operating . . . under *you?*" Travis ventured.

"Under the committee."

"Believe me, Travis," Collarman said, "encouraging alcohol abuse among the natives is not our objective."

"You're going to have to convince me," Travis said resentfully.

"That's precisely what we hope to do."

MacFarlane spoke. "Travis, our reason for allowing the Chamrais a liquor supply is based on necessity. It insures us that a potentially damaging secret concerning our region never becomes public knowledge. The Chamrais were the first to discover it, with incidents among their own. Then it extended to the town."

Travis regarded the doctor with impatience. "Cannibalism."

The room fell quiet.

MacFarlane went on. "Like a bad cold you thought wouldn't amount to much developing into pneumonia. It was something we thought was just an isolated occurrence . . . but it wasn't."

"Five cases so far," Trelevan offered.

Travis looked numb.

The mayor cleared his throat. "Now this is where it gets complicated. You see, Batesville is a town that's been dying a slow economic death for a number of years. Ever since our mill operations ceased. But none of us—here on the committee and a few others we've let into our confidence for practical concerns—was just going to sit back and let our community die. Through some complex financial maneuverings, courtesy of Mr. Collarman's office, we managed to postpone it year after year. But we still knew that was all we were doing: putting off what eventually was just going to have to be. Until we got together and looked seriously at our assets. Two in particular: a beautiful surrounding area and a crystal-clear lake with great fishing potential. Unfortunately—I'm sure because of our distance from provincial population centers—our tourist trade has been extremely limited. What we needed was to provide incentive. *Make* someone want to travel those extra miles. That was when we came up with the idea of building a luxury fishing lodge on the banks of Great Spirit Lake. Hotel, restaurant, souvenir shop, boat rental, and guide service—complete. And so far, from an economic standpoint, our venture looks promising. Morris—Mr. Collarman has had virtually no difficulty persuading investors. From outside the province as well."

"You didn't know about this—" Travis found he could barely say the word. "—*cannibalism* before you decided to go ahead with your plan?"

"No, we did. But as we said, after that first incident came to our attention we never expected it to happen again. An isolated case of madness, that was how we looked at it. But regardless, we still had to keep it under wraps. Surely you can understand when I tell you we wanted to avoid that kind of publicity. At that point we had made definite decisions regarding our enterprise and didn't want anything to discourage potential investors. Great Spirit Lake had to be kept as appealing as possible.''

Travis continued to listen, sitting without moving in his chair, looking as if in disbelief.

''By the time we discovered how serious this problem actually was we'd collected most of our backing and were preparing to announce publicly our intention to build.''

''You never looked for a reason as to why this was happening?'' Travis said.

Collarman was quick to put up his hand, as if he'd found a point with which to vindicate the committee. ''We paid medical men to fly up here,'' he said with emphasis. ''Paid them for *all* their services. But not one could even guess at a probable cause.''

''For all their services. They were paid to keep quiet?'' Travis surmised.

The silence that followed said all.

''What about him?'' Travis then said, gesturing to MacFarlane.

Collarman hesitated.

Jessup answered for him. ''Dr. MacFarlane has provided services in, uh, other ways.''

Travis nodded, again surmising. ''The falsifying of records?''

Jessup spoke with abruptness; it was important that the kid see there was a reason for every action the committee was ''forced'' into taking. ''What else could we do? Truthfully? If our . . . troubles were to become provincial news, which they surely would, we'd lose everything . . . not to mention having some very important 'businessmen' come down hard on us. Travis, there are millions of dollars tied up in this. Money that right now is not working to anyone's concern. But which soon has to be answered for."

There was so much Travis could say if he could afford to be just a little bolder. *Money working to no one's interest?* He doubted that. Very much. And he suspected "interest" was exactly the word.

"That's unfortunate," he said, still with not a whole lot of sympathy. "But as far as I'm concerned, that's not your major problem."

Again Jessup had a ready answer. "A lot of money has been spent trying to find the cause and, hopefully, a cure for this—*disease*. We certainly don't want to find ourselves faced with an epidemic, and, while that might sound premature, remember: it also hasn't lessened. It's just something that we have to handle ourselves. Without outside intervention."

"If the town dies, Travis, a lot of people lose. Not only will new jobs not be created, old ones will be lost by the score. What then for these people? Relocation to cities already plagued by mass unemployment?" This was spoken, solemnly, by Collarman, hoping to soften Travis by pointing out perhaps the most personal ramification.

"Something to consider, isn't it, Travis?" the mayor added, equally as solemn. "It's really the lesser of two evils, if you want to look at it that way. It's survival." He then spoke with enthusiasm. "And we can do it, Travis. My God, the future of Batesville looks brighter now than it

has for twenty years. But only because
sacrifices and compromises have had to be
made. May have to be made for a while yet. Tell
me . . . tell all of us it isn't worth it."

Travis didn't say anything for the next few
moments. When he did speak it was in a quiet,
contemplative tone. "What good is economic
survival if you can't control a threat which you
admit could conceivably reach epidemic pro-
portions? And how long before this does reach
other ears?"

Collarman said: "Your arguments have
been considered. The point is we couldn't do
anything different now if we wanted to—"

Jessup took over. "You've already pin-
pointed Dr. MacFarlane's main level of
participation. Falsifying death records, a very
serious offense. He'd go to jail for however
long—but worse, his credibility as a man of
medicine would be ruined."

Travis glanced at the doctor, thinking how
it was already too late to do much for his
credibility. MacFarlane caught his eye, read his
thought, and tried to remain unaffected. He
knew the mayor's using him as an example
wasn't just by caprice. He was making sure
there would be minimum opposition in the event
the kid decided against their offer.

The mayor concluded: "As for the rest of us
here, it goes without saying we wouldn't get off
any easier. And again, the bottom line, it would
be the town that would suffer. People who have
worked hard all their lives . . . people who have
believed in Batesville would be the true victims.
Understand when I say there can be no change
in our handling of the situation."

Travis shook his head, looked past Jessup

out the window behind him. "I still don't see how you've been able to keep it quiet this long."

Collarman said, perhaps a little too un-hesitatingly, "You haven't figured that out?"

Travis's eye caught the publisher's and in an instant he understood.

The *Clarion*.

How could he not have guessed? It all really fit so neatly into place. Why else did the paper instruct him to keep clear of the Chamrais reserve after Lloyd Caribou's rampage? As it had supposedly done earlier with Sharon. As *Robbie* had instructed. Robbie, he thought regretfully . . . he'd really come to respect her. and just who else was wrapped up in this web?

"We want you with us, Travis," Collarman said. "Everything's been put up front for you. We've taken a hell of a chance by doing so. I hope that gives you an idea of how much we want you to make the right decision."

"And if I decide I don't want any part?" Travis was curious to know.

"You have to make the choice, son."

Travis had the feeling he wasn't going to have much option in making his decision. As far as these men were concerned, his answer was given.

And it was, had to be, but not for the reason they thought. He'd go along with whatever the mayor and his committee wanted. For now. Then, when he had himself where he wanted . . . *he'd screw every last one of those bastards involved in the cover-up.* Blow the lid right off the machinations of the mayor's office.

Travis thought vengefully how they may have felt they had picked the right man to act as their puppet . . . but how soon they were going to regret their choice.

Because, regardless of what happened to her, *they* were the real killers of Nicole.

It wasn't until later that day that Travis made a further connection—one which he wished he hadn't. *Incidents of cannibalism. Nicole's disappearance.* The thought made him sick. But if what the committee was saying were true . . .

Lloyd Caribou.

Cannibalism.

Maybe a deeper connection?

Oh God, if there was, now he was going to find it.

He had to.

He owed it to Nicole.

49

Travis: "I don't know how I'd be handling this if I hadn't had that period of just not knowing. It gave me the chance to prepare myself. Because even though I tried to keep myself from thinking the worst . . . you can't totally ignore the possibility. When I did have to face the truth, it was almost as if there was the most natural transition of thought. I guess it's kinda like watching a loved one slowly die of cancer. Death comes almost as a relief because at least it's over. With Nicole . . . sure it's hard. But now I know."

Sharon, who was sitting on the couch beside Travis in her apartment, said, "I can't imagine what it would be like. Outside of my mother— and she died when I was so young—I've never lost anyone close to me. It has to take a lot of strength to make the adjustment. Strength I've always known you had."

Travis shook his head. "No, it's more the nature of my people to keep emotion inside. But don't be completely fooled by that. There are those private moments when I miss her so much I really think I'm not going to be able to go on. You always manage to survive, though, don't you? I think part of the reason is having someone to talk to. To collect the overflow. I know it's helping me. And Sharon . . . I do want to thank you . . . you know, just for being there."

"I'm always here for you, Travis." She reached across and took his hand in hers. He squeezed it. Tightly. Appreciatively.

"Thanks," he said.

"Have you thought of what you're going to do now?" Sharon asked. "You do plan to keep on at the paper?"

Travis hadn't told her anything about his being "approached," didn't plan to. He was practically certain Sharon had no involvement with the mayor's committee, but, despite her assistance in the past, on this one he was going all the way—alone.

"Not much else I can do," he answered simply. "Gotta keep busy."

"Staying on at the boarding house?"

"Yeah. For now."

Sharon then said, "You know, you don't have to."

"Huh?"

"If you find it hard because of . . ."

Travis understood. "No, that's not a problem. In truth, I don't really spend a lot of time there."

Sharon shifted a bit in her seat. "Look, what I'm getting at is that anytime you feel you'd rather not be there—" She patted the couch. "—there's always a bed for you here. No strings attached."

Travis wasn't quite sure what to make of

her offer, and so he just gave a smile and said, "You want to spoil me."

Sharon spoke gently, laying her other hand over his. "I think right now you could use a little spoiling."

For the next few moments they sat quietly. Then Travis started to rise. "I gotta go," he said.

Sharon experienced an inner chill. This wasn't what she wanted.

Travis caught her drop in expression and explained, "I've been here for most of the afternoon. You must be getting sick of me."

Sharon's features eased into a smile. "I—was going to ask you to stay for dinner."

Travis paused. "Dinner? Uh, what were you going to fix?"

Sharon paused. "Good question." Then: "How about we eat out? My treat."

"The cafe?"

"Best burgers in town."

Travis considered it. "Thanks," he then said, "but I don't feel like being on display tonight."

"Then we'll order out," Sharon suggested.

"They don't have a delivery service," Travis reminded her.

"Take out. How about it? We can walk down there and pick it up. I'll phone in the order first so we don't have to stand around and wait."

"Sure." Travis nodded. "Sounds good."

"Great," Sharon beamed. "Coats are in the closet."

As Travis thought about it, this could prove a productive dinner. Spending this time with Sharon might provide him with the opportunity to do some subtle probing and find out just how deep her knowledge of the politics of the town went.

50

Calvin Jessup sat alone in the gloomy dark of his office sipping on a glass of imported beer. He hadn't gone for dinner and probably wouldn't this night. He was listening to the faint breathing of the wind outside his window, though oblivious to the snow swirls carried with it.

He still wasn't comfortable with the committee's move. Perhaps it was because he prided himself on being an accurate judge of character that he remained convinced they had made a mistake. A major error that could, in all probability, come back to haunt them in a year, a week—*even a day*. Maybe the others were too caught up in their collective concern to see, but he'd certainly detected an insincerity to that Randall kid's acceptance earlier today. He seemed to give it just a little too quickly, especially after the mayor had noted that all preceding signs seemed pointed to a definite "no." It was as if the kid agreed to come in with the committee for reasons of his own. Such as maybe using this "in" to do some digging to find out more about their affairs.

That was exactly what the mayor had been afraid of. Now he was worried.

And thoroughly angered with his partners for forcing him to go against his better judgment.

Unfortunately, the damage had already been done. There was no point in again voicing his concerns with them. Any move now decided on would have to be carried out without their participation . . . or knowledge.

And Mayor Jessup found himself beginning to think seriously about just such a move.

51

Travis didn't begin asking careful questions until their dinner was almost finished. Mainly because he needed the time to think of the best way to broach them—without being too obvious in his concerns.

It wasn't that Sharon was uncooperative really. More uninterested. Talking about the town and, in particular, the mayor's office, seemed to hold no appeal to her tonight, and most of the answers she gave Travis found vague and unproductive. This pretty well told him that there wouldn't be much she could provide him with.

Travis left shortly after nine-thirty. It had been a long day and he was tired. Sharon had offered to let him stay the night, but this time he was adamant about overstaying his welcome. Besides, he just wanted to get home.

He told her he'd see her the next day at the office.

It was quite a lovely night. Peaceful. The wind had ceased and the temperature was just right for a brisk walk. The streets were empty, pretty. The light snow that had fallen earlier glistened softly under the bright starlight. Travis paused at the intersection and looked down the main road. The simple perfection of the scene reminded him of those little plastic snow shakers with the miniature village encased inside.

It also made him start thinking of Christmas.

For just an instant he experienced the warmth of good feeling.

Then he once more remembered.

Merry Christmas.

He was alone on the street but still clenched his jaw against the tears that were beginning to squeeze out of his eyes.

"Oh God," he said in a tremble as his wall of resistance crumbled.

The snow began to fall again.

52

The mill.

About all that Nicole was doing was surviving. She had no choice about that. "Living" as such had been taken away from her. Perhaps "existing" was more appropriate to describe her situation.

The days had passed—though after a while time had lost its meaning to her. She had lost hope of rescue. Had been forced to eat whatever "food" her captor was able to scrounge up. In short, she was sharing his life.

Although the passage of time had made her less afraid of him, the one fear that was constant, that she couldn't seem to rid herself of, was that most basic dread of any woman who might find herself in similar circumstances.

No attempt had been made. But sometimes the way he let his eyes fall on her . . . the way he moved toward her. It was as though the impulse was there, but there was just enough doubt . . .

The urge was indeed inside Lloyd, and it wasn't some twinkling of retained morality that kept him from taking her. He was held back partly by a memory that wasn't clear in his mind.

And he sensed a danger accompanying such an action. One that he feared as much as he feared anything.

Nicole was beginning to feel the effects of her confinement in other ways. Physically she was growing ever more fatigued. As a result, determination had given way to acceptance of her situation. She wanted to survive, but death was no longer looked upon by her as a black villain. Lately she had come to regard it as possibly her only escape route.

The mill was cold but, as with her captor, prolonged exposure had begun to numb her to its effects. Lloyd tried to keep her as warm as he could, but short of starting a fire there wasn't much he could do to provide comfort.

Boredom and periods of desperation had prompted attempts at conversation by Nicole. Lloyd never responded . . . even though Nicole felt it in her gut that he could understand every word she said. A few times frustration brought her to confront him with that suspicion, but still—no acknowledgment. Barely a flicker of expression.

And then Nicole would begin to cry and Lloyd would duck away: either to allow her privacy or because it was an emotion he wasn't able to handle.

It was both basically, although it was the tears he most wanted to avoid. He feared them because of what they might evoke in him. Thoughts that had become fragmented, shadowed images. Of a past that now might have existed only as a dream.

He didn't want the memory!

Wanted nothing to force it from the black clay of his unconscious where it had so long ago settled . . . though disturbances had occasionally rocked edges to the surface.

Perhaps his very existence depended on his maintaining it there.

53

As usual Robbie was the last to leave the *Clarion* office. Travis, secured in an apartment building foyer across the street, watched as her Mercury came around the corner and disappeared down the main street. He then rushed over to the back of the *Clarion* building and used his key to enter.

He was nervous about doing this.

It was a long shot, but he was hoping to find the name of just one of the cannibalism victims in the paper's files. He knew there would be no obvious mention; what he was chancing to come across was maybe a slight discrepancy in one (or more) of the obituaries. Something that only a searching eye might pick up on.

With the aid of a small flashlight he searched the obit file drawers for close to an hour—finding nothing. It was just too easy to fake a death notice. *Suddenly, peacefully, after a lengthy illness, accidentally.* Travis couldn't help believing that accidentally would be the least likely term for the committee to use. Then again, maybe its very obviousness provided a protective blanket.

Not many people had died of accidental causes in Batesville. At least not in the past two years, which was as far back as the records contained in this set of drawers extended.

He had no luck covering this route.

Maybe the lack of injurious deaths wouldn't give them much of a cover.

The cannibalism cases had to be buried somewhere within the more general, non-violent causes of death . . .

But this as well got him nowhere. Each obituary he studied was worded in the same computerized way: impersonal, matter-of-fact.

Dead end.

Travis was discouraged. Now he'd have to hope for another entry. If he could think of one.

He began putting the files back into the drawers, carefully, in their proper organization. Occasionally stopping to take a quick repeat glance through one. Just in case.

He flipped through some typed copy . . . and suddenly came to a stop. An iceberg of a chill swept through him as he stood, paralyzed, gazing at the name of

NICOLE RANDALL

A brief obit notice that had been prepared, but had not yet been printed. As if the paper couldn't wait for the news of the discovery of her body. Just like buzzards hovering patiently over their prey.

Travis clenched his teeth.

"Bastards," he gritted. "Cold-blooded bastards. Every last one of you."

54

The mayor was seated in the greasy back office of "Big" Roy Cohen's garage. For a man who placed so much importance on accumulating and maintaining life's delicacies, spending any length of time in such "lowbrow" surroundings was a test in endurance.

Roy was drinking cheap whisky that he poured into paper bathroom cups, one for each straight shot he consumed. The floor around him was littered with the hand-crushed cones.

The mayor was not drinking.

He cleared his throat before he resumed speaking. "As far as the committee's concerned, there's going to be no secret after the news of the boy's 'accident.' But I'm not losing sleep over that."

Roy tilted back on his chair behind a desk that was missing one leg and had to be supported by a stack of *National Geographic* magazines. The ample bulk of the man predicted an eventual similar fate for that chair which he was abusing.

He snorted. "Yeah, but I need a more solid guarantee, Mr. Mayor . . . for m'self. How'd ya just put it to me? A—a weakening of the links, wasn't it? Colorful language, Mr. Mayor, but still clear as a bell to me."

"I'm giving you a personal guarantee, Roy," the mayor said, fighting another grimace.

Roy lit up a vile-smelling cigar. He thought about it. Then he laughed. "Y'know, goin' down with class don't make it any more respectful. Ya still end up in the same place. Yeah, kinda like—what do they call it?—the least common denominator."

The mayor forced a smile, for added reassurance. "No one's going down, Roy. The committee will stick together on this just like it always has. There might be a few tense moments, but they'll be handled."

Again Roy stopped to consider. He made what sounded like grunting noises while he chewed on his cigar. Jessup half-expected to see the fat fuck start drooling. Damned if he could figure out how a man like him could be so respected and admired in town.

"An' money?" Roy asked.

"You'll be paid. Same as usual."

Roy twisted open his mouth, slowly shook his head. It was time for the lowbrow to do some bargaining with the big shots. "No, uh, I don't think so, Mr. Mayor," he said. "Let's consider this—a premium job."

Jessup felt his ire beginning to rise, but it was important he keep his temper in check; he was the one in charge here.

He raised a bit higher in his chair. "There'll be no more difficulty involved in this one than—"

"No, not in the execution," Roy interrupted. He thudded forward with his chair, then began rubbing a sausage-like finger through the dust which seemed to grow out of his desk like moss. "But let's just look at this increase as . . . a bonus. Or, if you like, a more substantial part of this guarantee you're offerin'. Just in case those 'tense moments' don't go away."

The mayor was beginning to lose the reins on his control. "I told you that's not going to be a concern," he said in a raised, irritated tone.

Roy just smiled.

The mayor waited for a few moments. Then he spoke more professionally again. "How much more?"

"Why don't you make me an offer?" Roy said with arrogance, confident that it was he who now held the upper hand. He was curious to see just how far he could go with this *man of importance*.

"I have no idea—"

Again Roy interrupted. "*You* have no idea?" he said with a mock incredulity. "You, Mr. Mayor, who's based his whole life around the making of money? Come on, I'm no fancy college student, sure, but you can't start handin' me crap like that. No sir, Mr. Mayor. Now I know you can make me a fair offer."

The problem was, and Jessup knew it, that Roy didn't have his sights set on a "fair" offer.

"You're talking almost like you've got something else on the brain," the mayor probed.

"Yeah?" Roy said, interested. "Like what?"

"Blackmail."

"No real need for that now, is there?" Roy returned simply.

Jessup's eyes narrowed. "You tell me."

Roy emitted a short laugh which was intended to wrap up this branch of the conversation. Then he said: "Y'know, if we find we can't come to mutually agreeable terms—well, you can always do in the kid yourself. Might find ya actually enjoy the 'workin' side of it. I'll tell ya somethin' I read lately . . . see if it maybe applies to this whole little talk we're havin'. It's got to do with this change in capital punishment in the States. This magazine I was readin' did an interview with a former death-house executioner —the guy, of course, was talkin' anonymously. Anyway, at one point of their talk the guy's asked his opinion about this option condemned men are given: death by injection. An' you know what he answered? He said that was the reason he left his job. The thrill was gone from it. Since most were choosin' that way to die, he was losing out on that immediate excitement of pullin' the switch to the electric chair. He no longer had that feeling of bein' completely in control of the last seconds of some sucker's life." He paused to look at the mayor, who wasn't looking at him. "Think about it. You know what they say about samplin' your own shine." He guffawed heartily.

Jessup's eyes snaped up at Roy; they were as cold and hard as metal. Roy just grinned. He poured some more booze into a fresh cup, offering a shot to the mayor, who didn't ease his glare.

"You'll get your price," he then said bitterly.

"Knew I would," Roy said, raising his glass in a salute. "*L'chayim.*"

55

To get anywhere in his hope to expose the mayor's committee required that Travis remain cordial and cooperative at the *Clarion*. This was particularly hard now, after his previous night's find in the obit file.

Although never directly approached by her, Travis could tell that Robbie knew he was in with the committee. She seemed to be coming out of her office more, throwing furtive glances his way. He caught them all, though he never let on.

It was a situation that filled him with impatience. Talking to Robbie might provide him with just the information he was looking for. But he couldn't chance making the move because of her obvious deep involvement with Jessup's group.

He wished there were some way he could subtly persuade her to come to him.

"Hey pardner, goin' for lunch?"

Travis looked up at Sharon. She was wearing a camel-colored Stetson, almost identical to the one he owned.

He was more taken aback than amused, even though he couldn't have brought up a laugh had he wanted to. He had to force his smile.

Sharon flicked the Stetson up over her brow. "You hang around someone long enough and his idiosyncrasies begin to rub off on you."

"We wouldn't be hard to pick out of a crowd," Travis remarked, just to say something.

"Well, how's about we double up and hit the chow trail?"

"Yeah, sure." Travis sounded hesitant.

He wished it were possible to ask her about Nicole's inclusion in the obit file. Whose idea it was, who wrote it. That he felt she did know.

Sharon more than knew about it. It was she who had badgered Robbie for permission to write it. Robbie hadn't even considered sketching an outline when Sharon had come to her. There was little question that Nicole Randall was dead, but preparing the notice before the official word was received had seemed rather ghoulish to Robbie. Sharon's insistence had been deliberately aimed to wear down the editor. And she had been convincing: claiming that preparing the notice at least would save them a difficult task later on. That argument had convinced Robbie and she had given her approval, though still with reluctance.

So Nicole Randall was dead. Writing up the notice had made it definite in Sharon's mind. Since it was only a notice it was composed in the typical style. But just typing the name NICOLE RANDALL above the paragraph had made this perhaps the most special piece of writing she had ever done.

Travis's reticence at lunch made Sharon think he was merely having one of his blue days. That was no problem; she could wait for such times to clear from his system. And in the meantime offer understanding, which she was in no short supply of. Travis made not the vaguest attempt to let on what was really upsetting him. He maintained an unaffected, though slightly thoughtful, expression all through lunch. He was holding the unlikely hope that Sharon might offer something just for conversation.

Unfortunately, anything she said had about as much value to him as her answers at dinner the other night.

In so many ways Sharon was becoming like excess baggage. A burden.

"Well, loose lips," Sharon said after their lunch was finished, "I hope I didn't bore you."

Travis wasn't much in the mood for her sarcasm either.

He glanced at her over his coffee cup but didn't offer a response. Another strained smile instead.

Sharon lit a cigarette, blowing her first inhaled smoke out of the side of her mouth away from Travis.

"Sometimes you're not the easiest person in the world to converse with," she said.

It was getting harder for Travis not to give in to the frown that was trying to work out of him.

Sharon paused, then spoke sympathetically. "Look, you wanna talk?"

"Not today."

"Then why'd you come with me for lunch?"

Travis shrugged. "Wanted to get out for a while."

"The way you're obviously feeling you'd do better to be on your own today," Sharon commented.

Travis felt a tightening in his jaw. "Let's just get off it, okay?"

Sharon started to slide out of the booth. "Sure," she said, more hot than hurt. She hesitated before getting to her feet. "Just remember, Travis Randall, you do have a willing ear."

She went to the cashier to pay their check.

Dammit, Travis thought, if only he *could* talk to her.

Chance had never played much of a part in Travis's life, but this afternoon it was as though fate had decided to give him a break—albeit a rather questionable one. Shortly before quitting time on this dull day at the paper, Robbie popped out into the news room and asked to see him in her office. Once he was seated before her desk she pulled out a manila folder which he recognized only too well. He was careful not to let anything slip by his expression.

"Travis," Robbie began with what he perceived as discomfort, "there's something in this folder my friendship for you tells me shouldn't be shown you—yet, but the editor in me thinks it only fair I do show it to you."

Travis kept his eye on the folder and tried to ready himself for the proper reaction with which to respond.

"This was written up several days ago," Robbie said as she removed a sheet of newsprint. She didn't know what else she could say and so just handed Travis the copy.

He took it, convincing in his tentativeness.

"Nicole's obituary," he said in a whispered tone.

"No. Notice," Robbie corrected, as if it really made any difference.

Travis again perused it. Once more he felt both his anger and his stomach try to get away from him.

Robbie watched his expression. He just sat there looking numb.

She made another attempt at an explanation. "Major media centers generally prepare obits of important people in advance: background details, highlights of their career. Updates are frequently required to include developments in later years. It's a necessary practice; it doesn't leave the news agencies dangling and rushing to put something together when a death does occur. Our doing that with Nicole was basically for the same reason . . . except somewhat more personal. When the final news does come it's going to be hard on everyone around here. Believe me, I know. I put Harold's obit together."

Travis, eyes still directed down at the paper, cleared his throat. "Yeah," he said lowly, his voice raspy. "But like you said, Robbie, this is only a notice. The obit itself still has to be written."

Robbie nodded, stepped behind her desk. "That could be put together now too."

Travis sat straight in his chair. "Nicole is dead, we all know that. But does she have to be buried before her body's even been found?"

"All I'm saying is that it could make it a little easier."

"Was this your idea?" Travis asked, waving the paper at her with not-very-well-restrained hostility.

Robbie took a minute before answering.

"No. But I approved it."

"Then who . . . *who did this?*" he demanded.

Robbie couldn't give a name. Even if professional ethics weren't involved, Travis's present state didn't warrant such information.

But it didn't have to be offered. It was clear. Had been staring Travis in the face all along. Maybe it was that he just didn't want to see. Didn't want to believe it.

His eyes were locked on Robbie's, his stare penetrating. "Sharon . . . came to you?" he said.

He wanted to know.

Robbie acknowledged, nervously. "But I gave the approval," she repeated with emphasis.

Travis remained seated. He tried to make some sense out of the kaleidoscope of thoughts that were spinning furiously inside his head. Random ones he grabbed: questions . . . Why would Sharon do something so deliberately cruel to him? How could she "bury" Nicole and in the next instant come on all fun-and-games with the quick talk and the Stetson . . . and the oh-so-sincere promise of always being there for him?

About the only thing definite Travis could form out of this jumble was that . . . Sharon was still the disturbed girl he once thought she was. That he had been talked out of believing she was.

He could control himself no longer. The confusion and rage were an overpowering combination. The expression on his face had become like that of one possessed. He was out of the chair and heading for the door.

Robbie moved round to the front of her desk.

"Travis?" she called after him.

He stopped at the door, turned to her.

"No one meant to hurt you," she said.

He looked at her for just a moment. At that face so "obviously" full of sincerity.

Then he slammed out.

Ben Quarry was the only one in the office, seated at his desk taking what appeared to be an important phone call. Travis glared at him. But it wasn't necessary he disturb him to find out where Sharon had gone. It was five minutes after five.

He grabbed his parka and Stetson from off the coat rack and hurried out.

56

The search for the missing Officer Byrant coincided with the RCMP's continuing efforts to locate the body of Nicole Randall. A week had passed before Bryant's cruiser was discovered at the far end of a heavily snowed-in path. The car had been abandoned while still running, geared in reverse, and had angled off the path until its rear fender had made halting contact with the stump of a tree. The fuel gauge registered empty.

And the driver's door looked to have been . . . *ripped* off!'

It was this more than the other baffling indicators that prompted speculation among Bryant's colleagues. And speculation not of a hopeful nature.

One relatively positive theory presented at the site was that the force of the previous week's storm was responsible for the damage to the cruiser . . . and that Bryant may have panicked and rushed to the more substantial shelter of the old mill. There perhaps becoming snowbound.

A search team would have to be sent out to check this possibility.

"What d'ya figure he was doing out here?" one young officer asked. "And why didn't he bother to radio in his position?"

"He was probably looking for Caribou," came a reply. "That sonofabitch has been a thorn in the whole department's side."

It wasn't that long of a walk to the sawmill, but the surrounding ground conditions were worse than anticipated, certainly not allowing for easy access, and none of the officers were prepared for the trek. Proper boots and protective outer garments were required, which necessitated a return to the detachment.

Sergeant Gary Connors was presented with their find. He agreed to the request for a search, but could only spare two men. Officers Reichert and Hovemeyer were assigned: the former a fourteen-year veteran, the latter a graduate rookie. Both were instructed to keep together at all times and to maintain radio contact with a unit that would be on patrol in Batesville. It would be long into nightfall before they would even begin their search; Connors didn't want to chance losing any more men . . . to the elements or whatever else might be out there.

Including Lloyd Caribou.

57

Lloyd wasn't relaxed tonight.

The perception he had developed and honed beyond his five senses warned him of a danger. He couldn't identify the enemy, however, and this made him unsure of how to respond.

Nicole, huddled in her corner, watched Lloyd. She had become attuned to his feelings and emotions through the development of her own sixth sense, and this evening she was once again filled with a fear of his unpredictability.

Lloyd's sense of peril heightened as the night progressed. He was now visibly demonstrating his apprehension: repeatedly rushing over to the eyehole that he'd cut in the wall to peer outside.

The night was still. On the surface as peaceful as a winter's evening could be.

But something was out there. Waiting. Something that meant to hurt them both.

58

Travis ran all the way to Sharon's apartment building, pushing himself even as the breaths had to be ripped raw from his lungs.

Once there, he burst in the back way and rushed upstairs, taking the steps two at a time. He wasn't allowing himself to think with rationality about this; he was incensed enough to throttle her at the door, and he wanted to maintain the feeling.

He came to the door. There, for the first seconds since leaving the *Clarion*, he hesitated. He raised his fist to strike the door, and just held it in position. Several good swallows of air, then he followed through.

Sharon had just finished dinner: half a tin of flaked tuna with two slices of unbuttered whole wheat bread. She was starting to undress for a shower when she heard the heavy banging at the door.

She walked over, re-buttoning her blouse as she went.

"Who is it?" she asked cautiously before removing the chain.

"Travis."

"Travis?" she echoed with mild surprise. She hurriedly unlocked the door.

Travis's greeting expression was more grim than angry. Sharon could tell right away that something was wrong. She wasn't comfortable with the feeling that accompanied that knowledge.

He didn't say anything, just stared at her with accusing eyes.

Sharon was actually a little hesitant, but she invited him inside. Asked if she could get him a coffee or something.

He stepped over her threshold, with the back of his hand closing the door behind him.

Then he spoke.

"You reminded me of something I never should have let myself think differently about." His anger was clear, though there was control in his tone.

"Travis?" Sharon said with wide-eyed, innocent concern. Her hands went up to touch his face.

"No. I don't want that," he said sharply as he brushed her arms aside. Then: "But that's what you've wanted all along, isn't it? Yeah, I guess I should be flattered. You really went all out to continue living this fantasy."

Sharon's face was a mask of troubled confusion. She continued to regard him with worry. But Travis wasn't blind any longer—he knew it was just a game to make him start thinking he was the crazy one. She was full of such games.

"I—I don't know what you're talking about, Travis," she said, struggling to keep sincerity in her voice. "Why are you saying this? Why do you want to hurt me?"

Travis nodded expectantly. "I forgot about your little episode at the reserve; you did a good job getting me to forget . . . and I guess I didn't want to lose that relationship we had established. It meant something to me. But all along I've just been part of this sick game you're playing. A friendship, Sharon, that's all it ever was." He finished with emotion, "I was satisfied with that. Why couldn't you be?"

Sharon had ceased hearing him. All she could think of was how wrong this was. Why was it happening? Now that there could be that chance at a future for them.

Why was he hurting her?

Not now.

Not when everything could be so right!

"What have I done, Travis?" she suddenly screamed, flinging herself at him with fists at the ready. *"Why do you hate me?"*

Travis grabbed her arms and began to apply pressure to her wrists. She was trying to fall limp into him but he held her up—kept her away . . . and continued to squeeze his grip.

"Ow," she whimpered. "You—you're hurting me."

Travis wasn't listening. His features were tight but expressionless as he started to slowly turn her arms inward, forcing her down to her knees.

"You're hurting me, Travis," she sobbed. "Please . . . stop."

And then her whole body tensed like a panther getting ready to strike and she looked up at him with a crazed grin stretched across her tear-stained face.

"No Travis," she said in a hiss. "If that's what you want, hurt me." She began to laugh—prolonged shrieking that abruptly became short, choppy cackles.

"I mean it, Travis. Hurt me. I—won't try to stop you."

Travis stiffened.

What in God's name was he doing?

He actually wanted to hurt her . . . and here she was begging him to do so.

He looked down at her. Her head was again bowed, lolling drunkenly. Travis's expression melted into pathetic bewilderment.

She had her arms wrapped around his legs—tightly, desperately. Then she started to lick his crotch region. And was moaning . . . with pleasure.

With disgust he forced himself free, and she fell almost comically face-forward to the floor. He slowly backed the few steps to the door, now regarding her with contempt.

"*Travis!*"

Then she spoke in a sensuous whisper. "Don't go. It's just us now. Just as we wanted it to be. No more Nicole. Nicole's dead, Travis . . . I wrote up her death notice."

Travis felt himself ready to vomit. At the moment there was a frightening saneness to her voice that made what she was saying all the more disturbing.

He fumbled for the knob, the moisture in his palm not enabling him to get an immediate firm grasp on it.

When he finally did get a grip on it, he yanked open the door. Rushed off down the hallway.

Sharon slithered out after, just past the

doorway, still talking in a whisper even though he was long gone.

"I love you, Travis. I've always loved you."

Sharon lifted herself from the couch where she had been sitting trance-like for the past half-hour.

She went stiffly to the bathroom. She turned on the sink faucets, filling the basin, and then began washing her face. She massaged the soap into her skin, finishing by splashing on warm water to rinse off the lather. She patted her face dry with a thick towel.

She walked into the bedroom, going over to the vanity table. She sat herself on the stool before the oval mirror and looked emptily at her reflection. Her hand, with widespread fingers, slid along the polished surface of the table for her make-up.

Just a smear of shadow. A stroke of liner. A faint smile came to her face.

She brushed on a whisper of blush. Gazed back at her reflection.

Lipstick. She had some open but chose a fresh tube. She rolled out the bullet, traced it along the curve of her lips—lightly but firmly. Again she regarded herself in the glass, gazing at her reflection for a long while, not altering her placid expression.

Then she rose off the stool. Now she was smiling—but at something very private. That she could share with no one . . . even if she could define what it was.

She padded into the next room, over to her stereo and record collection. Her choice was already made. She carefully removed her Barry Manilow album from the pile, just as carefully drawing the record from its sleeve and then from its cover. Holding it by its edges with her fingertips, she gently set the record on the turntable, and then she adjusted the switch to "automatic."

She returned to the bathroom just as music began filling the apartment.

She left the bathroom door open.

She again filled the sink basin with warm water.

She slid open the vanity above. Her hand reached in an came out with a pair of point-edged scissors. She opened them to their widest separation, turning one of the sharp edges deliberately inward, as if to use as a knife.

She was still smiling as she turned her right wrist inward to meet the steel. Initial contact was tentative.

She closed the fingers of that hand and tensed, making a tight fist. The tendons and muscles in her wrist bulged. She was certain she could see her veins throb.

In smooth harmony she lowered both her wrist and the scissors held firm in her other hand into the warm water.

Then she pressed the steel deeper into her flesh . . . and with a swift single motion drew it across.

There was only the briefest flinch in her expression. A psychological wincing. What she had heard was true: there was no pain.

She brought herself to gaze down into the basin.

Already the water was a swirling crimson.

Barry Manilow's melodic voice swelled in a crescendo.

An abrupt end.

59

Travis wasn't given a lot of time to dwell on his disturbing episode with Sharon. As soon as he got back to the boarding house he was given a message by Cora that Mayor Jessup wanted to speak to him. He had said that it was urgent. Cora seemed impressed that Travis would receive such a call, but Travis, although he might at one time been flattered to be personally sought out by the official, returned it only out of the most private sense of duty.

"Mayor Jessup, Travis Randall," he said into the receiver after the connection had been made.

"Travis, yes. We need you out at the Chamrais reserve. Right away." There was a practiced sense of immediacy to Jessup's voice: meant to convey urgency, but not excitement.

"Trouble?" Travis as well kept a deliberate base in his tone.

"We just got a call. We don't know exactly all the details but it sounds serious. Collarman's already on his way. He'll meet you out there."

"Okay," Travis said, and he hung up.

Roy Cohen was waiting for Travis in the winter dark, only a quarter-mile from the village entrance. He had angled his van off the pathway, but the rear would still obstruct the passage of Travis's car. To the kid, as he approached, it would look as though someone had either had an accident or gotten stuck in the deep snow that banked the side of the road. But no chances were being taken: even if he chose not to investigate, he would still have to leave his car to attempt to clear his passage.

Getting him out of the car—that was what Roy was depending on. The rest would be easy. Even setting up the scene so that it would look as though the kid's death were the result of an accident. Deciding on this particular route to make the "hit" was not only because of the solitude it provided.

Travis wasn't overly conscious of the blackness or the treacherous, winding curves as he negotiated the path to the village. The lonely ride to the Chamrais reservation evoked... other thoughts.

Nicole ... the business with the mayor's committee ... *Sharon*—all had caused him to forget what had been his central concern only weeks ago. He was wondering how sincere he had really been when he had made that vow to help the village. So much had happened to erode his determination—and even now, driving out there, he was really only carrying a personal vengeance through: "acting" his bit with the committee. He could be headed to any other neutral point in the province for all the effect this trip to the Chamrais village was having on him.

Then, in so many other ways, Travis Randall was no longer the person he was the day before.

Roy stayed well off the path, away from the reflective glare of any approaching headlights.

It was a clear, star-filled night. And not too unbearably cold. Of course, regardless, Roy was well-insulated against the weather.

He was smoking a thick cigar, flexing his powerful hand, the fist of which he was going to use to break the kid's neck. Just one quick, direct thump and the kid wouldn't even know what hit him.

Broken neck resulting from car crash.

At least that was the way the mayor would get Doc MacFarlane to write it up.

Roy heard the car approach before he saw the first intrusion of its beams. He spit out his cigar and crushed it beneath his foot. He then edged a little farther back.

Travis saw the tail of the van stretching across the path. He immediately thought that its ominous positioning was somehow related to whatever it was that was going on at the reserve.

He pulled Old Betsy off to the side, angling her so that the headlights would illuminate the scene. Leaving the car running, he then stepped out to take a closer look.

Only a few feet from the driver's door . . . and something occurred to him.

This van being here made the remaining distance to the reserve impossible to any vehicle.

And didn't the mayor say over the phone that Collarman had already driven out?

The van looked to have been sitting across the path for a long while. How could Collarman's car have passed through?

No, suddenly it didn't seem right to him.

He could pinpoint it exactly:

He was being set up.

He began to step back, toward the Pontiac. His eyes scanned the surrounding bush. He could see nothing, but Roy could watch him. The headlights put him in clear view.

His slow retreat told Roy that he suspected something.

Roy would have to act quickly.

Travis had just backed into the front fender of his car. His eyes still searching, he inched toward the door, his hand reaching out and curling around the handle—

The bushes opposite him exploded in a shower of snow as the massive form of Roy came barreling into the open.

Roy moved quickly and certainly for a man of his size. Travis had the door open and was beginning to lever himself inside when he felt a python-like grip on his arm, and he was next aware of being thrown into space.

The snow provided a cushion for his landing. Momentarily dazed, Travis regained himself quickly. His eyes locked on Roy, whose bull-like body was blocking any attempt at entry to the car.

Roy maintained an aggressive position for a moment.

Then he started to move toward Travis.

Travis scrambled to his feet, while doing so digging his hand under the snow surface and scooping up a handful of gravel which he tossed in a sweeping motion at Roy, catching him full in the face. Roy's hands went to his eyes.

Travis lunged at him, full force, with his elbow jutting out like a spear.

It was similar to ramming into a rubber tire, but the effect was there. Roy howled as he stepped involuntarily backward.

Travis didn't waste an instant. He knew that if the fat man were to get hold of him it would be like the fly in the spider's web. He repeated his move: pulling back a distance, then again rushing forward with the point of his elbow.

This time Roy was thrown back into the bush at the edge of the road. He landed hard, sinking into the snow.

Travis didn't wait to see what was going to happen next. He beat his path to the car. Locked himself inside—

Discovered that the car he had left running wasn't any longer.

Travis quickly switched the ignition. A sound like automotive diarrhea purred from the engine.

Travis tried again.

And again.

If anything, the sound got weaker.

He checked the fuel indicator, knowing that there was sufficient gasoline in the tank.

Reliable Old Betsy had finally, and most inopportunely, let him down.

He turned to look out his window . . . just in time to see a rock firmly gripped in Roy's heavy hand swing toward the glass.

Travis threw himself lengthwise onto the seat, just narrowly escaping the explosion. The glass shattered, showering him. But he still pulled himself upright to the opposite side and burst out through the passenger door.

He took off into the bush.

Roy, his hand covered in cuts from the broken glass, threw the rock into the bush and started after him. He was no longer acting with a greater sense of purpose; his moves now were governed by humiliation. The urge just to tear the kid limb from limb.

Travis followed the direction that would take him to the reserve. There was virtually no light to guide him through the heavy cluster of trees, and more than once his arms and shoulders rebounded off a heavy trunk. By the time he had made any distance he was throbbing with aches.

Roy remained in pursuit. His rage was complete. He threw himself free when he came into contact with the trees. He was grunting and breathing heavily as he pushed his way through the dark and the deep snow. Travis had agility working for him. But Roy had persistence.

Travis kept his eyes focused ahead, hoping to catch even a flicker of light that would tell him he was nearing the reserve. He knew he would be safe there; he wouldn't be followed *into* the village.

Roy was prepared to follow the kid into Hell if he had to.

And that was almost exactly what he did.

There was no cry, no warning. Just the sudden rising up of a silhouette against the night.

Roy had no knowledge of Chamrais lore. Perhaps if he'd had he never would have stepped closer, in a move of curiosity and challenge.

But there would have been no escape for

him regardless. The Windigo held dominion over this land—as it had since the beginning of time. Roy had ventured into its domain, by doing so allowing himself to be seized.

The creature took Roy in its grasp. The fat man offered token struggle, but by the time he was lifted off the ground he knew his fate had been sealed. The dark of the night provided a mask for the demon's horrific visage, but the knowledge of impending death had already numbed Roy to further shock.

He didn't so much as scream.

Travis continued to trudge through the snow, still unsure of the distance left to go to reach the village. Desperation, the will to survive, made him continue, but he didn't know how much longer he'd be able to push on.

A few more yards.

His legs finally became like rubber and he twisted into a collapse. He couldn't get up.

His heart felt like it was beating out of his chest, his lungs about to cave in with each contraction.

He listened hard for the approaching sounds of his pursuer.

And then he realized he was hearing— *nothing*.

For many long minutes only the winter's deep quiet filled his ears. A most peaceful sound.

Travis was given the opportunity to regain his strength. Then he once more tried to pull to his feet. Making it. He looked back in the direction in which he was being followed. Clear.

Believing he was safe now, Travis next experienced a climaxing of that feeling of revenge he was holding against Jessup and the committee. They had wanted him dead, they had failed, and now the next move was his. He still was without the necessary proof to expose them, but he was going to find some way to take advantage of his offensive position. He had to now—if only to stay alive.

There was no point in his attempting a return to his car. Could be that his pursuer was waiting there for him—expecting him to make such a move. He'd be better off just to keep on toward the village. Try to get an assist there.

As he continued his trek he thought of how much there was still to learn from the Chamrais. Information that, if he could garner their support, would put him in a position to disclose the operations of the committee.

How to persuade the Chamrais . . . that was the problem.

Travis walked. And walked. There was still no sign of the village. He began to grow concerned. He was sure he had been following the right direction. Unless earlier when he had been running he somehow had turned off course. If that was the case . . . then he was lost!

He was becoming increasingly more receptive to the cold. He wasn't sure if that meant his resistance was lowering, or if the night was indeed dropping in temperature.

It made little difference. He could freeze to death either way.

"Shit," Officer Hovemeyer puffed as he trudged his way through the deep snow drifts toward the mill.

"Tells you the kind of shape you're in, doesn't it?" Officer Reichert said with a smug smile. The elder RCMP was experiencing none of the distress his partner apparently was. Or at least he wasn't letting on.

Hovemeyer coughed. "Sure, and you know . . . which of us is gonna drop face first in the snow."

"Don't count on it, boy." Reichert thudded a closed fist heavily against his well-padded chest. "Like iron."

"That's what I mean. It's always you . . . in-shape older guys who bite it. And usually in the middle of some vigorous workout."

Reichert replied, "As long as I reach my climax first."

"You should hope, old man."

Their flashlights cut spears through the dark; the surrounding blackness was so thick they were reliant solely on the guiding of their beams.

"Shoulda waited until morning," Hove-meyer continued to grumble. "Hell . . . for all we know we could have already passed Bryant . . . lying somewhere back there in the snow. Can't see dick."

"If that's the case, then it really doesn't make any difference," Reichert said practically.

"Makes a difference to me," Hovemeyer retorted. "We could turn back and put an end to this torture."

"We're almost at the mill, kid," Reichert said, amused. "You'll survive."

Hovemeyer came to an abrupt stop. "Oh Jesus."

"What is it now?"

"All this walking musta loosened up some-thing. Man, all of a sudden I gotta take a super-shit."

"Yeah, you'd have to, wouldn't you?"

"Hey, don't blame me. Besides, you're not the one with the problem."

Reichert flashed his beam in a striking semicircle. "Well, you've got your choice of resting posts. Just don't take too long, huh?"

"Yeah." Hovemeyer moved quicker now, and with less effort than he had during their trek. He had begun to loosen the layers of clothing.

"Don't go too far," Reichert called after him.

Hovemeyer was in too much of a hurry to acknowledge.

Reichert followed the trace of his partner's beam until it settled low across the snow. With Hovemeyer away from him, the older officer turned his back—letting his raised shoulders sag and his taut facial muscles relax into the obvious signs of his fatigue. He struck up a cigarette which he puffed on fast and furiously.

"Hell," he then muttered in complete acceptance of his exhaustion, "can't take much more of this."

Hovemeyer yanked up his pants and then zipped up his skidoo suit. He felt a good five pounds lighter. Last time I go for extra helpings of spaghetti, he thought with resolve.

"Okay Reichert," he whispered as he went for his flashlight, "now we'll see who outlasts who . . . you old fart."

The soft snow made a mushing sound behind him.

Hovemeyer spun around and the beam of hs flashlight lit up the face of Travis Randall, rushing up to him.

Hovemeyer held steady.

"Hold it right there, you," he said softly.

Travis, breathless, waved aside his caution. "You . . . don't have . . . to worry about me." As he came to a stop: "But . . . I'm sure glad to see you . . ."

Hovemeyer regarded him no less suspiciously. "Maybe you'd better tell me what you're doing out here," he said.

Travis took a minute to catch his breath.

"Hovemeyer?"

Reichert came over to the two men. He too wasn't quite sure what to make of Travis. He looked to his partner for an explanation.

Hovemeyer shrugged his shoulders. "Just came out of the bush," he said.

"Oh?" Reichert turned to Travis.

Travis hesitated.

"We'd better take him with us to the mill," Reichert suggested. That they were going to want some answers later was clear, but the officer offered a more obliging explanation. "It's a ways back to our car."

Travis nodded.

"Cold?" Reichert inquired.

Travis nodded again.

"Well, we haven't far to go."

60

Mayor Jessup was in an uncharacteristically impatient mood.

He was alone in his office waiting for the phone to ring. The call from Roy Cohen—the simple "good night" that was their code for success.

The mayor again checked his wristwatch; it was close to twelve. It had to have been done by now. Perhaps Roy was having some difficulty rigging up the "accident."

There was a slow knocking at his door. Jessup stiffened, momentarily taken aback. And then his next thought was that it had to be Roy. Damn fool. Regardless of the late hour it was not a smart move his coming to the office.

Something must have gone wrong.

Before Jessup could acknowledge, the door opened.

Dr. MacFarlane stood there—and he looked somehow different.

"Stewart?"

MacFarlane walked all the way into the

dimly lit office, not bothering to close the door after him.

Now Jessup could tell what the difference was: he was drunk.

"My God, Stewart," he said with disgust. MacFarlane was a proud man—not one given to slovenly appearance or behavior.

MacFarlane slumped into one of the two chairs the mayor had positioned before his desk. His expression was troubled and this, coupled with his inebriation, drastically changed his appearance. He suddenly looked very much like an old, tired man. No longer composed. No longer in control.

This was a stranger sitting across from Jessup.

"It's time we admit defeat, Calvin," the doctor said in a slow yet perfectly even voice.

The mayor's eyebrows knitted in concern. "What are you talking about, Stewart? You're . . . you've been drinking."

"Yes," MacFarlane responded unhesitatingly. "And you'd do well to bury the committee with a good stiff one. Because it's over, Calvin. For you, for me, Trelevan, Collarman—all of us. We've lost."

"No Stewart," the mayor returned confidently. "We haven't lost."

MacFarlane's voice rose. "Why is it so hard for you to see? We've been kidding ourselves. Trelevan could see it. Collarman. And—now it's been made clear to me. Thinking we can beat this. I don't know what it is we're up against, but I do know it's something we can't fight. And we can't go on believing we can. You talk about working for the good of the town—everything we've had to do is for Batesville. If you mean that you'll see we can accomplish more by admitting our failure. Sparing lives, Calvin. Because we haven't just killed Trelevan's kid . . . Harold Foley. Those lives that were lost to this thing . . . while we knew what was going on . . . we're responsible for them too."

Jessup said nothing, just continued to regard the doctor with an unyielding expression.

"We have to save lives now," MacFarlane went on. "Not that we can ever make up for what we . . . *didn't* do. But it can still make a difference."

"We've gone too far," Jessup said simply.

"We have to admit the truth," MacFarlane shouted. "Alert people to the danger. Let them be responsible for their lives. It—it isn't our right. Never was."

The mayor cleared his throat. "I've never been a quitter, Stewart."

"Quitting? This isn't a hockey game. Tell me what we're proving. Outside of taking lives—and needlessly. Are we any closer to beating this thing now than we were at the outset?"

"We're closer to realizing an investment opportunity whose returns are virtually limitless."

"How can it benefit us, Calvin? We're encouraging more of these incidents by building now. Incidents that inevitably are going to reach beyond our boundaries."

"Perhaps," Jessup said, unconcerned.

"Perhaps," MacFarlane reiterated sourly. Then: "No matter which way you look at it, we're burying ourselves."

Jessup said nothing.

MacFarlane spoke softly. "You've still lost.

327

Collarman, Trelevan, and I . . . we're doing what we believe—what we *know* is right. I was hoping you could see it too. But I guess I knew you wouldn't."

The mayor still wasn't going to relinquish his authority. "And neither will you. Not when it comes right down to it."

MacFarlane shook his head. Then he said, "You've been right about one thing. We will stick together."

Jessup smiled. "Yes. We will."

61

They all heard the cry.

Reichert pivoted his light in its direction, aiming the beam level.

"*Geez-us*," Hovemeyer said in a quiet yet raised voice.

The three men stood motionlessly in the slight clearing—a lonely tableau.

"What d'ya figure that is?" Hovemeyer said.

Suddenly, and he didn't know why it came to him—why that long-forgotten piece of information pushed forward in his thoughts—Travis muttered, "Weetigo."

"What?" Hovemeyer said, turning to him.

"An old Chamrais . . . he told me—mentioned this spirit: Weetigo. I never gave it a thought at the time. Still don't know what it is, or why I'm thinking about it now. Except . . ."

"There's no truth behind any of those legends," Hovemeyer said quickly, but with unsteady resolve. "A wolf in heat maybe, but that sure isn't no Chamrais spirit."

"Come on," Reichert said, "let's get this over with."

The men moved on, just out of the clearing... and then Travis sensed it. He couldn't determine exactly what it was, but it was like some fourth entity was insinuating itself into the group.

Hovemeyer felt it too—though he wasn't going to say anything.

Reichert was receptive to it.

The presence seemed to be getting stronger.

Still, no acknowledgment was made.

Growing... growing...

Hovemeyer felt himself becoming overwhelmed by it. He'd broken out in a sweat.

Finally, in a whisper, he asked, "What is it?"

Travis and Reichert came to a stop. They glanced at each other, then focused on Hovemeyer.

"Can't you feel it?" His perspiration-glossed face was pleading. "It's with us—"

The young RCMP screamed as his head snapped back, with such sudden force that his neck was broken. He was then flung into the trees, landing spread-eagled.

Travis and Reichert rushed over to him. Reichert directed his beam downward.

Hovemeyer was twisting feebly in the snow, struggling to breathe. His trachea and a good portion of his throat had been ripped... *chewed* away, exposing severed tendons and muscles. With each attempt at breath blood bubbled out like a low-pressure fountain.

"Oh shit," Reichert sputtered as he knelt beside his partner, making a quick examination to see what, if anything, he could do.

Hovemeyer was dying.

Reichert switched on his radio and prepared to speak into it.

Travis, who discovered he couldn't watch a man die, had veered his eyes away from the scene. He heard Reichert make initial contact with a Batesville unit . . . and then a gurgling sound. He forced himself to turn in his direction—

Just in time to see the elder RCMP, his eyes wide with uncomprehending horror, being urged back into the darkness.

Travis scrambled to his feet, shot a panicked gaze into the black. But he could see nothing. Listened. Could hear no sounds. His eyes slowly circled the bush. Then, hesitatingly, he glanced down at Hovemeyer's stiffening body—locking on the radio attached to his outer belt. He'd never operated one before, but he'd have to learn fast. He had to complete Reichert's transmission. He scooped it up, switching the button to ON. Static. He raised the antenna, fiddled with the dial, all the while speaking desperately into it:

Hello . . . Hello . . . Is someone there? . . . Hello . . ."

Continued crackling.

Frantically: *"Hello! Can anyone hear me?"*

He felt the presence returning.

Coming for him!

"C'mon, damnit," Travis gritted, slapping the side of the radio with the inside of his hand.

Frustrated, he threw the two-way aside and again bent down beside Hovemeyer's corpse. He fought back a wave of nausea as he unzipped the officer's skidoo suit and reached his hand in at the waist. He felt about for the holster, and once he located it he snapped up the cover and withdrew the revolver.

He then straightened—and took a few slow, deliberate steps backward, at the same time raising and leveling the gun.

For a moment all around him was peaceful.

Travis remained in position.

And then the stillness exploded, the night closing in on Travis in a rush. It was as if the elements were suddenly unleashed in all their collective fury.

Travis began firing, wildly. He emptied the revolver, but his effort was futile. Whatever this was he was up against had defenses he couldn't hope to penetrate.

His only chance came with finding cover.

He was close enough to the sawmill to attempt to run to it, but the force called out all its resources to prevent him from completing the distance. Heavy, blinding snows whipped up in vortex-like effect, urged by the sudden *devil's-breath* winds. Tremors rocked the ground beneath him. Travis maneuvered, edging cautiously through the blizzard—straining his vision to make his way. Sounds like tortured cries carried to him on the wind. Shrieking laughs. Taunting sounds. Unnatural sounds.

Five yards? *Five hundred yards?* Travis was rapidly becoming disoriented. Distance was lost to him. As was direction. Had he stumbled off course again?

What was he leading into?

The cold intensified until it was biting through his parka.

The wind whipped at him like a chain.

The ground rocked.

The air screamed.

Lost in a sea of white.

His strength was ebbing.

He could feel the presence closing in ...
around him. Now he was entirely in its power.

Too tired, too weak, with no hope of escape,
Travis gave in to this overwhelming opposition,
collapsing face forward into the snow ...

Snow which continued to blow in on him,
burying him. Preserving him.

The fly in the web.

Consciousness trickled away from him. His
entry into oblivion was slow, but accompanying
numbness of feeling and thought made the
transition peaceful.

And then a sharp tugging sensation.

Travis couldn't recover wholly, though he
was receptive to the grasp which pulled him free
of the snow and began dragging him across its
powdery surface.

Momentarily receptive.

And then consciousness returned to a blur.
Reality dissolved into a haze. Travis had become
neutral to all around him. His very existence. He
was only vaguely aware of entering the internal
dark of a shelter. Numb to whatever warmth it
might provide.

A voice called to him from within its depths.

A voice that triggered a partial return to
awareness.

A hallucinatory dream?

A voice urging him into the beyond?

It was neither.

Just the sound of his moan had brought
recognition to her. She rushed over from her
corner, dropping to her knees, taking his head
gently in her hands and cradling it. Sobbing
with a release of what little fortitude she had
been able to retain.

"Nicole?" Travis said weakly.

Nicole was too convulsed with emotion to acknowledge. She continued just to hold him close.

Lloyd Caribou backed away.

He watched from a distance. This time, as she cried, he couldn't look away. Because this time he was watching her with an understanding. An understanding difficult for him to acknowledge—but the evocation was simply too strong for him to ignore.

So long ago . . .

The blackness inside the mill was nearly as impenetrable as the night itself. For Nicole, however, it was bathed in more light now than it had been in a month.

Travis was unable to recover immediately. He did so in stages. But he had regained enough control of his faculties to know that he was not imagining this moment.

Nicole was alive.

He couldn't stop the tears. "I—I thought I'd lost you," he said in a whisper.

Nicole just slowly shook her head. She was a shadow in Travis's eyes, but he wasn't asking for any more. Not right now. It had been too long.

Lloyd kept at his place. His fragmented thoughts were all coming together like pieces in an abstract jigsaw puzzle.

The moment these two were sharing, he had experienced . . .

Susan

Susan!

His mind erupted into violent, only half-understood images:

Blood!

A sharp, gleaming object repeatedly thrusting forward ...

More blood!

A veil of crimson staining his remembrances.

Lloyd couldn't respond with tears of his own. Not any longer. But an impulse was building inside him. An accumulation that would somehow have to be released.

With Nicole's help Travis had pulled himself into a sitting position. They were locked in a tight embrace.

The door and a good portion of the front entranceway imploded, the sudden funnel-like suction of snow providing a striking contrast against the black.

Nicole screamed as she and Travis found themselves caught in the center of the blast. Both threw up their arms to shield themselves from its lashing impact, at the same time attempting to rise to their feet.

Lloyd watched the two scramble off to the side, and then he squinted tightly as he looked out into the blizzard.

A shape materialized in the distance, cutting an exact form through the assault of snow.

It began to advance—its hulking, long-armed silhouette growing larger.

Travis forced himself to recover. His body still partially numb, he nevertheless worked his legs into motion, pushing Nicole in back of him and stepping cautiously in reverse.

Although not clearly defined, it was a creature out of a nightmare that was entering the mill. It was moving toward Travis and Nicole.

Travis glanced about for some form of weapon, but could see nothing. He took Nicole by the arm and backed deeper into the mill.

Lloyd saw his opening for escape. The creature wasn't even considering him. He could easily run out into the night. But he hesitated.

Travis's eyes continued to scout the mill for something he could use against this... *monster*. But even if there was a tool lying about, there simply wasn't enough light inside to expose it.

He glanced behind him. The ladder to the loft was only several yards away.

"Nicole, get up there," he urged, giving her a light nudge.

The girl couldn't move. Her horror had petrified her.

"Nicole," Travis said firmly.

Her eyes couldn't even shift to him; they were locked on their aggressor. Growing nearer.

Travis scooped his arm around her waist and forcefully dragged her over to the ladder.

"Climb, damnit!"

The harsh insistence in Travis's voice seemed to free Nicole of her paralysis. She started up, though hesitantly.

Travis waited until she was almost at the top, and then he hurried up after.

The creature's deep, throaty breathing told Travis that it was close enough so that he couldn't hesitate even for a moment. He locked his hands high around the parallel posts and hefted himself the height of the first four steps. He wanted to glance behind, but didn't dare. He pulled himself up another couple of steps. Nicole was watching from above. He couldn't see her clearly, but her expression was one of anxious terror.

Travis was only several steps from the loft. He was straining to the limit but again lifted a little higher.

His feet came down hard on the board—and snapped it.

Travis dangled in space, holding with all his strength onto the posts, frantically trying to kick his feet into contact with another base.

Nicole had heard the crack of the wood. "*Travis!*" she called.

"I'm—all right!" he shouted back at her.

He tried to pull himself up only a bit further . . . and then he felt the creature's huge hands wrap themselves around his legs—and tug.

His grip released from the posts and he was thrust backwards.

Nicole screamed.

Travis swayed like a rag doll in the monster's powerful grasp—torso and head flung back, arms spread out loosely at the sides. He knew there would be no chance for him if he attempted resistance and so made himself remain limp. Hoping that maybe the creature would think he was dead.

Nicole thought he already was. The scene below her was a shadowy blur but she could tell he wasn't fighting to free himself. Her horror and agony were almost overshadowed by her sense of injustice. How long she had waited for Travis—*only to have it end like this!*

Lloyd Caribou, in his own way, shared her feeling. There was so much he still couldn't bring himself to understand, but Nicole's tear-filled screaming evoked in him that sense of loss that he had come so close to recognizing.

He shot his eyes up to the loft.

"*Go!*" he shouted to Nicole.

Then he threw himself at the creature.

The suddenness of his attempt resulted in the monster's dropping Travis to the floor. Travis managed to prepare himself for the fall, landing in a roll rather than a flat hit. He raised with difficulty into a standing position and staggered back over to the ladder.

"Come on!" he yelled up at Nicole.

Nicole shakily descended the ladder. She had to feel for each step. Slowly. Carefully. Finally she came to the broken one and could proceed no further.

"Jump!" Travis urged.

It was still a ten-foot drop.

"Jump, Nicole!"

Nicole knew there wasn't a whole lot of time to ready herself. She just focused on Travis, who was holding open his arms, then screwed her eyes shut and let herself fall. Travis couldn't make a clean catch; instead he eased her into a less forceful collision. Her ankle still twisted inward on impact, though, and she cried out in pain as she collapsed into Travis.

Lloyd was entirely in the clutches of the creature. There wasn't anything Travis could do for him. The couple moved carefully into the complete dark of the far wall, Travis supporting his wife, and then edged along to the shattered entranceway.

Travis trired to shield Nicole from catching sight of the action at the front center of the mill. It looked as though the monster had begun to . . . *devour its victim!*

Holding Lloyd aloft by one shredded arm, the creature's large, almost luminous teeth had ripped away most of his shoulder. Blood, tissue, and chips of bone flowed in a river down the front of Lloyd's shirt. Only the neck vertebrae and a few remaining strands of fiber prevented the head from snapping off.

If there was anything to be thankful for in this moment of unrelenting horror it was that at least he was already dead.

The creature was absorbed in its meal. Travis and Nicole were able to make it to the opening. Travis's last glimpse was of the monster inverting the mangled body and, grasping it by both legs, effortlessly halving it.

Still keeping sure Nicole's eyes were averted, Travis escaped with her into the woods.

There had been no letup in the storm. Travis didn't want to admit to Nicole that he had no idea which way to go. He just held her close and ran.

"He saved us Travis," Nicole sputtered.

"It was Caribou?"

"Yes." Nicole had finally come to realize his identity.

They ran through the blizzard for what seemed an eternity. It wasn't possible for the night to be as long as this. The whipping cold, their fatigue, their strained muscles—nothing could overcome their determination to reach safety. What Travis had experienced that night had filled him with a surplus of resolution. He'd rather drop dead in the snow than surrender to weakness and again end up in that monster's grasp.

Nicole's firmness of will was based on the same conviction.

Finally, not so far in the distance, Travis's eyes made contact with a flash of light.

They had to be approaching the Chamrais village.

"We're gonna be okay," he said in a tired, raspy, but now optimistic voice.

Nicole looked up as he pointed out.

"The reserve," he said.

This last stretch seemed the longest. When they reached the village boundary they were on the verge of collapse. Not surprisingly, given the weather and the late hour, no one was outside. A couple of cabin lights were on, but Travis could think of only the one to go to.

"This way," he said to Nicole as he directed her to the cabin of the old Chamrais couple.

They pushed their way up the steps. Nicole's injured ankle was causing her unbearable pain and she leaned heavily on Travis for more support.

No lights were on here but Travis still banged furiously at the door.

Travis continued hammering. "Please . . . open up!"

The curtains parted slightly and the old man peered out. Travis gestured for him to let them inside. The man's face remained solemn, and he dropped the curtain.

He apparently remembered only too well.

"No! Please!" Travis pleaded. Then: "You were right! I've seen it . . . *The Weetigo!*"

For a moment, nothing.

And then the door opened. The man looked with seriousness at Travis.

"What you told me . . . about the Weetigo," Travis said. "It's out there." His hand stretched in the direction of the north bush they had just cleared.

The man beckoned them inside.

"Stand over by the stove," he said as he closed the door and bolted it.

"There's no time," Travis was quick to reply, even though he was just now beginning to feel the full effect of the cold. "Too much to do, and my wife—she's been hurt. We need a vehicle. To get into town."

The man said, "I have no—"

"You've gotta know someone who has," Travis cut him off impatiently.

"What you are saying about the Weetigo . . ." the man first wanted to know.

"It's at the sawmill," Travis explained. "Was there." A pause. "Caribou too."

"Lloyd?" the man said, his eyes sparking with interest.

Another pause. Then Travis said, "He's dead."

"The spirit?"

Travis shook his head. "It's more than a spirit."

The man turned away from him. "We have a truck. It's late. . . . I must come with you."

Travis wasn't going to waste time arguing. "Yeah, sure," he said.

The man got his coat. Then he walked over to the gun rack on the far wall and took down his rifle. Over to a set of drawers where he removed a box of cartridges. He took one out, opened the breach and slid the cartridge into the chamber.

"That's not gonna do any good," Travis remarked.

The man didn't respond.

As they walked to the door, Travis said: "Your wife. Shouldn't you tell her where you're going?"

"My wife has died," the man replied flatly.

They went back out into the storm. The heavy snow swirled in eddies. The man stopped on the porch for a moment, as if considering the wiseness of their move given the affected visibility. But then he waved Travis and Nicole after him and started for the northern edge of the village.

Travis wished it were possible to take just a moment to rest. To strengthen himself for whatever else lay ahead this endless night. But time was at a premium now. Each second had to count.

The middle-aged bald man at whose cabin they found themselves seemed understandably annoyed at their disturbance. The old man—perhaps wisely—avoided going into detail. "I need the truck," was all he said.

"Tomorrow," the bald man snorted, turning back inside.

The old man laid a quick hand upon his shoulder. "No, now," he said.

Travis spoke up. "We have to get into town. It's important."

The bald man looked neutrally at Travis, then his eyes shifted to Nicole—her tired, drawn face and her dirt-caked hair which hung flat and formless against her head. Her appearance alone seemed to convince him of their urgency.

"I'll get you the keys," he said, though still not entirely without reluctance.

"His truck?" Travis inquired.

"No," the old man replied. "But he keeps it running. The village has few vehicles."

Once they had the set of keys, they rounded the cabin and hurried to the half-ton. Travis helped Nicole inside and then, while the man tried to get it started, wiped the wet snow off the windshield with his elbow.

The man was flicking the ignition, but all he got from under the hood was a grinding sound.

"Check the battery posts," the man called to Travis through the window.

Travis yanked the hood release and the hood banged up. He reached into the cavity and felt about for the battery. There wasn't sufficient light to determine its condition.

The headlights flashed on. Their glow was dim.

Truck's not going to see them out of the reserve, Travis thought.

Checking the bulbs, he noticed that the reason for their dullness was that they were smudged with dirt. He wiped them clean with a handful of snow. This indeed strengthened their light.

The battery terminals were pretty badly corroded. Travis possessed minimal mechanical aptitude, but he didn't have to to determine this as the cause for the truck's hesitance.

The man was persistent with the ignition, even though by now it was obvious he was fighting a losing battle.

"Forget it, it's not going to start," Travis shouted to him.

The man climbed out of the cab and went over to Travis. He studied the situation with a shared ignorance.

"What about him?" Travis said, indicating the cabin with the bald man.

"He won't be of any help. Not till the morning."

"Well, damn, that's something I'm just gonna have to find out for myself," Travis said determinedly. He backed away from the hood and signaled to Nicole. "Stay in the truck." Then he rushed back around to the front of the cabin.

Only yards behind the half-ton, from within

the bush, two malignant eyes blazed red.

Travis hurried up the steps of the cabin. By the time the old man got beside him he was already slamming the door with his fist.

"Hey in there, open up!" he shouted impatiently. Then, turning to the old man: "You said there are other vehicles?"

The man shook his head. "Truck's the only one I'd trust to handle the road in this weather."

The door opened and the bald man stood glowering at them.

"Truck won't start," Travis told him.

"Nothing I can do now."

"Look, we have to get into town as quickly as we can," Travis once again explained. "Seems you're the only one who can help us."

"Not till morning," the bald man said, then he slammed shut the door.

Travis gave it a frustrated kick. He gritted: "No phones, no transportation. How the hell are we gonna get out of here?"

The shape moved ever closer to the back of the truck . . .

Nicole, still inside the cab, sat as if in a stupor. She saw Travis and the old man round the cabin and hurry toward the truck—

Then she saw Travis's face widen in horror.

She saw the old man, his own expression equally as set in shock, pull the rifle from his shoulder and level it in her direction.

"*Nicole, get out! Run!*"

Her eye caught a glimpse of something out the side window. She turned . . . and gazed into the hideous black face of the Windigo!

Its mighty jaws stretched open.

Before Nicole could erect, the door ripped open and a blizzard of snow consumed the interior of the cab—carrying with it a large gnarled hand which closed around her arm.

"*No!*" Travis shouted as he broke into a run toward the truck.

The old man fired off several shots in quick succession, but as the creature pulled the swooning Nicole entirely free of the vehicle he eased his finger from the trigger. He couldn't gamble on his aim.

Travis kept his distance from the creature, moving around it stealthily, looking for an opportunity to extract Nicole from its grasp.

The semi-conscious girl was feebly trying to twist free, but the creature was now gripping her in both hands.

The old man was inching toward another position, one where Nicole wasn't so easily a target.

His gunshots had brought some Chamrais men running from their cabins. A few carried rifles. Upon seeing this supernatural being they immediately raised their guns into firing position.

"No!" the old man shouted. "The girl!"

The creature emitted a long, fearsome cry. It seemed to be challenging the men. As if aware of its invincibility.

The activity carried yet more of the villagers out into the storm. Most had been shaken from bed and were in pajamas and slippers, though bundled in heavy parkas.

The men who brought guns were eager to begin blasting at the creature that continued to stand in complete defiance before them. Repeated shouts to hold back until the girl was free filled the air.

"It truly is a demon," the old man remarked to the ashen-faced fellow standing next to him. "I've emptied a cartridge into it and it's still on its feet.''

One Chamrais, impatient, inverted his rifle and, using it as a club, rushed at the creature. He swung once, powerfully—connecting, but the monster didn't flinch. It retaliated by striking out with its hand, sweeping the foolhardy young man back into the bush.

Travis still circled the creature, looking for his opening. The monster, however, seemed aware of its prize and was not going to let Nicole get away.

A shot went off—striking the creature's arm.

Then another.

It was as though someone had given the signal to begin firing. But no one had ... one over-eager Chamrais boy had decided to take the initiative.

"*For God's sake—NO!*" Travis shouted through the opening volley of gunfire.

But by now bullets were flying everywhere. Most slammed into the creature—to no effect, but many were wild. Nicole was nicked in the shoulder but she had again lapsed into unconsciousness and so could not feel her wound.

"*Stop!*" Travis continued to cry.

The men weren't listening. They were like a group possessed.

The old man, realizing that the situation could not be controlled, made the only move he could think of. He took careful aim of his rifle ... and fired off a single shot into the half-ton's gas tank.

The truck erupted in an overpowering blast—so blinding that the skies momentarily became like daylight. Nicole was thrown free just as a jet of flame hooked onto the creature, the accompanying spray of gasoline transforming it quickly into a living torch.

Then—an explosion.

Engulfed in flames, the monster walked through the circle of fire.

Every rifle at the site turned on it, blasting away.

The creature remained erect as the bullets tore into its body. A flaming sculpture, it seemed immune to the onslaught. But the men kept their guns in action.

Then, finally, the monster began to crumple inward. Another explosion—as if the fire had ignited something within.

Moments later . . . the inferno had consumed the monster entirely.

Guns lowered, the villagers watched the blaze in silence.

No one was really aware that the storm had ended.

The old man separated himself from the crowd and walked over to Travis, who was kneeling beside the prostrate form of his wife, cradling her.

"How is she?" the man asked.

"Alive," Travis said thankfully.

The man looked back at the fire. "I wish I could believe it was truly dead," he said pensively.

Travis glanced up at him, his eyes not comprehending.

The man explained: "We destroyed an incarnation, but the spirit cannot die so easily. I fear it has returned to the woods . . . where it will wait."

Travis shivered at the prospect. But he still said: "For now, though, it's over."

The man nodded, then returned his troubled gaze to the flames.

62

Dr. MacFarlane tended to Nicole. He treated her ankle and bullet-grazed shoulder and examined her thoroughly for the physical effects of her confinement. She was suffering from exposure and a vitamin deficiency, both easily treated. MacFarlane suggested a week of rest and the proper diet, which he would prescribe.

There was concern for Nicole's emotional state, however, and Travis knew that the best cure was for the two of them to leave the town. It was a move he was planning regardless. He wanted Batesville to be nothing more than a bad memory.

Two days had passed since the incident at the Chamrais reserve. They were two days in which Travis had made the preparations for their departure. What he didn't bother to do was officially resign with the *Clarion*. There was no point: he'd never use it as a reference. It would just be another reminder that he'd rather not have.

He was hoping to avoid Robbie when late

Friday morning he dropped in at the paper to clean out his desk. His feelings toward her were still uncertain.

Robbie, though, had been expecting Travis and made it a point to be in her office when he came in.

Their initial moments together were uncomfortable.

Robbie spoke first. She was uncharacteristically subdued, perhaps realizing that there wasn't much she could really say.

"I'm sorry things couldn't have worked out better," she said.

"It didn't have to turn out the way it did," Travis said in response.

"Yes, it did."

Before Travis could turn to leave, Robbie took him gently by the arm and said: "There's still the committee."

"Not for long," Travis replied.

"I meant that—as a warning."

"It's too late. They know it. Too many people are involved now."

"You're going to tell the story?"

"Someone has to."

"A lot of people are going to be hurt," Robbie reminded.

"I know. And I wish you weren't one of them," Travis replied sincerely.

Robbie smiled wanly. "I think all of us knew this time was going to come. Explanations won't do any good now, I know, but there were those of us who really believed everything we did was for the right reason."

"And if it's any consolation," Travis said gently, "I don't think Batesville is going to suffer all that much for it. The Chamrais, I know, are going to come out ahead. They have a lot more than just their heritage to be proud of."

Robbie offered her hand. "Good luck, Travis."

Travis accepted it. "Thanks," he said.

Travis went to the boarding house to pick up Nicole. The bus from Thompson would be making its five-minute stopover in Batesville at 2:15 P.M. There was just enough time for quick goodbyes with Cora and Rosa. Cora was happy for them. She admitted hating to see them leave, but was brimming with optimism for their future.

"You're going to do some wonderful things, I know," she said to Travis. To Nicole: "You're a lucky girl."

Nicole grabbed Travis's arm. "I've always known that."

"God bless you both."

Cora had asked a neighbor to drive them the few blocks to the bus depot. Once they arrived, the neighbor unloaded their bags on the transport cart while Travis went inside to get their tickets.

"Two for Winnipeg," he said to the clerk. "One way."

Then, as Travis turned to join Nicole outside, he saw four familiar faces staring at him: Mayor Jessup, Dr. MacFarlane, Mr. Collarman, and Mr. Trelevan. All looked appropriately somber.

Travis just nodded.

As usual, it was the mayor who did the talking. "Travis, there's still a lot that doesn't have to be said." His voice had an obvious paternal edge to it.

"It wouldn't make sense now not to say it,"

Travis replied, not allowing himself to be intimidated.

"And the town?"

"Batesville's gonna make it. If I wasn't so sure of that . . ."

"You really are?" Jessup questioned with suspicion.

"Don't have a doubt."

The mayor paused, then said: "I wish you'd think seriously about this move."

"I've never thought more seriously about anything. If I have one regret, it's for those people who really believed you—who really thought they were doing what was right. They're going to have to answer for a lot as well."

The bus hissed to a stop outside the front doors. Travis and Nicole were the only ones departing from Batesville, though there were a dozen or so people who had boarded in Thompson.

"I've gotta go," Travis said.

"Travis . . ." Jessup said, his tone firm.

Travis just looked at him, boldly, not hiding the contempt he felt for the man.

"The committee's still powerful," the mayor said, clearly as a threat.

Travis knew an idle threat.

He eyed each of the other men.

Their decision had already been made.

MacFarlane walked away.

Collarman and Trelevan followed.

The mayor turned to them, astonished. Yet he was determined not to lose his control.

"We have to remain together," he shouted as they walked out the door. "Especially now, can't you see that? We've put too much time

and effort into . . . just to give up. We have to
see this through! We have to fight! Make sure
that our office doesn't lose its credibility.
We . . . we . . .''

The men were gone.

Travis suddenly couldn't help feeling a kind
of sick pity for Calvin Jessup. The man was
destroyed. Such a proud man. And, perhaps
regrettably, Travis figured he'd never really
know whether the mayor truly believed everything he had done was for the good of the town.

He walked away from Jessup and collected
Nicole, and together they boarded the bus.
Travis was insistent they take seats right up
front. "I wanna know I'm out of this town as
soon as possible," was how he explained it to
Nicole.

The bus pulled away from the depot and
started out of Batesville by way of the main
street. Only once did Travis look back: when
they passed Sharon Crane's apartment building.
For just a moment he thought about her.
Wondered what would become of her. He still
couldn't help hoping she'd make it; he'd never
considered her much of a survivor.

But he and Nicole were survivors.

He was more sure of that than ever once the
bus crossed Batesville's southern boundary and
he knew they were on their way.

He took Nicole's hand in his and, smiling,
settled back to enjoy the ride.

PART I

The Chamrais

Perhaps more legend and folklore has come from Canada's north country than anywhere else in the world.

1

This is the legend:

The early days of November 1884.

A time when the communities of northern Manitoba were preparing for another long, cold winter. A winter that would surely isolate many of them.

The Chamrais Indians, who held claim to the vast expanse of land that extended west from the Wabowden River as far as the southernmost tip of Great Spirit Lake, made no exception when it came to tradition. Even with the first breaths of the fourth season giving warning, there could be no break in that which the Chamrais had come to regard as custom. Marie Dan understood this, as did her family (which included one of the tribe's elders), and so her preparations continued.

Within a week the young girl would be married. But first she would have to return from the journey that her mother, grandmother, and all the wives of the village had at one time taken.

She was to go off into the forest alone—the forest that encircled the village and broke at the banks of Great Spirit Lake. She would journey for three days and just as many nights, bringing with her the clothes on her back and small hand-stitched satchel into which would be placed only the tiniest amount of food. Enough to see her through her journey, but only if she was careful. On the fourth day she was expected to return with the sun. She would then be allowed a brief reunion with her betrothed, the purpose of which was go give the bridegroom the opportunity to make the final decision as to whether she had reached that level of strength the men in the tribe demanded of their mates. Rarely had it happened that marriage plans were canceled at this point, but in the event the bride-to-be was deemed unacceptable after her trek, she would be forced to leave the village in disgrace. Weakness was a quality not tolerated by the Chamrais.

Marie Dan was not ignorant of this possibility. She knew that love was of secondary importance in the unions within the tribe. She also knew that regardless of whatever feelings her beloved had professed to her during their period of courtship, he'd had it bred into him—as had all the Chamrais males—that perfect unity could be attained only when one could accept his mate as a spiritual equal. Marie Dan was determined to prove herself as such.

On that November morning of her departure, a sleet had begun to blow in from the higher ground, already visibly capped with a translucent layer of pre-winter frost. It was early when Marie Dan stepped from her cabin; the sun was just starting to wink over the eastern horizon. As was also the Chamrais custom, only the mother (or closest living female relation, or, in certain instances, a non-family member approved by the council) was allowed to be with the girl at this time. Even so, she could only go with her as far as the village boundary. She then had to turn back before the girl chose a direction in which to go. Tradition dictated that she must never be seen leaving the village.

It was Marie Dan's aged mother who accompanied her to the edge of the village. No words were spoken during this time, and neither was there a moment of affection between the two.

By noon that day the sleet had formed beds of ice throughout the muddy floors of the village, beds that were soon sheeted with the heavy snows into which the wind-urged sleet had developed.

John Redleather watched this threatening change in the weather and he grew worried. "Custom" among the males in the tribe was such that he was not supposed to voice concern for his betrothed during the three days of her "spiritual strenghtening." John's worry quickly grew into anger against that unwritten rule which forbade him to go out in search of the girl he loved.

By late afternoon a full-fledged storm had developed. Snow-driven winds shrieked outside the cabin, and to John, already overwhelmed with anxiety, it was the lost, desperate cries of Marie that he was hearing. He knew that if she wasn't dead yet she soon would be. It wouldn't be long before night would be upon her. The thought of his beautiful Marie perishing alone in the cold and the dark was too much for John to bear. He quickly bundled himself as warmly as he could in buckskin and then—against the protests of his family—burst out of the cabin into the blizzard.

In which direction did she go?

There was no way for John to know. For a moment he stood in the openness of the village center, swaying as wind blasted into him. He called out Marie's name, believing desperately that the sound of his voice might travel on the wind and carry out to her. Give her the hope that he was coming to find her.

By this time a few men had come out after him and tried to persuade him back inside the cabin. Their words had no effect and any attempt at physical urging was met with sturdy resistance.

Finally John ran off, defying both his people and nature. He disappeared into the forest.

All he could do was pray: pray that he had chosen the right direction to make his search ... that he could find the strength to reach his Marie ... and, most of all, that he would find her alive.

Already deep drifts of snow had wedged between the trees, slowing John's progress, tiring him rapidly. Yet whenever he felt himself weakening, craving but a moment of warmth and rest, he made himself bring to mind the image of Marie struggling alone somewhere out in these woods—terrified, hoping for rescue. And she would not have to feel disgrace. In John's eyes she had already done more to strengthen her spirit and prove her love for him than if she'd completed her journey. He would accept her. In every way.

If only now he could be given the

opportunity.

As the night deepened, the penetrating cold intensified. John tried to fight it from his mind, but he soon found its physical effects too overwhelming. His arms and legs were biting. As well, the continuous stinging brought about by the sweeping of the snow against his face (coupled with the eyestrain caused by his attempts to focus through the blinding whiteness) resulted in a headache that John found he could barely endure. But he had to continue . . . and somehow he found it in him to move on yet further.

Although his throat was raw, he still called out her name:

"*Marie!*"

He trudged deeper into the woods.

"*Marie!*"

And then, from off in the distance, traveling on the wind like an echo, he heard the voice of his beloved cry back to him. . . .

Winter had not yet officially come, but by the next day that season's unmistakable icy hue had fallen completely across the land. The sky was clear, as blue as it can get only in the northlands. But this clarity foretold a day of bitter cold.

The Chamrais village woke early, its people eager to see if sometime during the night their brother had returned. He hadn't. By noon several of the men unleashed their dogs and set out to find him. It was expected to be a long, difficult search; tracks made the night before had been swept clean.

Perhaps if the Chamrais had not been such persistent and adept hunters the sight that they were soon to be made witness to would have been spared them. Such, however, was not the case. Late in the day they came upon John . . . and Marie, by the curving banks of the rushing Wabowden River. John lay frozen in the snow, his arms locked in an empty embrace. Marie knelt before him, and when the men came upon the two her back was facing them. No sound escaped her lips but it appeared she was sobbing, mourning the death of the man that she had loved and planned to marry. It was only when the men stepped forward and around to face her that her real action was discovered.

Oblivious to both the cold and the sudden presence of the men from her village, Marie Dan continued to partake of the meal her dead love had provided her with—

She chewed into the fleshy underside of John's raised upper arm, ripping away the surface meat and consuming it as if she were enjoying a most elaborate feast. Her face was smeared with his blood, blood which had congealed obscenely around her lips. She'd already opened his stomach and devoured—wholly or partially—most of his internal organs, but frozen globs of viscera and distended ropes of intestine still lay strewn about the snow surrounding John's body.

The Chamrais prided themselves on their fortitude, on their ability to boldly face any challenge, but no amount of tribal conditioning could have prepared those eight men for that moment which preceded the raising of the rifles and slow pulling of the triggers. It was a moment that none of them had ever come close to experiencing before—not even in their worst nightmare. But when they stepped over to

Marie's bullet-ravaged body and noticed that the satchel of food she had been given was still slung over her shoulder, its contents untouched, they came to the realization that the true cause of this horror was something not one was unfamiliar with.

No one said it, but that single dreaded word implanted itself in each of their thoughts:

Weetigo!

PART II

Batesville

2

Travis Randall had serious doubts about the Pontiac making it. With over eighty-five thousand miles reading on the odometer, it still had its original engine, and just lately all manner of unsettling noises had been coming from under the hood. Sputters, coughs, and farts—sometimes a horrendous combination of all three—foretold the impending death of Travis's beloved automobile.

He was a sentimentalist, but he knew his wife Nicole had had the right idea when she had made the suggestion back in the city that they unload the Pontiac (while they could still squeeze a few bucks out of her) and leave the driving to the bus. After all, she had reasoned, they weren't exactly going to be traveling just down the block. Old Betsy, death-rattles and all, was going to have to carry them more than three hundred miles. It just didn't make sense to whip a dying beast.

But Travis argued; Nicole, as usual, gave in . . . and now here they were: alone on a seemingly endless stretch of provincial highway. They'd passed the two-hundred-fifty-mile mark, and from this point on each mile they rolled they considered a gift from St. Christopher.

Finally they were off Highway 6 (this was an accomplishment), now going northeast on Route 391, passing road signs that identified Button and Dunlop, communities that both Travis and Nicole were just now discovering. Once they blinked and found that they'd both entered and cleared Dunlap, Travis turned to his wife, smiled with confidence, and remarked: "I think Old Betsy's gonna see us through."

Nicole looked at Travis, her expression a clear sign she had yet to be convinced.

Travis tilted his wide, camel-colored Stetson up off his forehead. "You're gonna jinx us," he said jokingly.

Nicole sighed. "We've been jinxed ever since we—correction, *you*—decided not to part with this buffalo while it was still worth something."

"Aw, come on, Nicki." Travis patted the sun-faded dashboard affectionately. "You're not being hardly fair. She's gotten us this far. She's not going to let us down now."

Again Nicole responded with her "convince me" expression.

"Unbeliever," Travis said in a mock-pious tone.

Nicole glanced out the window, then she turned back to her husband and said with a wink and self-assured smile: "We're not there yet."

No, they weren't there yet, and as Travis's

mind begun to drift he thought how that perhaps applied to more than just traveling distance. Travis, as was his nature—the nature of his people—had been displaying outward calm, but he wondered what really would be waiting for him once he and Nicole reached Batesville, a town that until three weeks ago neither had even known existed. A new job—one which he'd trained for but had never worked at. Not in a paying capacity. After two years of community college, studying Communications with a major in Journalism, and earning fairly respectable marks (considering that during his first year three-quarters of the stuff he'd handed in had come from sources no more reliable than his own imagination), he had graduated, and now he was embarking on Phase One of his chosen career: the rural reporter. But just what would there be to report in such a town? he'd begun to ask himself. A town that not only was bordering on Eskimo communities, but which had also decided to dispense with pretense altogether by tacking a "-ville" onto its name. Travis certainly had visions. Interviewing old Mrs. Jenkins to get the "inside story" on what it feels like to be the proud owner of a 300-pound porker that had just given birth to a half-dozen hale and hearty piglets. Reporter's comment: *Mother and children doing well.* Facetious? Maybe. But still, totally possible copy.

Regardless of the flippancy of his thoughts, Travis did appreciate having this opportunity to "get his feet wet." He knew that, even though sacrifices had been made, he had to start somewhere. School had drilled it into him that he wouldn't so much as be considered for a position on a city paper without experience. And if covering pig births and cattle-grading festivals was going to provide him with the credentials he needed, well, that was how it was going to be.

Nicole as well understood this, and that was why she had agreed to give up the security of her government job so that she could be beside her husband as he began his career. Immediately it meant an almost ridiculous cut in income, but since both had agreed that Travis was going to eventually be the sole breadwinner in the family, it was a period of struggling that would have to be endured.

On this day Nicole was as proud as she could be of Travis. She knew better than anyone that he hadn't had an easy time of it. It was no simple task for a junior-high dropout to adapt to a post-secondary educational environment. Only dedication and determination had gotten Travis through those two years. But, as he had told Nicole on more than one occasion, he had never had any doubt that he would make it.

Of Cree descent and raised (if that was the word for it) in perhaps the most destitute section of Winnipeg's central city, Travis had had two strikes against him right from the beginning. But he had been strong in his determination not to let that stop him from doing something worthwhile with his life . . . especially after watching a brother who had let his bitterness get the better of him drop in the street with two police slugs in his gut. Not that Travis had ever kidded himself that he'd be traveling an easy route. Lacking education, he had had to grab whatever job he could find, and certainly none were what could be termed glamorous. He had found himself hopping around quite a bit—running the gamut from gas pumper to shipping-box maker in a casket company—but there had never been any real advancement. perhaps there never would have been . . . if not for Nicole.

She had come into his life at a time when he was battling daily urges just to chuck it all. He couldn't see himself ever accomplishing anything of consequence, and the combination of burning ambition and poor prospects had driven him to despair. It was Nicole who had kept that weakening spark of faith alive. She had breathed on it, fueling Travis with new confidence. She had seen something in him that he really could no longer see in himself, and when he had halfheartedly proposed to her during the intermission break at a drive-in movie, she had surprised him with a quick acceptance.

During their first year of marriage Nicole had managed to draw out of Travis a natural creative talent: the ability to write effectively. He had explained that he had been composing prose and verse for most of his life but had never seen any opportunity to earn money from it, and so had just let the talent grow stagnant while he had tackled the mundane realities of life. Nicole, however, had seen a way to combine the two. She had suggested a career in journalism. Travis had pondered the idea, decided he liked it, and, with Nicole behind him in every way, enrolled at college as a mature student.

That decision had led to now. . . .

Today he was actually beginning his "career" (something so impressive about the sound of that). A career that had been made possible only by the belief and support of his wife. That was why he was determined to make this work. For Nicole as much as himself.

3

Batesville was not one of Manitoba's larger towns, but neither was it merely a pinprick on the provincial map. Its geographic center was located on a rise that stretched nearly two and a quarter miles in an easterly direction; residences began on the north and south slopes and then spread out more numerously on the flat ground that extended to heavy forests.

The town had been founded by American settlers in 1876 and in many respects still appeared stuck in that era. There was nothing very modern-looking about the structure or design of its houses and buildings. Almost all were of the most basic kind of architecture: wood-framed or with plain brick fronts. Telephone poles and a smattering of television antennas were two of the signs that put Batesville in the present, but there were few paved roads and most of the travel done on them was either by foot or bicycle.

Industry was practically non-existent in Batesville. For a number of years following the

24

Second War War a sawmill had operated successfully outside the town, but contracts had ceased during the mid-sixties when Flin Flon and Thompson mining operations had expanded and Batesville had lost much of its manpower to the lure of bigger dollars. Unable to meet many of its deadlines, the mill had lost orders and had never been able to persuade those important customers to come back. Currently the town depended on its retail outlets, although it also relied—to a lesser extent, though the potential existed for expansion—on its fishing and tourism industries.

Neither Travis nor Nicole uttered a word as Old Betsy chugged and generally gave her all rolling up the rise onto the town's main road. The expression on both their faces was as if they couldn't believe what they were entering. Granted, neither had held high expectations, but they weren't exactly prepared to drive through a time warp either.

It was Travis who finally broke the silence with a sigh. "Well, we knew it wasn't going to be much."

Nicole could only give a weak nod. Suddenly she found herself thinking about winter. For six or seven months she could look forward to literally being trapped out here. She shuddered. Not an attractive prospect for someone who had spent her life surrounded by the concrete comforts of the city.

Perhaps it was because of all the raising-of-the-dead racket Old Betsy was making, or maybe it had something to do with the people of this town being quick to take notice of strangers, but a lot of hard stares came Travis and Nicole's way as they drove slowly up the street. Suddenly Travis couldn't help thinking of Nicole and himself as a modern-day version of Bonnie and Clyde, driving into the one-dog town to rip off its general store.

In an attempt to lessen their uneasiness, Travis said, "How come I'm half-expecting to see Rod Serling standing at the side of the road?" He then went into a passable Serling imitation. "Consider Travis and Nicole Randall. Little do they realize that a seemingly innocent job offer from a small Manitoba town is, in reality, an invitation to . . . The Twilight Zone."

Nicole grinned and then joined in by whistling the repetitious opening notes of the show's theme.

All of a sudden serious, Travis said, "Think we're gonna fit in?"

Nicole stopped the whistling, hunched her shoulders, and replied simply: "We're going to have to."

And she knew that was the truth. She had encouraged this move, and so, regardless of what her immediate impressions were of their new home, she wasn't going to say anything that might start them off on the wrong foot.

Travis pulled Old Betsy into one of the angular parking spaces in front of the square, gray-bricked building that housed *The Batesville Clarion*. It was a compact, two-storied structure and, besides the town's sole newspaper, two other businesses obviously operated there: a printing shop and a combination card and gift store. As Travis walked up to the front of the building and took note of the glass-encased directory at the outside entrance, he discovered yet a forth tenant: *Collarman Investments*.

"Investments?" Nicole muttered as she came up beside her husband, taking his arm. "What's there to invest in around here?"

"Boredom," Travis replied. Then he winked and said: "One thing's for sure, though. Won't take long and I'll know everything there is to kow about this town."

Nicole glanced along the main street. "Shouldn't take long at all," she mumbled.

They went inside and the strong, almost claustrophobic smell that greeted them left no doubt in their minds that they had entered a printing establishment. There was a nauseating combination of ink and press-cleaning solutions. They walked down the narrow, wood-paneled hall that about midway along had open doors on either side. On the left was *Kromack Printers*, across the way the card and gift store—with a large front window opening it up to the outside. As they neared the back they noticed that the hallway there opened the width of the building, allowing a much more welcoming rear entrance-way. A spacious coat room stood at the side of a stairway that led to the second floor. A hand-made cardboard sign in the shape of an arrow was angled upstairs. *Batesville Clarion* was printed in handscript in the center of the arrow. A more professional-looking sign nearby bore the manufactured gold legend *Collarman Investments/Second Floor*. The two signs looked almost to be in competition with each other, and if that was the case the newspaper obviously lost.

When they got upstairs the found themselves standing in the front office of the newspaper. Travis felt a little embarrassed. Behind this reception area was ... *the news*

27

room?

There were only three desks, each one not much bigger than the ones Travis had sat behind in journalism class. A quick scan of the typewriters sitting atop each revealed how antiquated they were.

At this time only one of the desks was occupied: a youngish girl with long, straight chestnut hair and plain looks was seated at it. She appeared as bored as she could be, lightly fingering the keys on her machine and crushing a cigarette butt in an ashtray that was already close to overflowing. Travis walked over to the counter that separated the receptionist's station from the rest of the office, and said a pleasant hello to the girl.

"Uh, I'm supposed to see Robbie Wade," he then said.

The girl's expression was dull. And then, as though a spark had been ignited, her face brightened.

"Oh, you must be that new guy from Winnipeg," she said, getting up from her desk—apparently eager to do so. She walked over to Travis with an extended hand.

Travis met her hand and smiled. "Yeah, Travis Randall," he said in introduction. "And my wife Nicole."

"Did you just get in?" the girl asked, speaking to Travis but now flashing a smile at Nicole.

"Yeah, drove in not five minutes ago," Travis answered.

"By car? That's quite a long way."

Nicole playfully rolled her eyes at the girl as if to say, "Tell me about it."

Travis shook his head. "It wasn't that bad.

We gave ourselves a couple of days' travel time."

"Yeah, and the gods were with us," Nicole added in humor.

The girl then introduced herself. She was Sharon Crane.

"Hi Sharon." Travis took another slow look around the office. "So, what do you do around here?"

"At this exact moment, whatever comes up." She began listing off her fingers. "Receptionist, editor, reporter, researcher . . whatever I'm needed as. Things are quiet now but the cliche still applies."

"Which cliche is that?"

"Jack of all trades and master of none. You'll find out soon enough what I mean."

Travis nodded.

"As with the rest of us you'll do some of it all," Sharon explained. "The best way to describe it is like this: you're above nothing at the *Clarion*. And that includes cleaning your own typewriter."

Travis drew a breath. "Well, it's not like I didn't expect this. Words of wisdom from my journalism instructor: be prepared for anything when working for a small-town paper."

"Best way to learn. Anyway, Robbie will fill you in more when she gets back."

Travis looked at Sharon a little strangely. "She?" he asked cautiously.

Sharon wore a knowing smile. "*Roberta* Wade."

Travis turned to his wife and snapped down the brim of his Stetson. "Sonofagun, and all this time we thought Robbie Wade was a guy."

"*You* thought she was a guy," Nicole

29

corrected. "I just never bothered to contradict you." She then winked over to Sharon.

"Well, I can tell you with certainty she's a woman," Sharon said. "But don't let that get you thinking she doesn't know how to run a paper."

Travis rocked his head, still taken aback. "Uh, how long is she going to be gone for?"

"Not long," Sharon replied. "She just went across the street for coffee."

Travis looked at Nicole. "Maybe we should go over ourselves?" he suggested.

"I could go for a drink. My throat's parched."

"Good idea," Sharon added. "There's something about a first-time meeting with your boss outside the office that isn't as intimidating."

"Is that something I should watch for?" Travis asked with suspicion. He'd never worked under a woman before and, although he didn't think of himself as a male chauvinist, really felt quite unsure of what to expect.

"No," Sharon responded with a castaway tilt of her head. "She's pretty easygoing . . . as long as you bring her an earth-shaker of a story at least once every six months."

Travis said, and not entirely lightly. "Why do I feel that's probably a lot more difficult than it sounds?"

Sharon winked at him, reacting with humor to his not-very-well-hidden uncertainty. "You're catching on fast, lad."

It was called the Batesville Grille (why not? Travis thought), and it looked to be the only lunch-counter eating establishment in the town. It was four in the afternoon but the restaurant was filled to capacity. Of course, as soon as

Travis and Nicole stepped inside, conversation dulled and all but a few sets of eyes focused on them. Travis smiled uncomfortably and for some reason couldn't stop himself from giving a cordial wave. Neither it nor his smile was returned.

Nicole sidled up to him and whispered out the corner of her mouth, "What's the definition of paranoia?"

"They, uh, just have to get used to us," Travis said, also through the side of his mouth.

"I think that's going to go both ways."

With Nicole close beside him (as if she were expecting one of the grease-coats who were in the majority in the cafe to make a sudden grab for her), Travis walked over to the busy serving counter. While standing there waiting to be acknowledged he tried to guess which one of the customers was Robbie Wade. Within seconds he was sure he'd picked her out—sitting in a far booth with two others whose backs were to him—but he still wanted to save himself some really unneeded embarrassment and so waited until he could check with one of the serving personnel.

"Excuse me," he finally said, politely and not a little shyly, to the bony-faced girl who was ringing up an order at the cash register. (A sign was taped to the back of the machine which read, in floating lyrical script, HAVE A NICE DAY.) The man who was settling his bill was one of the "gronks" and he didn't hesitate to give Travis a pissed-off look.

The girl jerked her head in acknowledgment to Travis but rudely refused to give him so much as a glance.

Travis, however, remained pleasant as he

asked, "Could you tell me where I could find Robbie Wade?"

The girl grunted, handed her customer his change, and again jerked her head, this time off to the side—in the general area where Travis's guess was sitting. He didn't bother asking the girl for a more exact answer, thanking her instead and starting over to the booth.

The woman he believed to be Robbie Wade, he could tell right away, was one of those true professional types who would probably sacrifice any kind of personal life to advance her career. She had that . . . frustrated look about her. Tight. Still, there was no denying she was an attractive lady—had to be at least in her middle thirties—who obviously took great care in preserving herself. Her shoulder-length auburn hair was softly curled and highlighted with just the proper amount of blonde frosting. She had a naturally pretty face, one not reliant on a mask of makeup. What little she wore only accentuated what was already there. Her skin had a definite glow to it as if she exercised regularly, which, judging by the shape of her body, she clearly did.

Another thing Travis took note of. From the moment he first spotted her she hadn't seemed to stop talking.

He didn't barge in on the conversation she was having with her two companions. He merely stood with Nicole next to the booth and waited to be acknowledged. Robbie could see Travis wanted to talk to her but had no intention of stopping herself short. She was a woman who finished what she started.

Nicole's first impression of Robbie Wade was not particularly favorable. She detected a snobbishness about her. Then again, at the moment her impression of Batesville as a whole was such that it could be stuffed into a sack and dropped down a well.

Finally Robbie finished what she was saying, her closing words raising a polite stream of laughter from the two men sitting opposite her. Nicole quickly perceived a transparency to their response and couldn't shake the tag "brown-nosers" from her next volley of thoughts. Which was kind of sad. Both men were obviously employees of Robbie Wade's who, judging by their appearance, had been probably working in journalism before she was even born.

Robbie held her coffee cup to her lips. She looked first, neutrally, at Nicole . . . and then her gaze shifted to Travis.

"Travis Randall, right?" she said, and her tone was as indifferent as her expression.

Travis nodded, smiled, and out of courtesy removed his Stetson. The hair that poured out was black and greasy . . . and just as long as Robbie's.

"Miss Wade?" he inquired.

"If you like," and now she smiled. "But most people just call me Robbie. Informality helps in this business, especially in a community of this size."

"I can understand that," Travis said with another nod. He brushed his hair back.

Robbie next introduced Travis to her two companions. Nicole was right in her guess, both were *Clarion* employees: Harold Foley and Ben Quarry. The brief employment bio Robbie then provided revealed to Travis that both had been staffers for over a quarter of a century. Re-

porters ... though Travis remembered what
Sharon had said and realized the vagueness of
the title.

After Travis introduced Nicole to the group,
Harold and Ben excused themselves, explaining
that they had to copyedit some material and
prepare for a town council meeting respectively.
Robbie then invited Travis and Nicole to sit
with her.

Looking for a conversational starting point,
Travis remarked: "Copy editing?"

"Ominous sounding, isn't it?" Then Robbie
smiled reassuringly. "Really it's no big deal.
Remember who we're writing for. All we ask for
is legibility, rudimentary grammatical and
punctuational ability."

"Grade-school qualifications, huh?" Travis
joked, and then in the next instant wished he
hadn't said that.

Robbie's smile broadened. "Oh, you'll have
your work cut out for you, don't worry about
that. Our news room consists of exactly five
people, including myself, and in October
Harold's going to be retiring and the publisher
is adamant about not refilling the position.
Gives you some idea of the budget we're
working with. As well, even though the past
couple of weeks have been slow locally, our
reporting isn't confined to Batesville activities.
We cover a seventy-five-mile radius, reporting
on events that happen in all the communities in
that circle."

"Get up to Thompson?" Travis asked.

"We cover Thompson but don't have a circulation there. Although we do get special
orders."

The waitress came over. She was that same

skull-faced girl who had been so "helpful" at the counter. Robbie called her Jennie. Travis and Nicole both ordered large Cokes, and Robbie persuaded Travis to try the pie as well. House specialty; apple. Nicole claimed she wasn't hungry, despite Robbie's offer to pay. She stayed with her soft drink. Robbie ordered another coffee.

"Well, I know it's too early to have formed any kind of solid opinion," she then said. "But from what you've seen so far, what do you think of our town?"

Travis and Nicole exchanged a look. They had giveaway smiles on their faces but before either could commit to an answer Robbie let them off the hook.

"I know," she said with a slight laugh and wave of her hand. "I'm not originally from around here either. I still can't get used to the virtual isolation—geographical and other-wise—but I have found the best way to cope with it is by keeping yourself busy." To Nicole: "Speaking of which, are you going to be looking for anything?"

"After we get settled, yeah, I'd like to."

"What about volunteer work?"

"It's something I'd consider, but ideally I'd like to be able to make a few dollars to help us along."

Travis added, "These next months in particular are going to be tight."

Robbie nodded sympathetically. "Well, I have to tell you there's not a whole lot of opportunity up here. Don't take offense, but your getting hired by us, Travis, was really just a matter of fortuitous timing. Your application landed on my desk within an hour of our having

to hire somebody. But I'll keep my ears open. If
I hear of anything I'll mention you, Nicole,
that's a promise."

"I'd really appreciate it," Nicole said
gratefully. Her opinion of Robbie had started to
shift a little more to the favorable side.

"Nicole was with the Federal Government,"
Travis put in. "Clerk-typist with Health and
Welfare. Just in case you're asked."

Robbie tossed a wink. "I can be quite a persuasive salesperson."

Travis wasn't expected to start work until
the next day, and so after they were finished
getting acquainted with Robbie they started for
the boarding house at which they'd be staying.
Both were hoping this would only be temporary,
until they could save enough cash to put a down
payment on their own place. But with the money
Travis would be earning such a move wouldn't
be until sometime in the future. Which was
another reason Nicole was anxious to find work.
Any kind of work.

The boarding house was on Valgard Street,
though there was no street sign identifying it.
As a result, Travis found himself chugging up
and down the town's gravel roads searching for
it until he finally grew frustrated and asked
some freckle-faced kid on a bike for directions.
Naturally he wasn't saved the embarrassment
of being any farther than a block from it.

The house was on the corner of Valgard,
where the street intersected with Portnoy—this
avenue visibly marked since it was the town's
second most-traveled route.

It was without question the most impressive residence in Batesville. Built in a quasi-
colonial style which stood as a tribute to its

original owner's heritage. And Travis and Nicole would soon discover that its current proprietor was the granddaughter of that American prospector who had become one of the founders of the town. He had been named Russell Bates.

Cora Bates saw the Randalls approach the front porch and she met them at the door. She looked to be somewhere in her seventies but still possessed a face that Travis believed must have been a man-stopper in its day. Cora Bates, however, had never married. She'd lived her entire life in her parents' house, caring for them when they were older, and when they finally died and Cora was in a position to live her own life, she was already too set in a pattern to consider changing things.

Both Travis and Nicole felt immediately at ease with Cora. She exuded a pleasantness and cheerfulness that would make anyone feel comfortable. She invited them inside and after offering coffee or tea—which they both declined—took them on a tour of the house. She was a spry old woman and moved with a briskness that many a younger person would have a difficult time keeping step with.

The house was spacious but warm. The furnishings were of a Victorian design, and when Travis inquired as to their age and place of origin, Cora explained that all the pieces had been imported from Europe over sixty years before.

In a town that had been battling economic despair for nearly two decades, the house stood as an anachronism.

They learned that there were three other boarders in the house: another couple, retired, and a Batesville-based salesman whose travels rarely permitted an extended stay. As well, there was a live-in housekeeper, and Travis and Nicole were given an introduction to her as they entered their room. Her name was Rosa, and in some ways she could have been Cora's sister, only it was apparent that her years of service had taken from her any cordial disposition she may have at one time possessed. She had a face that seemed to be screwed into a perpetual frown.

Later that evening, after a delicious dinner of broiled chicken breasts and mashed potatoes, Travis and Nicole decided to go for a walk around their new neighborhood. The town seemed as quiet and still as the night itself and both of the young people were caught up in the tranquility of the moment. They strolled along Valgard—not talking much—up to the main street. But they chose not to continue, sparing themselves any stares and oblique glances.

Finding a bench alongside the road, the two sat for awhile just watching the night. The subdued lights of the town shone in a misty haze behind them. There was a bit of a nip to the air and Nicole snuggled into Travis. He wrapped his arm around her shoulder and drew her even closer. He then took a deep, long breath. It was as if he wanted just to swallow the air.

"Y'know, I think I'm changing my tune," he said.

"What do you mean?" Nicole asked quietly.

"I was meant for this kind of life. Fresh air, open land. There's such a freedom to it all."

"You're an Indian, the country's in your blood," Nicole kidded.

"That's probably true." Then, softly, he said to her, "I just hope you're not going to find this change too difficult."

38

Nicole responded with a smile. "It's what we have to do, isn't it?"

"That doesn't tell me how you feel."

Nicole sighed. "I'll make it, honey. But it is—different out here."

"That's not the word for it." Travis pointed to the sky, which was clear and filled with sparkling gems. "I mean, you just have to look at the stars. In the city you never see them like this. Out here it's as if you can almost touch one." He paused, then said quietly, "Reach for a star and carry it in your heart."

"What was that?"

"Oh, it's just something I heard once. A long time ago. It's part of a rhyme that has to do with . . . with dreams coming true."

Nicole thought about that for a moment. "It's kinda pretty."

Travis gently closed his hand over hers. "I've reached my star," he said.

Nicole looked up at him and she was smiling.

"I'm not being cute," Travis was quick to add. "Everything I am and anything I might someday be is because of you."

Nicole didn't have to say anything in return; the feelings she had for Travis were reflected in her eyes, so round and warm. She was a beautiful girl at any time, but to Travis at that moment—either because of their surroundings or the enormous love he was feeling for her—she couldn't have been bettered by an angel.

4

Batesville was too small a community to have its burial grounds within its boundaries. Consequently, the Batesville Cemetery was located two miles north of town, off the gravel road that ran parallel to Route 391. The cemetery entrance was so thickly tree-lined that passage was often not without difficulty. Particularly during the summer months when foliage was at its heaviest.

As with many rural graveyards, upkeep was never of chief importance to the town officials. It was their reasoning that the community's limited budget could be put to much better use servicing the living. A groundkeeper was employed, but cemetery maintenance was just one of his many duties, and when he did travel out to the graveyard it was usually only to open or close another six-foot hole in the ground.

Bill Meyer had been busy in town all that day, and so had to clock in overtime to get a grave dug for the next day's burial. Travis and Sherry had already returned to the boarding

40

house and had bedded down for the night before Bill had reached the end of his digging. The plot of earth was nearly hollowed, but he was still looking at another half-hour's work leveling off the walls. Maybe longer, since he was now solely reliant on the feeble light provided by his lantern, which would have to be shifted frequently if the job was to be done right.

Bill climbed out of the hole, took a look at what was left to do, and said simply, "Screw it." He still had that long walk back into town to consider. He could always come back early the next day and get the job finished before the procession arrived at ten-thirty.

And that was what he was going to do.

With a determined thrust he embedded his spade into the mound of moist earth at graveside. He then wiped his hands against his coveralls and carried the lantern back to the shed at the far corner of the cemetery.

He was admittedly a little uncomfortable being out there at night. The familiarity he felt in the grounds during the daylight hours was missing, replaced by an almost threatening gloom. He found himself more receptive to the noises and stirrings that went on around him. All manner of unidentified night creatures sounded in the bush. The tree leaves would rustle like the folds of a shroud whenever a periodic breeze caught them . . . sounding to Bill as if someone, or some *thing*, was clearing them . . . heading right for him.

"Whoa!" Bill shouted, determined to put a stop to this paranoia before he pushed it too far. Hearing his own gruff voice rise above the other sounds did make him feel a little more relaxed. It reminded him of who really was in charge here.

"Better be careful before I piss m'self."

He laughed at this. But he remained un-
aware that he was carrying his lantern much the
same way he would a club—high at his side,
ready for swinging.

He lowered the lantern by the door of the
shed and inserted his key into the rusted padlock. He had a hard time getting it to open
again, and as he cursed the damn thing he made
a mental promise to take himself down to
Boyle's Hardware the next day and pick up a
new padlock. Charged to the town, of course.

Finally the lock snapped free and he
removed it.

He lifted the lantern and went inside.

He began rummaging around the shed,
trying to remember where he'd hidden his bottle
of scotch.

He was not inside more than a minute when
he heard it. A shrill, echoing cry that came from
somewhere out among the graves. Bill stood
without moving and waited for . . . whatever
that was to sound again.

The wind maybe?

When he next heard the wailing he knew at
once that it was not the wind. At least not any
wind he was familiar with. It sounded somehow
alive. Emanating from one distinct source, yet
surrounding the shed. Growing closer.

Bill's throat closed. He took a few tentative
steps over to the open door, not hesitating to
grab the pitchfork from its place on the wall. He
brought himself to call, though dryly, "Whoever's out there better be gone by the time I
come out! Cemetery's off limits after dark!"

Then he waited. For some response. Perhaps

the sound of running feet. Anything. But whatever it was that was outside the shed responded with silence. As if it too were waiting. Bill tightened his grip on the pitchfork and inched a little closer to the door.

"Ya still out there, are ya? Ya'd better start doin' some answerin'!"

His free hand groped behind for the lantern which he'd placed on the shelf by the door. As Bill moved it, its dull yellow light shifted and distorted the many shadows painted in the corner, unnerving him yet more.

He swallowed and tried for communication one more time, forcing it all out of himself.

"Old Bill's comin' out just now! Don't wanna see no one. I mean it. No one!"

He stepped outside, but for the first few minutes stood with his back against the door. The lantern dangled loosely from his arm but the pitchfork was poised to ventilate the first thing that moved. He started away from the protection of the shed.

His light touched on no form more menacing than the nearest tombstone. Slowly he turned in a half-circle.

The ground behind him moved. He spun around, jabbing the darkness with his pitchfork. Nothing. He held his position, though, remaining in a defensive stance.

"C'mon!" he shouted, though his voice was wavering. "I—I'm waitin' for ya!"

Then, piercing the night like the razor-sharp blade of a knife, came the prolonged shrill cry that again seemed to come at Bill from every direction.

Some powerful, unseen force took control of the pitchfork and sent it flying out of his hands.

It landed several yards deep in the bush. Bill felt a large, clammy hand close around his shoulder. His urine spilled. He raised his lantern and turned himself slowly around . . . and gazed up at the black, frost-bitten face of a true demon from Hell.

The quiet of the night shattered with his screams.

After services in town, the funeral for Thomas Gwynne moved out to the cemetery. It wasn't a large procession; outside of the lead car and the hearse there were only four other vehicles accompanying the deceased on this, his last ride. Not that Old Man Gwynne would have been hurt or disappointed by the turnout. He had probably expected it. A farmer from the next-door community of Lyddal, his circle of acquaintances had consisted of just those few Batesville merchants with whom survival required he do business. And of those who were attending today, probably most were looking for nothing more than getting out of work for half a day.

The cars arrived at the cemetery at ten-forty. William Trelevan, the director of the Trelevan Funeral Home, couldn't understand it when he saw that the mound of soil at graveside had not been properly covered with greens. Apparently, the lowering device had not been set up either. The mortician gritted his teeth; he knew about Bill Meyer, knew him as a man who cherished a drink. But he'd never let that interfere with his duties before. Now it obviously was starting to.

Trelevan stopped his car just past the entranceway, leaving the following vehicles to idle on the tree-bracketed gravel path, out of view of the grounds. He jumped out of his Caddy and instructed his teenaged assistant who was behind the wheel of the hearse to rush over to the shed and start laying the greens over that obscene hill of root-laden mud. He then himself went over to the car which contained the deceased's brother and sister-in-law and came up with a fast excuse for the delay. He explained that his car had gotten stuck in a mud rut and that his man had gone to get a shovel to dig him out. Both seemed to accept his story and the stream of apologies that accompanied it and, as Trelevan started back to the cemetery to see how the kid was doing, he breathed a sigh of relief. Nothing worse than bad publicity for a funeral home. But by then he was so incensed at the outright negligence of Bill Meyer that he decided to demand that the council terminate the maintenance worker posthaste.

Trelevan found his assistant standing ashen-faced by the open grave. The two sections of Astroturf that he had dragged over lay in a careless heap at his feet. The fingers of both hands were still curled, in an empty grasp. He was looking off, open-mouthed, to the far side of the cemetery. Trelevan, annoyed beyond endurance at this point, called to the kid twice while storming over. When he finally got along-side him, the mortician roughly spun him around by the shoulders.

"Why the hell haven't—"

His assistant's head slowly turned back in the direction in which it had been facing.

That was when the flushed, tight-faced Trelevan followed his gaze. . . .

His own bottom jaw unhinged.

At the eastern edge of the cemetery lay the

jaundiced and bloated body of Bill Meyer. He was sprawled beside the gaping mouth of another grave, one which he had apparently opened with his bare hands—they were raw and bloody. This grave, however, had been occupied. The corpse of an old woman had been pulled from its coffin and was lying exposed in its own earth.

Rather what was left of it was.

Most of the body was gone. It had been ripped apart, as if by the claws of a wild animal. Gnawed, broken bones and layers of flesh were scattered abut the gravesite. The body had been embalmed and so there was no blood splashed about. Only a red-tinged yellowish juice that was dripping like melted ice from Bill Meyer's wrenched mouth.

5

Travis spent his first hours at the *Clarion* watching his assigned guide, Sharon Crane, go about her duties. This not only gave Travis an idea of how things were done at the newspaper, but also allowed him the chance to get comfortable in his new surroundings.

He watched Sharon type some copy (like him she was a hunt-and-pecker, but still managed about forty words a minute), and then rode with her to Earchman, where she was doing a followup on a shooting accident.

They were back in town by eleven and, after they dropped her notes at the office, decided to go for an early lunch.

The Batesville Grille was packed and again the stares came Travis's way. Much to his disappointment, they were unable to seclude themselves in a booth and had to remain on view at the counter.

Sharon reached for a menu, but Travis just leaned forward and let his eyes wander. His companion asked, "Aren't you interested in eating?"

Travis smiled. "Sure. It's just I don't need that. All I ever eat in places like this are hamburgers."

"Doesn't that get boring?"

"Nope. To tell you the truth, I could probably live on 'em. Besides, I figure that's the one food you can't go wrong with. And if you do, well, that tells you the kind of restaurant you're in."

Sharon called across the counter to the Oriental cook. "Better be careful with the hamburger today, Freddie. You've got a real connoisseur of the cow here."

Travis chuckled, only a little embarrassed. He then mused, "Quality control at McDonald's. That's a career I never considered."

"Ph.D.'s only need apply."

Travis saluted her. "Exactly."

After they placed their lunch order (all this talk about hamburgers prompting Sharon to ask for one), Travis said to her, "So tell me, have you been a Batesville-ite all your life?"

"I should be so lucky," Sharon said sarcastically. She drank some of her water and then lit a smoke. "Seriously, no. But not much better. I was born on a farm in Wordsworth, Saskatchewan. Ever hear of it? Lived all my life in the country and in small towns—you know, where the population never exceeded twelve thousand. No, that's wrong. I had a taste of the city once, for about two months. When I was all of five and my mother died. I was shipped off to Regina to live with my aunt—really my dad's cousin—until Dad changed his mind and took me back."

"That musta been rough," Travis said.

"Oh, I don't blame my father. He had a large spread to look after and just didn't feel he could do that plus adequately raise a pre-school-aged daughter."

"Any brothers or sisters?"

"Two brothers. They were quite a bit older, though, and could help Dad on the farm. You know, to this day I still think it was those two who talked Dad into bringing me back. They'll never admit it, though."

Travis smiled.

"Oh, those two guys have always been super-protective of me. God, I can't begin to tell you how many potential boyfriends they either intimidated or just plain scared off. It was like being raised by *three* fathers."

"And your dad never remarried?" Travis inquired.

"He's never even come close." Sharon's smile was almost rueful. "I guess that explains why I grew up to be a tomboy."

"I don't think you're like that," Travis said. He then pointed to her cigarette. "Except maybe . . ."

"You don't like to see a woman smoke?"

"I don't like to see *anyone* smoke. But, yeah, I do suppose the male chauvinist in me comes out when I see a girl with a cigarette. But then, hey, I try to follow the motto 'Live and let live.' "

Sharon took a deep, defiant drag. "Well, that's good because I don't have any desire to quit."

Travis hunched his shoulders. "At least you're honest."

"Anyway," Sharon said, "now that you

know my file, what deep, dark secrets do you have in your past?"

Travis looked at her. He tried to speak jokingly but there was still a hint of seriousness in his voice. "Me? I don't have a past."

"Really? The man who was born yesterday, is that it?"

"Yeah, something like that."

Sharon leaned over closer to him. "And what if I told you I don't believe you? That I think you're harboring some terrible secret that you're careful about anyone finding out."

"I'd say, go lighter on the mystery novels," Travis said with a grin. "Look, seriously, there's just no way I can talk about myself without making it sound like I'm going off on a sympathy trip."

"The rags-to-riches story?"

"More like rags to rags," Travis winked. "But I'm making progress."

"Working in Batesville is progress?"

Suddenly there was shouting in the street. Heads in the cafe turned toward the window just in time to see a few scattered pedestrians rush from the road onto the sidewalk. A moment later a careening half-ton sped past the window, its tires raising an explosion of dust. The truck was filled to capacity with young native boys who were whooping and swearing and just generally doing everything they could do disrupt the quiet of the town.

Those who were standing in the pickup section of the truck were struggling to hold their position and balance as the vehicle went sharply from side to side, as if the driver were trying to throw some off. Surprisingly, no one had yet fallen over.

Travis left his stool and joined a few others at the window to watch the truck's progress. Sharon stayed at the counter, clearly uninterested. She struck up a fresh cigarette.

When Travis came back over he was shaking his head. His expression was not one of amusement.

Sharon glanced casually at her watch. "Eleven-twenty. They're getting started earlier."

"What do you mean by *started*?" Travis asked her.

"They looked sober to you?"

A sour note had been hit with Travis. He didn't turn on Sharon, but his voice was firm. "They're kids. I didn't see one who looked to be older than seventeen."

"There aren't any age laws with those people," Sharon said neutrally.

Travis didn't appreciate her apparent indifference. Or reference to "those people."

He said, "So let them kill themselves or somebody else?"

Sharon took offense. "Hey, I don't like it anymore than you—"

"You're a reporter, Sharon," Travis challenged. "And what about the police?"

"Our closest detachment is forty miles away," Sharon said tightly. "Sometimes they patrol Batesville. But we can't get them to come speeding out here every time those kids go on a joyride."

"Maybe not. But they could find out where they live. Talk to them or something."

"They know where they live. They're from the Chamrais reservation, maybe twelve miles northwest, by Great Spirit Lake. And y'know

what else? The whole tribe's nothing but
drunks. That's the way it has been for as long as
I've been here."

"And they're allowed to go on that way?"
Travis couldn't believe that.

"Oh, Federal agencies make their share of
inspections, but it's the same as with other
reserves where liquor isn't prohibited. If things
have gotten a little out of hand, our Government
representative gives them a slap on the wrist
and tells them to be good. Then, of course, once
he leaves . . ."

"So why don't we do something?" Travis
suggested with enthusiasm. "You and me. To
hell with the bureaucrats. There's a definite
story there. And, who knows, we might even do
some good."

"Robbie won't let you do it," Sharon
answered simply.

Travis became a little annoyed. "How do
you know?"

Sharon took a breath. "Because I've tried to
get the story. And not just once or twice. I've
lost track of the number of times I've
approached her. No matter how different the
angle, it was always a flat no. That's why I
maybe seem a little callous, unfeeling. It's
frustration because my hands are tied."

"Wait a minute. You mean to tell me that
Clarion considers a stupid hunting
mishap . . . *that happened last fall* more
important than a community of people openly
killing themselves?" Travis found his voice
raising and brought himself under control. "Not
to mention their posing a threat to the people of
this town."

"That about sums it up," Sharon said,

rocking her head.

"Man, there's something definitely wrong here."

"Look, Travis, just a word of friendly advice. This is your first day at the paper. I know you want to prove yourself, tackle that big story right off the bat. But don't start upsetting things. You're not going to last long, guaranteed, if you do."

Travis wasn't buying any of that. "I made myself a promise when I got this chance that I wasn't going to mess up. By the same token, it's my responsibility as a newsman to find out if that's the way things are run in Batesville. And if they are, I've gotta find out why."

6

"There's little doubt that the major cause of death was botulism. But I'm also sure that a good portion of his digestive tract has been damaged." It was Dr. Stewart MacFarlane who was speaking, Batesville's sole physician. He hadn't had to dissect the cruelly twisted and grimaced body of Bill Meyer to reach his conclusion. The gravedigger had, after all, all but completely consumed a three-month-old embalmed corpse.

William Trelevan had seen many terrible sights during his years as town mortician, but the body currently stretched out before him ranked up there with the worst. He was visibly sickened. Old Dr. MacFarlane, on the other hand, had carried out his brief examination in Trelevan's basement embalming room with professional detachment.

The mortician was glad to finally see the doctor pull the sheet up over the corpse. Of course, *his* work with it was still to come.

MacFarlane spoke without emotion.

"Official cause of death: heart failure. I've been treating the deceased for arteriosclerosis for a number of years."

Trelevan nodded; it was what he'd been expecting. "Meyer had no family," he offered. "There won't be any questions asked."

"Good. Then the rest is up to you," Mac-Farlane said, indicating the body on the slab with a slight jerk of his head.

As if he had to be reminded. Trelevan tried to maintain an unaffected expression, but he knew he wasn't fooling the doctor for a minute.

MacFarlane walked across to the sink. He sprinkled a generous amount of disinfectant on his hands and scrubbed them vigorously under hot water.

Trelevan said, "There is one concern. My assistant Keith was with me. It was he who helped me move the bodies out of sight."

MacFarlane continued with his hand washing.

Trelevan continued. "I told him not to say anything until I first cleared it with the proper authorities. But that's only a Band-Aid. He's not going to forget what he saw."

The doctor pulled out a couple of paper towels from the dispenser. "Perhaps I should talk to him," he said as he began drying his hands, almost making a ritual out of doing so.

Trelevan's eyes locked on the doctor's. "And say what? This isn't something any one of us can afford to have hushed up just temporarily. What we need is . . ."

"A guarantee of permanence," MacFarlane finished.

Trelevan chilled at the implication. But he still muttered, "Exactly." He then turned away and spoke his frustration through clenched teeth. "God, what are we up against? How much longer does it go on?" He turned back to the doctor. "You're a man of medicine. Explain it!"

Both knew that he couldn't. But MacFarlane wasn't embarrassed by Trelevan's outburst. It was his desperation showing. The desperation that they all were feeling.

He spoke calmly, but not in response. "Jessup's going to want to see us, know what the situation is. We'd better have some answers ready."

7

Later that day Dr. MacFarlane sat in the mayor's office on the second floor of the Municipal Building. As he'd expected, Calvin Jessup, the town's elected official for the past eight years, had requested an emergency meeting with him and William Trelevan as well as Morris Collarman—who ran the investments enterprise. All three men held a seat on the town council, but this was not a council matter.

MacFarlane was the first to arrive, and precisely on time, and so, finding himself alone in the spacious office, he quickly became rather annoyed. He was a man who did not like to be kept waiting; he made it a point to always be punctual and expected the same consideration from others . . . and that extended even to those people who made appointments with his office.

Mayor Calvin Jessup was a man who truly enjoyed the finer things in life, and this was reflected in his office design and atmosphere. His mahogany furnishings were upholstered in quality leather. A faint but distinctive aroma of the best pipe tobacco always lingered pleasantly in the air. It was an office that seemed to welcome only the most important . . . of which there were too few in a town like Batesville.

Perhaps its impressive ambience was not appropriate given the town's current economic status, but, besides the fact that no complaints had ever reached the mayor's ears, all the trappings were paid for by the mayor himself. He was a former city lawyer who had amassed considerable personal wealth before embarking on his political career.

Mayor Jessup's taste for the good living extended even to his drinking; that in itself was not so unusual until one considered that the only beverage His Honor cared for was what many termed "the poor man's drink"—beer. The mayor, however, still managed to rise above the average by drinking only imported ales. The finest beers brewed in the countries that specialized in such: Germany, France, England. and he was careful when it came to his stock. Only on the most special of occasions—or with the most valued of friends—did he share a glass. To the casual guest he almost always offered domestic beer.

Dr. MacFarlane was perhaps the only person with whom the mayor frequently opened his stock. The good doctor should have felt honored to be considered so highly, but Mac-Farlane was never the type to take note of such, in his own words, *trivialities*. Whether he drank exotic beer with the mayor or not, he still spoke with the man on the same level he would with anyone else. Without the slightest hint of deference.

Mayor Calvin Jessup was a man who ex-

pected—even on occasion *demanded*—respect.
He had been known to respond quickly to those
who failed to recognize this. There were less than
a handful of people in Batesville with whom he
allowed himself to relax. No titles, just an open
casualness that existed between the brothers or
the closest of friends. But to the average citizen
of the town he remained "Mister" or "Mayor"
Jessup, or, better yet, "Your Honor." He
believed it was the deliberate stoicism and
aloofness that had kept him in office all these
years . . . unlike his predecessor, for whom easy
familiarity had indeed bred contempt. His
people liked their top official to tend to their
matters with a tough, unflinching approach, un-
hampered by emotion or sentiment. And the
mayor may have been right. The town might
still not have recovered from the economic
slump which had been plaguing it ever since the
mill closure, but it was generally agreed by the
citizenry that, with a lesser man handling their
affairs, Batesville would have died eight years
before. When it had reached the crisis point.

Unknown to the community—and deliberately so—was the fact that Calvin Jessup was
working closely with a private committee on a
blueprint, not to just get the town back on its
feet, but to turn its economy completely around.

Dr. MacFarlane was part of that committee.
As were the other two businessmen who were
called to this afternoon's meeting. By four
o'clock all three were seated in the office, not
speaking. When Jessup finally entered ten
minutes later, he headed straight for his desk
without so much as a greeting. He looked grave,
and this was understandable—a similar look
presented itself on the face of each man in the

room.

The mayor placed on his desk a brown paper bag which contained either a late lunch or early dinner. MacFarlane knew what their discussion was to encompass and was frankly surprised to see Jessup—a man with a known delicate stomach—make an attempt at eating.

Jessup hadn't had a meal since that morning, however, and even then had only wolfed down a chocolate-frosted doughnut and coffee. Once seated comfortably at his desk he went to work removing the two roast-beef sandwiches and coffee from the bag. The sandwiches he unwrapped with care. When his meal was spread out before him, he spoke his first words.

"We'll talk while I eat." It was a redundant statement, but an opening typical of the mayor.

He then made an attack on his lunch before directing his attention to MacFarlane. The mayor had the uncanny ability to make his individual contact so complete that others who might be in the room couldn't help feeling nonexistent.

"This can be handled without complication?" he said over a swallow. He passed a nakpkin around his mouth.

MacFarlane nodded. "I've already written out the death certificate. Bill assures me there's no family or anyone close to him to get curious."

"Well, at least we lucked out with that," the mayor said bitterly. To Trelevan: "What about the condition of the body? An open casket will serve us better."

"Some cleaning, a little makeup. Aspiration," Trelevan said quietly. "No one should be able to detect anything . . . out of the ordinary."

Jessup's appetite seemed genuinely unaffected by this discussion. He went to work on Sandwich Number Two.

"So Bill Meyer died of natural causes."

"Heart failure," MacFarlane offered.

"Heart failure." The mayor nodded with approval. "We can display his body at the funeral and there'll be no one to start asking questions. Good."

"There is something else to consider," MacFarlane said.

The mayor focused on him.

"Bill's assistant. He was with him when the body was discovered."

The mayor paused for a moment. "Where is he now?" he quietly asked Trelevan.

MacFarlane answered for him. "He's been given the day off."

Jessup looked critical. "I don't know if that was the best move, William."

Again MacFarlane spoke. "For the moment I don't think we have anything to worry about."

"You're sure, Doctor?"

Doctor? The only time Jessup called him by his title was when they were together in public or he wanted to press the seriousness of some issue.

But MacFarlane didn't twitch. He saw the eyes of Trelevan and Collarman on him and wasn't about to give "His Honor" the opportunity to squeeze him into a corner.

Sensing this, the mayor's gaze shifted to Trelevan.

The mortician was uncomfortable with the whole conversation. Even though he pushed to keep his voice steady and firm, his nervousness seeped out with each word.

"MacFarlane's right. For the time being we shouldn't have any problem. I told Keith that this was a matter that had to be handled properly, by the right people."

The mayor appeared none too convinced. "For the time being," he echoed. He looked at each of the men and then spoke a little less tightly. "I suppose that will at least buy us some time."

"I'm going to talk to the boy," MacFarlane said. "Try to convince him that what he saw was just an isolated case—of some insanity. And that since there's virtually no chance of recurrence there's no need to upset the town."

The mayor stifled a belch and sat back in his chair. "All right," he said. "But if it looks as though we're going to have trouble with him, I want to know."

8

News traveled slowly throughout the town that Bill Meyer, the maintenance worker, had died. Everyone knew the man, yet no one could truthfully say he'd known him. He was remembered by the community as a loner, a settled transient. When people heard the news that day in late May, it was invariably greeted with a sympathetic "that's a shame," and then was quickly forgotten. It was doubtful that even one of the townsfolk had enough concern to inquire as to how old Bill had died.

Travis was in the *Clarion* news room when he overheard Ben Quarry make passing mention of the death to Sharon. Five minutes later she found herself assigned the duty of putting together an obituary.

As for Travis, he had spent most of that afternoon in a state of impatience. Although he concealed it, he was becoming obsessed with the idea of writing a report on the alcohol abuse apparently so prevalent on the Chamrais reservation. He wanted to approach Robbie Wade and just see for himself if she really was so dead set against doing the story. Unfortunately, he knew Sharon was right. He was the new kid on the block; like it or not, he wasn't going to earn any brownie points by making waves his first day on the job. Still, if he wanted to do something that just might make a difference in the lives of these people, he couldn't wait too long. The Chamrais situation would first have to be examined . . . and he was thinking of maybe doing some investigative work on his own time to get the ball rolling.

There could be no denying that Travis's sudden and overwhelming interest with the Chamrais problem stemmed from his exposure to his own people's alcoholism and resultant irresponsibility. Although he personally had had a life-long aversion to liquor, he'd seen only too clearly the effects it had on others. He had spent most of his early years watching a race drink itself to virtual extinction. And he had too-vivid recollections of other consequences: fights, robberies, incidents of vandalism . . . even murder. It wasn't enough for him to want to avoid such a lifestyle; he felt an obligation to do his part to improve, however little, their situation.

He was given a reprieve from his thoughts when Sharon came over to his desk. "Wanna come with me while I research an obit?"

Travis shrugged. "Might as well. My turn will probably come soon enough."

Researching background on someone like Bill Meyer required a bit of legwork, but it wasn't difficult. Their first stop was at Dr. MacFarlane's office, where the nurse-receptionist filled them in as to the cause of death, which was such that it would lead off the obit: *After a lengthy illness* ...

They then walked down to the Municipal Building, where they were given access to Bill Meyer's job application. This was so the paper could quote some employment and educational history. It was a scantily completed form, with limited information and many unfilled spaces. Travis couldn't help thinking how in a city a job form like this would be laughingly buried at the bottom of the pile. Up here, however, it had gotten a man work.

Even if more information had been available, the obit wasn't going to be much more than filler size. Only the most basic facts were included in Sharon's notes, and back at the office still more paring would probably be done. Bill Meyer just wasn't that important a person.

On their way back to the *Clarion* Sharon took off on an odd line of discourse. "Funny thing, isn't it? Just yesterday morning I saw Bill Meyer sitting in the cafe having his breakfast, looking no different than usual. Yet within hours ... Do you ever wonder if the person suspects it?"

The image of his brother being shot down flashed across Travis's mind and he experienced a sudden chill. He didn't respond to Sharon's question ... which he wasn't even sure wasn't rhetorical. He just pretended not to hear.

Sharon continued, lost in her thoughts. "I mean, well, I don't want to get morbid or anything, but when you really think about it ... who knows where you or I'll be at this time tomorrow? A car could just now skid up out of control over the curb. We could trip down the stairs at the office. Or maybe one of us could drop dead right here on the sidewalk. On the surface I guess no one really knows when his time's gonna come. But then . . . maybe you are given some hint, a premonition. You might not know how to read it, but something's setting off a warning."

Travis was blunt when he said, "We're all gonna die soon enough. Oblivion or immortality, I'm not in any hurry to find out. Or curious to discover what precedes it."

"No, I guess no one is," Sharon agreed. And then her voice became distant as she added, "Unless it's something you've planned."

Travis trembled outwardly as another shiver shot through him. He turned and looked at Sharon, who appeared still absorbed in her thoughts. And he suddenly felt concern for her. He'd picked up the way she'd spoken that last remark, and it didn't sit well with him. Not at all.

9

That weekend Robbie Wade threw an informal dinner party at her house on Unger Avenue, which was near the eastern edge of the town. She lived in an unpretentious bungalow similar in design to almost every other house in Batesville—its chief distinction being the two enormous elm trees that stood guard in the front yard.

Robbie planned this Saturday night gathering as an opportunity for Travis and Nicole to get to know on a social level some of those people with whom Travis would be dealing. Among others, everyone from the office was invited and expected to come: Harold Foley and Ben Quarry with their wives; Sharon, who would be coming alone. Robbie as well would be without a date (she had a steady boyfriend but he worked up in Thompson and wasn't free this weekend.) Collarman, whom Travis had discovered was not only an investment advisor but also the owner and publisher of the *Clarion*, didn't commit to a definite yes, but said that he'd try to make it. He did, however, at Robbie's request, pass on an invitation to the mayor. His Honor, though unable to make the dinner, said that he'd drop by for a drink later in the evening.

It was a buffet-style dinner with quite an elaborate spread. An impressive array of cold cuts, tossed salad with a choice of dressings, peas and carrots or corn, mashed potatoes lightly sprinkled with paprika, and, for the main course, rare prime rib of beef. Dessert (which was sliced strawberries laid out on a cloud of vanilla ice cream) would be served later.

Travis and Nicole arrived at the requested time, seven o'clock, and still were among the last to show. Only the Foleys and the Mac-Farlanes had yet to arrive of those who had given a definite acceptance. Travis had brought along a bottle of Black Tower, but when offered a drink asked only for a root beer. Nicole had a bourbon, which she would probably be nursing all night. No one had made a comment about Travis's not drinking, but Robbie at least thought it admirable. It was rare to see an Indian around these parts, she thought, not belting back the booze.

After the MacFarlanes arrived (only scant minutes after seven so the doctor could still be held to his rule of punctuality), a call came from Harold Foley. His wife had suddenly taken ill, he explained to Robbie, and they'd be unable to come. Although outwardly understanding, Robbie wasn't surprised by the call. Nor was anyone else at the party. That sweet, elderly couple was in reality two of the most vicious and frequent domestic battlers in Batesville. Many a pre-planned evening had been canceled at the last moment because of a fight that would develop between Harold and Marge, and usually from the most passing of comment. This had been the situation for years, but, miraculously, they had never let any of their brawls affect their marriage. Their philosophy seemed to be that, as soon as a fight was finished, forget it. Indeed, no grudges were ever held.

The call was received as a joke by everyone in the room, with the natural exception of Travis and Nicole. Robbie tried to explain the humor in it to them, but unless one really knew the Foleys something was missing in the translation.

By eight-thirty, dinner and dessert had been eaten. The meal had gone well and Travis and Nicole began to feel relaxed with their new neighbors.

Something that Travis detected, however—and frankly it troubled him—was Sharon's virtual ignoring of him and Nicole. She had started out in her usual friendly mood, but as the night progressed she had begun to grow more distant. This bothered Travis because he could say in all honesty that Sharon Crane was his closest friend on the paper. No, his closest friend *in town*. They'd spent a lot of time together the past few days, and now it seemed almost as if she were deliberately avoiding him. It made him wonder if maybe he'd done something to offend her . . . although he was certain he hadn't.

Of course Sharon had been doing a fair bit of drinking that night. A gin-and-something mix mainly, though she'd had two glasses of wine with dinner. Non-drinkers always have an eye for the amounts consumed by others, and Travis, for reasons of his own, had an eye that was particularly sensitive.

He wanted to go over to where she was sitting and talk to her, but he didn't want to chance starting something. He didn't know her well enough, and if she were keeping away because of some personal problem, he didn't think it his place to start probing.

The mayor dropped by for his drink at nine-thirty. Not surprisingly, with his presence the party took on a more formal air. It had been a more-or-less subdued gathering to start with—polite conversation and all—but now the mood became almost somber. The mayor did seem anxious to meet Travis, however, and the young man felt a glowing sense of importance when he shook the official's hand. Jessup still was Jessup, however, and didn't stray from professional cordiality. Their brief conversation consisted primarily of his inquiring about Travis's background and, of course, his impressions of the town. It was only later, when Jessup had a few minutes alone with Dr. Mac-Farlane, that he admitted, and not with a little displeasure:

"I didn't know they hired an Indian."

No, the mayor was not thrilled by this discovery. Outside of one or two minor laborers in Batesville, the only Indians the town had any contact with were those from the Chamrais reservation. And, outside of their periodic roughriding into town when high on the sauce, the citizenry had nothing much to do with them. Which, as far as Mayor Jessup and his three-man committee were concerned, was for the best.

Jessup went so far as to say to MacFarlane at the tail end of their conversation: "Tomorrow

I'm going to have a talk with that damn fool Collarman. He knows the situation. Where does he get off pulling a jackass move like that?"

MacFarlane was walking the mayor to his car when he asked, "You're anticipating problems?"

Jessup stopped short. He was neither a tall man nor imposing in appearance, but he never left any doubt who was in charge. "What do you think?" he said, and his tone was harsh. "I've already gotten word that this Travis knows about the Chamrais situation."

"That shouldn't be a concern," MacFarlane said calmly. "That's something Morris has been able to pull the cover over for years."

"Yes, but he's never had one of *that* type working for him before," Jessup was quick to answer.

"And you really feel that's going to make a difference?"

"Don't you?"

MacFarlane didn't answer.

"Don't be naive, Stewart," the mayor said as he slid into his car. Before he shut the door he turned to the doctor and pointed sharply at him. "Maybe you'd be wise to keep one thought in mind. If the truth should get out, it's you, my friend, who's going to suffer the most."

MacFarlane stood firm. "That sounds almost like a threat, Calvin."

"Oh no, I don't have to threaten you. You know as well as I where each of us stands."

MacFarlane conceded that. "Still," he said, "it's going to look suspicious if Morris fires the kid before he's even worked his first week."

"I'm not thinking of termination of employment as the immediate solution," the mayor explained. "I just want a little pressure put on him. Friendly pressure, mind you. I want to make sure that his reporting assignments are of the most innocuous kind." As if for emphasis he added: "Damnit, this is how it's going to have to be."

The doctor turned away for a minute and gazed up into the night. The sky was clear, though indicating the approach of some cold weather, and stars twinkled magically, as they always do when viewed in the country.

He then looked back at Jessup and said, "We just keep getting ourselves in deeper."

"That's true," the mayor said with a rueful nod. "But at this stage it's the only way to continue handling our dilemma."

"Still, it makes me wonder. What do you figure would be the reaction of the people in this town if they discovered the truth? And how far four of its most prominent and trusted citizens would go to insure secrecy was maintained."

"I know we're pushing it close to the edge, Stewart. But so far our luck has been holding out. And so long as it does . . ."

MacFarlane muttered the rest for him. "We just keep on going."

10

Saturday night.

And in the Chamrais village, where for the most part the cheapest form of weekend celebrating had been going on, violence had erupted.

Two men were going at each other as a stark-naked girl stood terrified in the corner of her family's cabin. One of the men was Frank, and he was the brother and protector of the girl, Susan. The other man, the more aggressive of the two, was Lloyd Caribou. He was engaged to marry Susan, a marriage that had been arranged by their parents. Earlier in the evening an argument had started between the two, fueled by Lloyd's habitual drunkenness, and as tempers rose Lloyd stormed out to get even more loaded. When he returned he beat Susan and tore her clothes off. Her cries had brought her brother running from the back of the cabin, but he found himself faced by a crazy man, one who was holding him off with a beavercoon-skinning knife. Frank was careful, circling, waiting for his opening ... and once he found his way in a

73

vicious fight ensued. Lloyd remained in control of the knife and wasn't hesitant to use it against the man who up until that moment he had always regarded as a brother. The blade repeatedly made contact with Frank, slashing open his shoulders and arms. Soon Frank was saturated with blood, his upper body covered with wounds of varying severity, but he himself was now like a man possessed who wouldn't surrender. He continued rolling about the room with Lloyd, trying to remain oblivious to his injuries. And still the knife cut into him. Susan was numb beyond screaming at this point. It was like a nightmare. She was watching her brother being killed . . . by his best friend and the man she was engaged to marry!

Finally the struggle ended up in a corner where it subsided. Susan, to her horror, saw that the reason for this was that her brother had gone limp.

As Frank rolled off Lloyd onto the floor, Susan regained her voice and started to scream. Her eyes were transfixed on all the damage her fiance had inflicted upon Frank's body. His torso was a bloody mess, filled with oozing puncture wounds. As her screams continued to rattle the cabin, Lloyd panicked. Without considering his next move he rushed over to Susan and shut her up the fastest way he could. He slit her throat, from ear to ear.

He then heard the rush of footsteps approach the cabin. Now they were coming up the stairs! Lloyd bolted out the back way, still keeping a firm grasp on his knife, desperate enough to use it again if he had to. His path into the forest was clear, and he continued to run until he was lost among the trees.

It was a forest thick with the covering of nightfall.

After running for what seemed the better part of the night, Lloyd stopped to rest under a tree. His chest felt so heavy he was sure his heart was about to burst. But at least he had given himself the distance to afford these moments of rest. And, perhaps reluctantly, to think.

His brain was still clouded and filled to exploding with alcohol, but his earlier numbness had left him. Physically he felt every pain: from the pounding pressure in his head to each spot where he'd been punched and kicked by Frank. Emotionally he was subject to the suffering— that indescribable pain—that came from realizing what he had done to two human beings. To the two people he'd loved most in the world!

And the realization that he was now a wanted man.

He began to cry.

What could he do? Where could he go? There was no one he could turn to.

In his gut he knew that he should just return to the village. But he couldn't. He couldn't be sure of what would be waiting for him if he did. What he'd done was senseless and cold-blooded . . . and an act of violence against his own people. They might not wait to turn him over to the law. Their rage might be such that they'd revert to the custom of their forefathers and exact their own retribution.

But even if they didn't . . . even if they were to hand him over to the Mounties . . . he couldn't see himself surviving in a prison. He'd been a free man all his life. He'd really rather be dead than spend any time in confinement.

Lloyd rose from the muddy mound on which he'd been sitting. He tried to look out into the night but found that he could barely penetrate its blackness. It was as if he were in a prison cell at that very moment. Surrounded by four cold walls. His mind slowly began leading him to believe that was where he indeed was. A prison cell. Of his own making. Alone.

If . . . if only he could make it until day-break, then maybe this nightmare might not seem so hopeless. He knew that his thoughts were betraying him, leading him to take full advantage of the murky solitude of the moment. His conscience, or whatever one chose to call that divorced inner urging, would do all it could to prevent him from surviving until the tangible comforts of morning.

Perhaps he was trying, vainly, to escape those thoughts that he could no longer keep a grasp on when he broke into another run. His action was governed by no apparent direction of consciousness. It was as if he just had to keep moving. Faint, darkly indistinct images blurred past him as he ran. Continuing into that mirror of blackness, with reality still at a nightmare level. There was no end in sight for him. A perceptible but insubstantial blockade, was, in Lloyd's mind, a doorway to nowhere.

And worse, tomorrow they would find him.

But he still had the knife!

He demonstrated that security by thrashing the air before him with its blade—still stained with crimson, though he was no longer able to determine its significance. For at that moment Lloyd was conscious only of escape, from outside forces and from himself.

The forest was as dark as the grave, and he ran.

Sounds both real and imagined surrounded him, and he ran.

He ran until he finally cleared the forest and found himself standing on the shoulder of a familiar stretch of road.

A road that would take him to just outside Batesville.

PART III

The Calling

11

The streets were dark, and he couldn't identify them.

Gray buildings lined them; abstract, windowless edifices that bent and melted as though being reflected through a series of funhouse mirrors.

Sounds came to his ears slowly, only they weren't sounds he could associate with where he was. Or identify. They reached his ears as if through a jet drum. Hollow sounds—like some metallic heartbeat.

Steadily growing louder.

He ran through the shifting streets, trying to release himself from the deafening reverberations. But no matter which way he turned, the sounds remained with him.

And a voice formed within.

A voice which held a memory, but one he couldn't immediately recognize. It was calling to him. To him specifically. He knew where to go ... and although the street scene didn't change he followed a direction.

At the end of the street, in a shadowed cul-de-sac, it suddenly appeared: a white-shrouded figure standing with its back to him.

He wanted to stop, not progress any further, but his feet were betraying him—controlled by an inner urge that he had no power over.

Or was it the street itself?

It was!

It was the street that was driving him forward!

It had become like the slimy, slippery scales of a snake . . . and it was throbbing. With a life of its own!

The figure standing ahead—still at the same distance—slowly turned to him.

He didn't want to see, yet he couldn't look away.

Now it was facing him. Fresh blood dripped from a bullet wound in the upper left cheek. The eyes were closed, the skin colorless and waxen. But it was still unmistakably the face—

Of his brother!

"Travis," it rasped in a voice pulled from the grave. And as it spoke his name the shroud slid off, revealing a long vertical row of autopsy stitches. A lower torso that was a grotesque splotchy pink from poor embalming.

Its arms went out for an embrace.

He screamed. He was still racing toward it . . . *and now it was growing nearer!* . . . and already he could feel the morgue coldness that radiated from those outstretched hands.

And then there were a series of sharp explosions.

Gunshots!

The dead thing's expression melted into one

of sadness and, no longer aware of its brother's presence, it turned and drifted off toward the source of the shots.

"*No!*" he found himself screaming. "*Come back!*"

He saw a row of uniformed officers, lined up in firing-squad precision. All had their .38's drawn and were firing steadily.

No! This time the sound didn't come.

He saw the bullets enter and exit the body, each carrying on it a piece of still-pulsing organic flesh.

Little by little the body dissolved in the gunfire, until soon only the head continued forward. Bullets repeatedly slammed into it but to no effect.

Once more he heard his brother's voice.

And then a baby crying.

The row of officers was gone.

The buildings were gone.

The streets were gone.

He was now standing in an open field where the sun shone brightly and he was surrounded only by warmth and peace.

The grass was high and he began to wade through it. There were the whitest, fluffiest clouds in the sky and they moved with him. He felt good, as contented as he ever had in his life. He didn't recognize where he was, but somehow that lack of knowledge wasn't important. Not now. He was too overwhelmed by the freshness. The purity. There was no congestion here. There was only himself, and, for as far as he could see, the fields.

He walked the same line for a long while.

And then he hit a rock.

He was more disappointed than annoyed.

These fields were unspoiled. He bent down to pick up the rock and carry it with him out of the field.

As he took it in his hands he knew something was wrong. Whatever he held was moist, and it throbbed beneath his touch.

He hesitantly raised it clear of the grass.

Then, with soundless horror, he saw that in the cradle of his hands lay the still-living head of . . . *Sharon Crane!*

The eyes were open. A sad smile stretched across the lips.

"Travis . . ."

Travis's own eyes bugged open and, greeted by the darkness and momentary unfamiliarity, he shouted out just once. It wasn't enough to wake Nicole, however, who was folded up in the fetal position beside him.

It took several minutes that seemed like hours, but Travis found himself returning to ground level. To the base of reality. He was comforted to feel his wife next to him—asleep, snoring softly. A couple of good restoring breaths, then he went about the business of waking Nicole.

She was deep in her unconsciousness—probably a dreamless sleep, Travis thought with envy—and not responsive to her husband's gentle urgings. He had to practically roll her out of bed to get even a stir out of her. A groan required a near shout of her name.

By this point, though, Travis felt more in control of his situation, could tell himself he'd only been dreaming. A bad dream . . . a *nightmare*, but nothing more. This time, when Nicole submerged back into her coma, he allowed her to.

Sleep wouldn't come rushing back to him, so he quietly slipped out of bed and walked around the room a bit. Dream or not, he was disturbed by it. How could he not be? He'd never before been wakened by the memory of what happened to his brother those many years ago. *Never.*

And equally as unsettling was Sharon's appearance in that bizarre fantasy. What, if anything, did she represent? His brother was dead. But was there some—connection?

What about Sharon?

12

Moments before Travis had responded to the climax of his nightmare, Sharon had returned home to her apartment in the heart of town. She had been the last to leave Robbie's party, helping Robbie get a start on the next day's cleaning. Robbie had then returned the favor by driving Sharon the several blocks to her own place. There was a working cordiality between the two but not what one would call a tight friendship. Perhaps because of this, Sharon had thanked Robbie for the ride but hadn't thought of inviting her inside for coffee.

Sharon was glad to be home. She poured herself a glass of wine, drew all the curtains in her suite, then dropped a record onto the stereo turntable. Not a moment after she switched the needle arm to automatic she forgot what selection she chose.

She was briefly taken aback when Andy Williams's mellow crooning caressed the speakers.

She may have surprised herself but, given her mood, her pick was appropriate.

Sharon Crane was a girl who placed a lot of value in music. She had a wide assortment of albums, and each matched an emotion. Or could free her from one.

Her most consistent sentiment had been loneliness, not the type of mood relieved by Andy Williams's songs about loves-that-were or loves-that-could-be. And before this moment, unless she had wanted a good cry, these types of records had received limited play. Feelings of loneliness had been overcome by more up-beat—less overtly romantic—music.

But then, until just hours ago, she had never had the reason to believe that anything was going to change for her. Certainly not the way it had begun to change.

When she had first begun experiencing those feelings of transition it had actually scared her. She hadn't been sure how to respond to them. Not that a physical yearning for love was new to her; she'd felt that way before. But, of course, it had been different. Different so much that it had ashamed her. She had never wanted it to be that way, but she was like a prisoner unto herself, having no control over her desires.

To this day she still didn't know why she had allowed herself to actively seek out those encounters, a few of which she had willingly let develop into full-fledged affairs. Oh yes, she couldn't deny there was a strange pleasure in the arousing of new sensations. But where it mattered there had never been any sense of ful-fillment. In her mind she was still a freak. Be-cause of that, any of the relationships that might have had the chance to develop into some-thing potentially more meaningful, had been cut off—and always by her. She'd been beaten, verbally abused as a consequence, but each time the separation had been one she felt she had to initiate. She had been torn between her physical wants and her own sense of what was right. It had never been an easy decision, and that was why she finally had to discourage contact altogether. Her body continued to crave that kind of sexual commitment, but she had resisted every impulse. To compensate, she had attempted to enter into a "normal" relationship. The men had been there, but intimacies had been awkward and *never* satisfying. She had tried—oh God, how she had tried! She had encouraged every type of individual experimentation, no matter how kinky (as if perversion should have been a concern to her anyway.) Complete subjugation or aggressive participation, she had never come close to experiencing what she had before.

Rather than giving acceptance to what she was—surrendering to her proclivity—she had made the decision to permanently avoid further involvements. This meant a denying of the release she still hungered for, but she would also spare herself the mental torture that had on more than one occasion driven her to consider laying the razor against the wrist. A feeling that she'd still not completely overcome.

Tonight, however, maybe the past could finally be laid to rest.

Tonight—and she couldn't explain why it had happened—she had felt a wanting for someone that was so new to her she didn't know how to handle it. A desperate wanting.

For the first time in her life . . . *she had the burning desire to make love to a man.*

But she needed that man to be Travis Randall.

13

Robbie Wade hadn't been asleep an hour when the phone in the kitchen began ringing, pulling her from bed. As she trudged her way down the hall she glanced at the luminous hands of the wall clock.

"Wha—" she muttered miserably. It was just before three.

It was her boss, Morris Collarman, on the line and he was calling from his office at the *Clarion*. He spoke to the point, without amenity or apology.

"There's been an incident at the Chamrais reserve. I want you there right away." Collarman had a high, reedy voice that invariably rose a few octaves whenever he got excited. It was near dog-whistle pitch this morning.

Robbie wasn't awake enough to immediately grasp the significance of the call. All she was interpreting was something about her going out to cover a story.

Her voice remained groggy. "What's so important that I can't send someone else?"

"You're not listening to me, Robbie—"

A yawn. "And you're surprised by that? Do you know what time it is?"

Collarman spoke deliberately. "There's been a murder at the reserve. Do I have to spell out to you what that means?"

These words penetrated Robbie's brain and she felt herself coming more awake—but not pleasantly, with a gradualness that carried her from one darkness into another. Similar to the sensation of not really waking from a nightmare.

"MacFarlane's on his way," Collarman said. Then, with emphasis: "The police are already there. You know what to do, Robbie. I'm counting on you."

Robbie had reached full awareness now but found that she couldn't respond with anything more than an "okay." After Collarman hung up without a goodbye, Robbie held her place for just a few minutes longer, with the buzzing receiver still clutched in her hand. It had to happen, she thought. Even though she and the others kept reinforcing the belief that time would work for them. The moment had come, and unless the situation was handled properly, a lot of people could find themselves in the worst possible light.

She pulled into the reservation shortly after three-thirty. It was alive with a carnival of flashing red lights, the expected activity going on in the village center. She saw William Trelevan's hearse backed against one of the cabins, its loading door open. Most of the people of the village were milling around it, the kids peering inside tentatively. As if expecting something to jump out at them.

Robbie didn't make it to the steps of the cabin before she was stopped by a burly young RCMP, one who had "rookie" written all over him. Efficient to the letter. At his request she presented her credentials, but he remained suspicious, hesitant to give her clearance to enter. He went to his superior, who, at Robbie's insistence, checked with and got a positive identification from Dr. MacFarlane.

A glance passed between Robbie and MacFarlane once the editor entered the cabin. It was much more than a casual look of recognition and acknowledgment. It was the kind of eye contact two people might exchange when sharing the most intimate of secrets.

Trelevan's look to Robbie was more obvious, and reeking of concern. Robbie was quick to pass over him, and she focused her attention on the bodies. Both were sheeted, ready for transport, but evidence that their deaths had been brutal stared her in the face. The floor planks were awash with blood, puddles and smears, as if at some point the bodies had been dragged around the room.

Trelevan's assistant wasn't with him this morning; when it came time to remove the corpses he needed the help of one of the Chamrais men. Robbie watched them cart out the first body, and while doing so she felt her legs begin to grow weak. She regained her composure by turning away and starting toward the doctor, who was closing up his examining bag and preparing to leave.

He didn't look up at her, just said, "We'll talk later." His tone was brusque, efficient.

Before Robbie could utter something in response, he was gone. She understood why

MacFarlane didn't want to offer any information at the moment, but that also left her wondering why Collarman had insisted on her running out here at this ungodly hour if she wasn't going to get immediate cooperation.

To at least get some details, Robbie talked to the sergeant she had dealt with earlier. He was impatient, clearly not a fan of the press, and volunteered nothing beyond the base facts: the killer's identity was known, though not his motive. He had not yet been found but was believed to be somewhere in the surrounding woods. A thorough search would be launched with the coming of daylight.

Having said all he was going to, the sergeant went back to his duty, leaving Robbie to watch the hearse drive off. She glimpsed Trelevan behind the wheel and he still had a worried frown on his face. She could well understand why.

Robbie didn't even try to get back to sleep once she returned home. Her head was reeling and she knew the best way to clear out her thoughts was by going for a run. She quickly slipped into her jogging outfit and went out through the back door. It still wasn't light, and with a killer on the loose she decided to avoid her usual route, which would take her a couple of miles outside of Batesville. She instead stayed within the boundaries of the town and made her run in a circular direction.

She knew that where she really should be headed was the paper. No doubt Collarman was still sitting there waiting to hear from her. But what information she had wasn't so urgent it couldn't wait an extra hour. Besides, she needed this run. Already the fresh, brisk air that she pumped into her lungs was chasing out clouds in her head. After a quick shower she'd be able to tackle Collarman and whatever else lay ahead. And she knew it wasn't going to be pleasant.

She was running alongside the gravel ridge that provided a natural border for Batesville's easternmost tip when she became aware of a car following her. When, after several moments, it maintained its distance, Robbie at first put more effort into her pace, and then, defiantly, slowed. Though she didn't stop.

The car pulled up beside her. It was the mayor's sedan.

Robbie built back up into a brisk jog. The passenger window slid down electronically, exposing Calvin Jessup's troubled face.

As with Collarman there was no preceding amenity, just bluntness: "Have you talked to Morris yet about the way you're going to handle this?"

Robbie puffed, "You can't downplay murder."

"You know damn well that's not my concern," the mayor snapped. "What I'm talking about is the Chamrais situation in general. We can't afford for there to be any upset."

Robbie brought herself to a gradual stop and then looked inside the car, which braked as well. "There's not much we can do there either," she said, leaning against the hood. "This is the kind of news that'll bring in reporters from all across the province. They're going to dig up anything that has even a remote connection with what happened."

Jessup shook his head. "Not necessarily. Not if the *Clarion* runs interference for us."

"And how do you suppose we manage

that?''

"Simple. Who do you think these reporters will go to for background?''

"So you're suggesting we downplay any accusation that might be made by the reserve?''

"*If* an accusation should be made.''

"I know what you're saying," Robbie acknowledged. "But even the slightest suggestion of the town's involvement could provoke a large-scale investigation. We're talking on a Federal level. And if that happens not even an earthquake could cover up all that's been done.''

"I'm fully aware of what the ramifications could be," Jessup said, sounding annoyed. "But we also can't let ourselves become so overwhelmed by long-term consequences we start to overlook our immediate concerns. This has to be handled carefully, one step at a time.''

"I know what has to be done," Robbie said with a straight face, and this time it was she who sounded annoyed.

"There's no question in my mind. Enjoy your run.''

The power window hummed up and the car drove off.

Robbie watched it go. She was now standing alone bathed in the first light of dawn.

14

By noon that Sunday news of the incident at the Chamrais reservation had circulated throughout Batesville. Some people responded with shock, some with an I-wondered-when-that-was-going-to-happen attitude. The one reaction that was consistent, however, was fear. A fear not familiar to most of those who lived in the generally uneventful community. Two brutal murders had been committed, and the killer had not been caught.

The RCMP, with the assistance of volunteers, had been combing the woods since five-thirty that morning, covering each foot of ground with the expert thoroughness that had become synonymous with its name. Although not about to speak prematurely to the news media, Sergeant Gary Connors was confident that they'd have Lloyd Caribou by nightfall.

Efforts by the police and provincial news teams to collect information from the Chamrais were not successful. Speculation persisted; no amount of probing could get the people of the village to admit that alcohol could have been a factor in the killings. About the most anyone would commit to was that Lloyd Caribou had always been a hothead. The kind of person who was destined to some day kill somebody.

Monday's papers tagged Lloyd Caribou "The Mad Dog Killer."

Tuesday, and Lloyd Caribou remained at large.

The mayor's special committee had hoped to tone down the *Clarion*'s coverage of the incident, but the public demanded as much information as was possible to get. Terror still rocked the town, but within days this was tinged with a strange sense of excitement. "Mad Dog" Lloyd Caribou had become almost a celebrity in many people's eyes. It seemed as if most everyone in Batesville wanted to be somehow involved.

Travis Randall was feeling outrage. He'd yet to begin his personal investigation into the Chamrais reserve problem, and, although the weekend bloodshed seemed to be his opportunity to get "officially" involved, orders from upstairs made it clear to him that all matters pertaining to the story were to be handled by *Clarion* veterans Foley and Quarry.

Sharon picked up on Travis's dissatisfaction and again felt it necesary to impart a word of caution. She invited him to her place for lunch.

Travis was hot to burning. He'd been on the verge of a virtual eruption ever since that morning. He finally had met his employer, only to be told conclusively by Collarman that he was to have nothing to do with the Caribou affair. Or with the Chamrais.

Sharon took him up to her apartment and offered him a beer. Feeling as he was, Travis was almost tempted to accept it, but declined. Sharon then went about preparing grilled-cheese sandwiches.

"We should have picked up some potato chips," Sharon called from the kitchen.

Travis, on the couch, didn't respond.

The opening bites of their lunch didn't produce conversation, but as Travis neared the end of the sandwich he hadn't tasted he found he couldn't keep his thoughts inside anymore.

"Those are my people," he said bitterly. "I can get more out of them than Foley or Quarry could ever hope to."

Sharon tried to remain noncommittal. "Maybe. You might have a kinship with the Chamrais, but on the other hand Harold and Ben are journalists with years of experience behind them. They know how to probe: what questions to ask, how far to pursue, and when to stop. It's a skill that takes more than a few days to perfect."

"What you're saying is it's a skill that can't be learned in a classroom?" Travis challenged.

Sharon answered back. "That is *not* what I mean and you know it. You wanna know something else? I'm getting just a little tired of you taking out your professional frustrations on me."

"Oh, so that's what I've been doing?" Travis returned, again with defiance.

Sharon's voice remained calm, yet firm. "I'm not exactly sure what it is you've been doing. All I know is I don't want to be the recipient of your hostilities anymore."

Travis became quiet. The defensive

expression was gone from his face and his eyes had darted off to the far side of the room, away from Sharon's stare. Contemplation made him see that she was right. About his behavior at the moment at least; he was truly ignorant of any past transgressions. Sharon didn't speak either, and neither was she in the mood to finish her lunch. She regretted blowing up at Travis . . . not that she didn't feel she was justified. But the way he was just sitting there, with that look of a wounded animal—how could she not feel guilty?

She spoke first, trying to signal a truce. "You're sure you wouldn't like a beer?"

Travis shook his head. He wore the trace of a smile.

Sharon sighed. "You know what our problem is? We're too much alike."

Travis looked over to her, interested.

"It's the truth," Sharon said. "I could tell from the first time we met. We're both self-sufficient . . . or, as my father would call it, pig-headed."

Travis still didn't say anything, though his smile had widened. Sharon pushed away from her side of the table and walked over toward him. Slowly.

"But we do have one difference," she continued, and her voice took on a subtle new inflection—one which, had Travis been paying closer attention, he wouldn't have recognized. "Where I maybe cover it with cynicism, you're not afraid to show your sensitivity. I like that, Travis. Really like that. I've never known that many truly feeling men in my life." She was standing beside him now, her hand reaching to take his. "Most seem to want to hide it, by playing this macho role. That's not you. And you know something, Travis Randall? To me *you're* a real man."

As soon as their fingers made contact Travis's whole arm stiffened. His eyes shot back to her, but they were curious rather than accusing. He let her take his hand, rub her fingers smoothly alongside it. But he did change the direction of their conversation.

"You're right about my being pig-headed, no argument there," he said. "Remember when I told you that day at the restaurant I made myself that promise not to screw up on the job? Well, I define that as doing my work to the best of my ability. Right now I see a situation where I know in my gut I can do some good . . . and I look at that as a calling."

Sharon continued to hold onto his hand, resisting the temptation to tighten her grip.

Travis said to her, "You know what I'm talking about?"

Sharon nodded, then she said: "But what you're saying doesn't make sense. You say you want to do the best you can at your job, make it really work for you, yet you're willing to challenge those people who control the opportunities."

"It's not ambition so much, y'know. It's just that I keep my promises. Even those I make to myself."

Sharon didn't want to initiate another argument, and so said nothing further. She lowered her gaze to the table where their hands were joined. Her fingers remained gently in motion until she felt Travis begin to loose from her hold. She didn't want that physical connection to break, and for just an instant she struggled against it.

And then she released him.

Her eyes rose, met Travis's. She was about to mouth an apology, even though she wasn't embarrassed or ashamed. But the way he was returning her look seemed to tell her that she had nothing to be sorry for.

At least that was how Sharon read it.

15

Ever since coming upon that gruesome scene at the cemetery almost a week before, Keith Samuels—a first-year university dropout who had traveled in search of fame and fortune and instead found himself working as a glorified janitor in a Batesville funeral home—had been unable to rid himself of the memory. It seemed to be with him all the time and was beginning to affect both his personal and professional life. Trelevan, of course, had been the first to pick up on this. Even after Dr. MacFarlane had had his talk with him, the boy had remained more lost in himself than was right. This began to concern Trelevan. He could sense a buildup inside Keith, something that sooner or later he was just going to have to release.

Another worry of Trelevan's was Keith's being seen at the hotel pub every night since their horrible discovery. He'd talked to the boy and, despite assurances that Keith was handling himself properly, knew that there *was* a problem. One which would have to be dealt with immediately.

Mayor Jessup met with Trelevan late Tuesday afternoon in the mortician's office. Trelevan hadn't gone into detail over the phone but did tell the mayor his seeing him was a matter of urgency. When Jessup arrived he was quick to show his impatience. He was not a man who appreciated mystery . . . or enjoyed the cheerless surroundings of a funeral home.

Trelevan looked like one of his cadavers: his eyes were pouched and his skin coloring wasn't healthy at all. It was clear he hadn't been doing a whole lot of sleeping lately. Although Jessup made no remark about his appearance, he couldn't help associating it with the overall weakening of character he'd been detecting in Trelevan as of late.

The mortician further strenghtened the mayor's doubts by opening the top drawer of his desk and withdrawing a half-empty bottle of rye whisky. He poured it straight into two paper cups, one of which he unsteadily handed to Jessup.

"Sharing an afternoon drink is by no means an urgency," the mayor said, not hiding his disapproval.

Trelevan downed a good mouthful of his rye. He grimaced, then added some more to his cup.

The mayor spoke bluntly. "Why am I here?"

Trelevan clenched his teeth. "I'm sorry. I'm hesitating for a reason. Because I know what's going to have to be done . . . and I only wish there was some other way."

Jessup sensed right away what the problem was. "Your kid?" he asked softly.

Trelevan turned to him. "I just don't feel

he's going to be able to keep quiet much longer."

"What about MacFarlane? Didn't he talk to him?"

"It seems to have made no difference," Trelevan said.

"Has he said or hinted that—"

"No," Trelevan cut in. "But other signs are there." Another quick swallow of his drink.

The mayor glanced into his cup. "Bill," he said seriously, "you know this kid better than anyone. I want you to answer me honestly—you know how important this is. Do you really feel it's something we should worry about?"

Trelevan hesitated only for a moment; he nodded. "I wouldn't have asked to see you if I didn't," he answered.

The mayor then took a pause. "All right. You knew from the beginning that each of us had to be prepared for this eventuality. But I will say this. Although there's no getting around what has to be done, we are in the best position we could be."

Trelevan was nervously rubbing the lower part of his face. He wasn't aware of how closely Jessup was watching him.

He said, "Considering how up to now we haven't had to take this step, I can't see your reasoning for saying that."

"I'll give it to you in two words," the mayor said. "Lloyd Caribou."

Trelevan looked surprised. "What? Use him as a—scapegoat?"

"Well, if we have to," the mayor responded calmly. "He is there."

Trelevan shook his head. "You know what another murder's going to do, one involving Caribou. It's going to stir up everything we've been trying to tone down, bring back the news media and—"

"We only have to worry about that if his disappearance becomes a concern, which it shouldn't," Jessup was quick to reassure him. "From what you've told us, Bill, the kid's alone up here: no family, no close friends. So what if he's suddenly gone from town? And if anyone should ask, all you have to say is that he decided to look for work elsewhere. Didn't care much for being an apprentice undertaker." He took the first sip of his drink. "Who could blame him?"

Trelevan spoke as if in a daze. "But if curiosity should get too great . . ."

With a disturbingly casual shrug the mayor finished, "Then it's suddenly been discovered that on his way out of town he got waylaid by Caribou. Why not? The man's a psychopath, isn't he?"

Trelevan glanced at his cup, saw it was empty, and tossed it into the wastepaper basket. "I can't believe I'm going so far as to discuss this," he said with self-reproach.

"Believe it," the mayor said. He put the remainder of his drink off to the side. "Because this involves you every bit as much as it does MacFarlane, Collarman, and myself."

"When are you going to do it?" Trelevan asked tentatively. "How?"

"Those are details I don't want you to concern yourself with," Jessup said with a friendly smile. "You'll have enough to do answering inquiries—if they should come up."

16

Lloyd Caribou himself was surprised that he
had managed to keep ahead of his trackers. For
two days he had stayed buried in dense brush
close to the edge of town, never venturing in but
maintaining a proximity that gave him some
idea of what the activity in Batesville was like.
Tuesday night he backtracked, heading in the
direction of the Wabowden River—more specifically, the old abandoned sawmill. After its
closure in the mid-sixties, the mill had been
explored frequently by Lloyd and his buddies.
He knew it well. He figured that it had already
been checked by the Mounties and so was
chancing that it might be, at least temporarily, a
good place to take refuge.

He waited until it was dark before he
approached it. He had spent the final moments
of light crouching stealthily in the surrounding
bush, making a careful check of the riverside
structure. In case some men were stationed
around it.

It was clear.

Lloyd had to maintain a cautious step as he moved about inside. There was no light to guide him as he proceeded further into its depths. He progressed solely by memory. But that was how it had to be. Even if he'd had a lamp or flashlight it couldn't be used. Any glow might be noticed outside and alert the police to him.

The floorboards creaked beneath his feet with a dull echo, and more than once Lloyd spun around, not entirely sure that he was alone.

Finally he came to the ladder that reached the fifteen or so feet to the loft. Lloyd started up it, wondering if the aged steps would support his weight. The sounds that accompanied each advancement gave every indication that they wouldn't ... but he did make it to the top. Surplus lumber had been kept up there and logs, uncut, still remained. He felt his way between two high rows of rotting timber. He nestled in as deep as he could and then lay down to sleep.

It was not a sleep that came easily, nor would it go uninterrupted.

17

The doors to the beverage room of the Batesville Hotel remained open till one, though on week nights business usually cut off around ten. After 8:00 P.M. on any night its clientele never swelled, but there were always those workers who enjoyed getting away from the home scene and swapping talk with their buddies.

Keith Samuels had only discovered the hotel pub a week before, but had since become a regular customer. He'd been kept working at the mortuary until after eight the last few nights, but was still seated at his usual table by half past. It had become his routine just to sit off in a corner by himself and get loaded on double rums.

On this particular night he was doing just that. As well as again giving serious thought to quitting his job. Not only was being around death so much beginning to affect him, he also knew that for so long as he kept in this business—in the *town*—he'd never be able to lose *that* memory. And more than anything he wanted to forget.

Keith left the pub at eleven. Three doubles was his limit—and enough to block his thoughts so that he could sleep. His apartment was only several streets from the hotel, a distance he could manage no matter how much he was feeling the liquor.

Because of the hour the streets were empty. Tonight the skies over Batesville weren't clear. A ceiling of angry clouds hovered over the town, producing a chill that Keith wasn't protected against.

Or maybe was it something else?

He was smoking a cigarette and humming softly as he made his way along, trying to keep from the forefront of his thoughts an image that for some reason not only hadn't dimmed after that night's "numbing" session, but had actually become more vivid.

It was as if the ghoulish scene at the graveyard had been stamped indelibly into his memory. He began to doubt that liquor would work its magic anymore.

Suddenly, he was very sober.

Very uncertain being on these streets alone.

Although he still had a couple of blocks to go, he reached into his pocket for his apartment key, pulled it out, and held it firmly. His doing this gave him an odd sense of comfort.

He felt relief when he saw the glow from the front porch light of his apartment. The place was as close to a dump as he'd ever been in—miserable landlords! But at the moment it was the most welcome sight in town.

Keith's suite was on the second floor, the stairs to which were around the back. By now his key was poised ready to fit into the lock. He rounded the back of the building, entering that one brief stretch where light did not reach. Where tree foliage and shadows plunged the pathway into pitch blackness.

Keith hurried his step. Just to get inside.

He had only a glimpse of the unfamiliar vehicle idling quietly, headlights off, in the alley. There was someone seated at the wheel, but he was seen only as a silhouette.

Tree leaves rustled anxiously behind Keith as though a rush of wind had just passed through them.

He experienced one final, consuming cold sweep.

And then a heavy hand clamped over his mouth as an arm locked tightly around his throat. Struggle was useless. In an instant the boy felt the hand slide away from his face over to the side of his head, thrusting it, full pressure, against the opposing force on his neck.

He never heard the snap.

18

Although the manhunt continued, the passing of a month had succeeded in eroding much of the town's interest in Lloyd Caribou. Mayor Jessup and his committee were pleased by this drop in public concern, just as they were starting to breathe easier with the virtual disappearance of the killer. Absolutely no progress had been made by police land and air search parties; it was as if Caribou had simply vanished off the face of the planet.

Daily news items about Caribou continued in the *Clarion*, but they had been receiving less space with each edition. It was only an obligation the paper was trying to ease out of.

Travis Randall took note of this descent into indifference. It was becoming increasingly more dificult for him not to confront Robbie and find out why the *Clarion* was maintaining such an attitude. It seemed that where the Chamrais were concerned, the adage "Ignore the problem and it will go away" was practiced.

Nevertheless, Travis was playing it smart.

On the surface he had become a most cooperative and uncritical worker on the *Clarion*'s
payroll. He'd assumed this guise ever since his
cheese-sandwich lunch with Sharon. If he
wanted to have the chance to do his bit he'd
have to play the novice until he collected enough
facts to prove to his employer that he had something to say. Present information that couldn't
be ignored or swept under the table.

And Travis knew it was out there.

Something else that he wasn't comfortable
with was his feeling that there was more to the
Lloyd Caribou incident than was publicly
revealed. The constant knotting in his gut told
him that the *Clarion* had access to that information but for reasons unknown was not
going to print it.

With all that Travis had had on his mind
lately, it wasn't surprising that he had become
inattentive to Nicole—who had not only this to
deal with, but her own feelings of general
boredom as well. For someone who had worked
steadily right from high school, inactivity—
coupled with the small-town pace—had to take
its eventual toll. In Nicole's case, this had
happened in little over a month. She did her best
to combat those periods when the moods
became extreme, but they were hitting her with
increased frequency. She gave thought to
finding a hobby, but nothing she considered
really filled her with interest. All she knew was
that she didn't want to give in. She didn't want
to find herself saying something that would
cause guilt in Travis and start affecting his
work.

Unfortunately, keeping those frustrations
under control was a task she wasn't sure she

was up to meeting.

When Travis came home from work that night she felt she had to say *something* to him. Just to let him know a little of what she was feeling, without complaint. Finding the proper moment wasn't without difficulty. Dinner time had become a quiet period for the two; if Travis had anything to say he preferred not to voice it in the company of Cora Bates and whoever else happened to be at the table. Nicole shared this feeling, which was why she was hoping to have some time later on to talk.

Travis disappeared after his meal, soon to be found by Nicole sitting alone in the den reading that day's edition of the *Clarion*. She closed the door and went to sit beside him on the wing-armed chesterfield. She noticed immediately a look of displeasure on his face as he flipped through the pages of the paper.

Although he hadn't gone into detail, Travis had expressed to Nicole, mildly, his dissatisfaction with the way the paper handled many of its stories. As he had put it, they were "copping out on their responsibility."

"Junk. Worthless bird-cage liner," he said through clenched teeth. He slapped the paper onto the ornately carved coffee table and flopped back heavily into the chesterfield.

Nicole knew he was bothered, and, because of that, anything she was hoping to get off her chest would have to take a back seat for now.

"Why don't you tell me what it is?" she said softly, patiently.

Travis looked at her; his face was strained, as if he'd been staring into the light too long. He didn't want to concern her with his problems, but he also felt he needed an outlet. Otherwise he'd be pushing for some kind of a breakdown.

He paused a moment before proceeding.

"I didn't want to say anything," he then said. "I was afraid you might think only a couple of days into the job and already I was getting a bad attitude. But it's been building in me ever since that first week. Maybe you've been able to tell."

"No," Nicole lied.

Travis wore a knowing smile. He laid a hand over her knee. "Nicole, I don't know if it's paranoia or what, but I can't shake the feeling there's some kind of cover-up . . . or something not entirely up front going on at the office."

"What? Like a conspiracy?" Nicole asked, and she couldn't be completely serious about it.

Travis's expression soon convinced her that he was.

"That's a heavy word, hon," he said. "I don't think I'd take it that far. But I can't help believing they're trying to keep something from getting out."

Nicole waited for Travis to continue.

He took a breath, then said: "All I'm fairly certain of is that it has to do with the Indian tribe outside of town."

"The Chamrais?"

"Yeah," Travis said.

Nicole thought for a moment. "What could there be to hide?"

"Besides whatever preceded Lloyd Caribou's rampage, I don't know. But anything connected with that reservation the paper either sugarcoats or ignores altogether. Tell me if I'm wrong, but a responsible news agency doesn't do that. Or oppose any reporter who wants to research the situation."

"Has that happened with you?" Nicole asked with concern.

"No. The big shots at the paper don't know anything about my wanting to tackle that story. They just took it upon themselves to call me in and tell me to keep my nose out. And Collarman was so damn uptight talking to me that it makes me feel all the more that something's not right."

"So what are you going to do?"

Travis scratched the back of his head. "I know what I should do. Hell, what I should have been doing already. But I guess I really am a little afraid of overstepping my bounds. I know for a fact that if the paper found out I'd be kicked out the door, and that would be it for my journalism career."

"What could you do that'd be so terrible you'd lose your job?"

"There's nothing terrible about what I want to do," Travis said adamantly. "It's just they wouldn't go for it: my doing some private investigating around the Chamrais reserve."

There were a few seconds of quiet.

"Why does that sound dangerous to me?" Nicole said uneasily.

Travis was quick to dismiss her fear. "Probably because you're thinking about Caribou. But he's nowhere around the village, I can tell you that."

Another moment of silence.

Travis said, "No, the only worry I have is, like I said, the paper finding out."

That was enough, however, for Nicole to retain her doubts. "Is it so important that you start thinking about this—now? Why can't you wait until you're in with the paper a little tighter? Give yourself the chance to build up some security first."

Travis spoke impatiently. "Because it's like someone not bothering with a spark he sees falling into a pile of dry leaves. It soon gets to the point where you've got a fire blazing out of control." He thought about this, affected by the metaphor. In a voice just above a whisper he said, "I think I've just convinced myself. I know I've gotta do it. No more putting it off."

"But what if the paper does find out?" Nicole argued.

"I've just got to handle this carefully enough so they won't."

Travis could tell this determination of his was affecting Nicole negatively.

"Look, this is important," he said gently. "I can't tell you how important it is."

Nicole said nothing.

Travis took her by the chin and gingerly turned her head toward him. "You've always been beside me. I need to know you're there now."

Nicole's eyes shifted downward. "Maybe if I wasn't so unsure . . ."

"Let me tell you something. Don't ever think I don't appreciate all you've given up for me. A good job, the closeness of your family. Geez, I uprooted you from the only style of living you've ever known. Because of that, as far as my job is concerned, I'm not going to be careless. But part of what I've found so appealing about doing the type of work I do is having the power to affect changes, wherever those changes should be made. If I can't make use of that . . ."

Nicole's expressive eyes were on her husband now. "This really does mean a lot to you.''

Travis got up and walked across the room. He stared at an antique Old World globe that was mounted in the corner. He gave it a slight twirl.

He said, "I haven't told you, but lately I've been having a lot of thoughts about my brother. They seem to have really started that night of Robbie's party. For some reason, I dreamed about him. It was some dream. That's never happened before. Especially never how he . . . Anyway, the dream's stayed with me." His jaw tightened. "That tells me just one thing. No matter how much I want to forget, I can't ever let myself.''

19

The old sawmill had been reachecked by the Mounties just once since Lloyd Caribou had chosen it as his shelter. Lloyd had expected the search to return to it and so the day after moving in had started to work on a hiding place. Remembering that there was no cellar under the floor, only soft earth, Lloyd chose a corner where the light did not reach to rip up four of the planks and dig his own "grave"—just deep and long enough for him to lie flat within whenever he heard the mill being approached. He had practiced the routine of getting into the hole and re-planking it enough so that the procedure could now be accomplished in minimal time.

He hadn't ventured very far from the mill in the past week. Occasionally he would feel himself starting to suffocate and would have to step outside for a breath of fresh air, but this was done mostly at night, and his distance never exceeded the nearest bank of the Wabowden.

He'd had plenty of time to think: mainly about what was going to happen to him. Would he continue like this? Or would they eventually catch up with him? He knew that, whatever, he couldn't stay in hiding forever. Already it was beginning to affect him. The loneliness. The constantly reacting to shadows and sounds. Shadows and sounds that, for the most part, existed only within the confines of his mind. Yet he still knew what would be waiting for him if he turned himself in. And the prospect of prison was no more appealing now than it had been at the beginning of this nightmare.

He'd come across a coil of rope up in the loft and had found himself repeatedly drawn to it. Then one day he set about cutting off a section and, unconsciously, looping it into a noose. A noose which he fitted around his neck . . . and slowly tightened.

He didn't get very far, even though by the time he removed it he was drenched in sweat and his heart was racing. He then spent the next hour crying. He thought how wrong it was: that he could so easily murder two people he loved yet was unable to snuff out the life of the one who deserved to die.

There were so many moments lately when he just wished that could be.

20

Travis called Nicole from the cafe Tuesday noon to tell her that he would be late coming home that night. He was driving out to the Chamrais reservation after work to talk to some of its people. No, this would not be done with the *Clarion*'s knowledge. Nicole still came across as understanding, but there was no way she could shake the apprehension from her voice.

She knew that, from what Travis had said about his nightmare, his helping the people of the village was a way to finally deal with his brother's death. It was, simply, something he had to do. And she had to let him do it.

Travis had been no different than usual that Tuesday, and so was quite surprised when, ten minutes before quitting time, Sharon came up to his desk and said in a conspiratorial whisper: "Do you want some company?"

"I thought you'd given up," Travis returned.

Sharon winked. "I'll see you outside."

Robbie was leaving the building just as the

two of them climbed into Old Betsy. She saw them drive off together but thought nothing of it, obviously believing that Travis was just giving Sharon a ride home. She waved a cordial goodnight to them, and Sharon waved back. Sharon didn't seem a bit concerned that Robbie saw them together, but Travis thought that was a bad way to begin their investigation. He figured it was something Robbie might call back to mind if suspicions should start at the office.

Sharon suggested a quick dinner at her place and Travis, though anxious to get started, agreed. They stopped at a corner market to pick up hamburger fixings.

The meal was prepared, wolfed down, and then they started on their way.

The drive out of town was quiet. Travis appeared lost in thought, munching absently on an apple, and Sharon didn't disturb him. She lit a cigarette, the smoke of which she exhaled out her open window. If Travis were more receptive at the moment he would have appreciated her consideration.

It was when they turned onto the gravel rise that would lead them into the village that Sharon broke the silence.

"Have you given any thought to what you're going to ask them?" she said.

Travis suddenly looked caught. "You know something, damnit, I haven't." He slapped the palm of his hand against his forehead. "Oh, that's great, Randall. You finally get out here and now you're going to end up tongue-tied."

"Just play it by ear," Sharon advised. "With the convictions you have you shouldn't have any problem."

Travis nodded. "Thanks," he said, but he

still wasn't entirely convinced.

"Besides," she added, "don't forget I'm here."

Travis turned to her. He smiled; that was reassuring. "Yeah. Thanks again."

"You're welcome."

Night comes early in Batesville. It was only after seven, late June, but the light wouldn't be with them much longer. The density of the woods on either side of the rolling, man-made path made the route darker than it actually was, with only occasional bursts of orange cutting through from the west.

Finally they came to the reserve, which, at first glance, looked deserted. Not a soul in sight.

Travis soaked in what he saw in this expansive clearing. Frankly, he was surprised—and pleasantly. He was not expecting the village to look as clean and orderly as it apparently was. There were no signs of the alcoholism that he'd heard ran rampant here.

"I sure didn't picture this," he said in a mumble to Sharon.

"What? Good or bad?" the girl said as she prepared to light another smoke.

"I've seen how some of these villages can go to seed when drinking isn't prohibited. You'd never guess there was a problem here."

"Well, there is," Sharon said.

Travis parked the Pontiac at the southern edge of the village, against a clump of bushes. He and Sharon then got out of the car and walked into the center of the clearing.

"How many people live here?" Travis asked.

Sharon shrugged her shoulders. "I'm not sure. Probably under a hundred."

Travis just shook his head.

Two oil drums serving as smudge pots were smouldering with branches and dead leaves. Travis sniffed in the smoky, autumn-like air; it was a smell he'd always savored. Sharon stood beside him, close beside him, with her eyes scouting about. This was her first trip to the reserve as well.

"I guess we should knock on a door," she suggested.

Travis nodded.

They started toward the cabins, Travis continuing to breathe in deliberately. Sharon was amused by this. She kept thinking of a misplaced Indian just now reawakening to his origins.

"Hello," a gruff voice called from behind.

Travis was at the first step of one of the cabins when he turned around.

A native man dressed in a neat buckskin jacket and well-worn blue jeans was walking toward them. He looked to be about Travis's age, though there was a deep maturity to his face that the average person in his twenties didn't possess. Good-looking, with the features only slightly marred by a prominent aquiline nose that gave him the appearance of a hawk.

He had just cleared the bush, but if he had been hiking, it didn't show in perspiration or shortness of breath. At the moment this fellow looked as fit as anyone Travis or Sharon had ever seen.

Travis met him halfway.

"Clint Rogers," Travis said in introduction. Casting a thumb over to Sharon, he added: "And that's—"

"Lori Evans," she finished.

"Name's Marv Nelson," the man then offered. He squinted. "You two reporters?"

Sharon stepped over to the two men. "Is it that obvious?" she said.

"Don't take no psychic ability," Marv sniffed. "Lately hasn't been much of anyone else around here. 'Cept the Mounties."

Travis and Sharon both gave a knowing nod.

"Yeah, I was just out doin' a little huntin' for Caribou," Marv said with a throaty chuckle. "Figure I got a better chance of trackin' him than the police. They might have all that fancy equipment and all, but Lloyd 'n' me grew up around here. Know these woods pretty well. I might be able to guess his moves."

"No luck obviously," Travis observed.

Marv was unoffended. He grinned broadly—revealing two rows of teeth badly in need of dental work—and said: "Even if I'd had, you don't think I'd say anything now, do ya?"

"I dunno. Would you?" was Sharon's response.

Marv's eyes and grin fixed on her.

Travis asked, "What would you do if you did find him?"

Marv turned his attention back to him. He brushed back his thick black hair, at the same time pointing admiringly at Travis's Stetson. "Don't know," he answered thoughtfully. "Can't ignore the fact he is a friend of mine. But what he did . . ."

"You aren't exactly prepared for a run-in," Travis said, taking notice of his empty hands.

"Oh, you mean why ain't I carryin' a rifle or somethin'?" Marv said casually. "No need. From what I hear Lloyd's not armed either.

Well—" He reached inside his jacket and withdrew from a concealed sheath a menacing-looking hunting knife—one which, judging by its gleam and general appearance, he took expert care of. "—he killed with one of these so I guess he's not completely defenseless."

"Anyone else from here looking for him?"

"The hunt's kinda dwindled. First coupla days everybody was trackin' him. Hah, it was kinda like when we had that Sasquatch sightin' about five years back. Now—oh, there's still a few. Guess I'm the only one makin' a career out of it, though. Hey, how come you're not writin' any of this down?"

"Do you want us to?" Sharon asked.

"Makes no difference. Just seems kinda unusual, that's all."

Travis coughed. "Well, Marv, to be honest with you we're not here on assignment."

For the first time Marv regarded them with suspicion. "Oh?"

Travis shifted uncomfortably. "Look, is there some place we can talk?"

Marv sniffed. "Ain't that what we been doin'?"

"Caribou's only part of the reason we're here," Travis admitted.

"I guess we can go over to my place," Marv offered, though not without the faintest trace of reluctance. He then looked Travis and Sharon over thoroughly and said, "Suddenly I got a real funny feelin' about you two."

Marv lived alone in a shack just about a quarter mile from the village center. It was not accessible by vehicle and so the three had to push through some of the densest brush to reach it—no problem for Marv, but for the two

124

reporters it was sometimes comparable to wading through quicksand.

By the time they reached the shack it was already dark. Travis knew they'd have to impose on Marv later to guide them back to the village.

It was truly a hovel—providing shelter but not much more. There was only one chair in the whole of the shack and that was positioned at the eating table, which stood in the center of the room. Indeed, furnishings were practically non-existent, and the few pieces that there were had been crudely fashioned—most probably by Marv himself.

"Unassuming," Sharon remarked.

Marv was at the basin washing up. "Not what you'd call the glamorous life, is it?" he said with a gentle laugh that didn't betray embarrassment.

"To each his own," was Sharon's muttered comment.

Marv turned to the two, who were seated on the area rug on the floor. He rubbed his hands dry against his jeans. "Lemme tell you somethin'," he said, and he was speaking specifically to Travis. "Sure it's not much, but it's a way of reminding myself of who I am. Keeps me connected to the way our life used to be. To the way it *still* should be."

Sharon felt a familiar speech coming.

"I'll give ya a history lesson," Marv said as he pulled out the chair and raised a leg on it. "The Chamrais people held a lot more land than what you see in the village. That's always been the communal center, but it's been a constant compression . . . kinda like they're tryin' to squeeze us out of existence. Hell, you think I'm supposed to be where I am? I'm crossin' their boundary by exactly ten feet, and that's intentional. No one's said anything, and I'll be damned if I'd do somethin' about it if anyone did."

"Is there a lot of bitterness in the village?" Travis asked.

Marv ripped his thumb at himself. "As compared to me? Hardly. People learn to accept what they got."

"Then why do you—"

"I just feel that some things shouldn't be forgotten. And I also know how far the powers-that-be would go if they thought they could get away with it. No one's doin' us any favors."

Travis nodded, paused, then pushed out: "Is that why there's a problem with drinking in the village?"

"Drinkin?' I wouldn't know nothin' about that," Marv said dismissively.

"You keep to yourself that much?" Sharon said with disbelief.

Marv focused on her and his eyes told her in no uncertain terms that there were some things he didn't appreciate having said. Especially remarks made in an accusing tone.

Sharon was not the type of girl to be easily intimidated, but Marv's look quieted her.

Travis could see that neither of them was going to have an easy time getting Marv to open up about activities in the village, and so decided that he had nothing to lose by just coming straight out with his concerns.

"Okay Marv, straight on the cuff. I'm still new to the community and this reporting bit, but I've heard about—and to an extent seen for myself—what goes on in the village. With alcohol.

Maybe it's because I am inexperienced that I can't shake the feeling there's a lot more happening with the Chamrais than what appers on the surface."

"Sorry, can't help you there," Marv said rather too quickly.

Travis's lips drew inward. He couldn't understand this guy's obvious recalcitrance. His next reaction surprised even himself.

"Damnit!" he exploded. "Are you some kind of hypocrite or what? You just finished giving a speech about how the Chamrais—your people—are being driven to territorial extinction, but you won't help us reach a solution to one of the contributing factors! How the hell can these people stand up for themselves if, for the most part, they're out of their heads with liquor?"

Marv remained amazingly calm. "Hold on, friend. Any complainin' I was doin', I was doin' for myself. What's happened to the rest of the village they let happen, pisser that it is. Like I said, they've grown passive. I'm the only shit-disturber of the bunch, and again, it's only for me, and even then I don't holler loud enough for anyone to hear me."

"Then your apathy's worse than anyone else's," Travis accused.

Marv's eyes narrowed. "That's pretty aggressive talk."

Sensing trouble, Sharon whispered to Travis: "Why don't we just say goodbye?"

Travis ignored her. He'd made his stand. He rose to his feet and stared defiantly at Marv. "Would my challenging you prove how serious I am about doing something for the village?" he said.

"Travis, sit down," Sharon practically begged.

Marv was now regarding him with amusement. Just to illustrate a "friendly" warning he casually picked up an inch-thick piece of board from under the table and snapped it in two. "You don't have to prove nothin' to me, fella," he then said. "I know you've got a bee in your bonnet. I mean, what you want to do is admirable. It's just that I'm not interested, that's all."

"So you do admit there is a problem?" Travis said.

Marv's crooked smile remained intact. "You're readin' into things that just ain't there."

Sharon: "Travis, we're not going to solve anything by—"

"You're full of shit," Travis said flatly to Marv.

There was a twitch and slight drop in Marv's smile. Still his voice was level. "It's gotten dark. You've got that walk back to your car."

Travis held his position. His expression remained taut.

"Look, do ya want me to hold the door open for ya?" Marv said, now beginning to sound irritated.

Sharon stood up. She took Travis by the arm and gently tugged. But he wouldn't budge.

Marv slowly started over. His smile had completely disappeared.

"Travis," Sharon pleaded, tugging at his arm a little more forcefully.

"I said you're full of shit, Nelson."

Marv floored him with his first punch.

21

It was the last time she'd let herself be talked into going on a holiday outing.

Marilyn had known Brent for only two weeks, but during that time she'd formed the impression that he was the kind of guy who would treat a girl with class—perhaps believing that there were still some women left who appreciated life's delicacies.

She'd never be so quick to form impressions again.

The elegant candlelit dinner became beans cooked over an open fire. No formal wear here: blue jeans and heavy flannel shirt, and camper's boots in case she stumbled across one of nature's dropping grounds.

Ah yes, the great outdoors!

Well, maybe she was partially to blame for this. Then again, he'd certainly painted a more appealing picture than the one which she currently found herself at the center of.

Nature lovers, rejoice! she thought facetiously. There is life beyond your downtown shopping centers.

But paradise?

They had a camper trailer, but it wouldn't be used on this excursion. As evidenced by Brent's lying snuggled in his sleeping bag by the campfire reading some bible-sized paperback (which he'd barely cracked the cover of.) Marilyn felt as far removed from civilization as she ever had in her life.

The night had never seemed so lonely.

So dark.

She poured herself another cup of coffee. God knows how many she'd had tonight. She was admittedly using it as her companion. For, as attentive as Brent had been to her in the city, she could in no way compete with that to which his heart really belonged. Jealous? Hell yes, she was.

"Coffee?" she asked him.

Brent couldn't completely pull himself away from the page he was reading. "Huh? What?" he mumbled.

"Coffee. Do you want a cup?" she repeated.

"Uh, no, I don't think so," he answered again in a mutter as his eyes slipped back to the book.

"I'm not going to last," Marilyn said under her breath.

Still, she went over to the fire and sat on a stool across from Brent, at first watching him (slowly) turn pages and then looking off into the night. Empty. Not a star in the sky. No wonder she felt so claustrophobic; it was like being in a box.

"Mind if I turn on the radio?" she asked.

She was unable to decipher Brent's grunt.

But, she figured, a grunt can mean a yes as

much as it can a no, and besides . . . to hell with him.

Marilyn got up and walked to the trailer, taking long, deliberate steps as if stretching her leg muscles. The radio, powered by a portable generator, was perched on a leveled tree stump. She switched it on, then fiddled with the tuning dial, trying to escape the static, and hit just the right station. When she did, she turned up the volume accordingly, though remaining respectful.

She checked her watch. Ten o'clock. If she were back in the city she'd probably be pampering herself in a hot tub. Or enjoying herself on a more "civilized" date. She kept telling herself to make the best of this, but it wasn't easy.

Back over to Brent. He was never going to finish that damn book.

If it wasn't so dark she'd go for a bit of a walk.

(Yeah, a walk to the highway and then hitch-hike home!)

"Bren—" she found herself beginning, then she stopped herself. She really had nothing to say.

Suddenly she felt her bladder giving a familiar signal. With all the coffee she'd consumed this night, it didn't surprise her. But with the woods being as dark as they were, she wished it didn't have to be.

Again she was up from her stool. She glanced around the camp area and decided that her best bet would be to go park herself behind the trailer. She'd have her privacy, yet wouldn't be too far from the protective light of the fire.

Brent didn't see her leave, and she was glad

of that. In her mind there was something . . . *primitive* about relieving yourself outdoors. Not something that the average person would find attractive or appealing—

Who said Brent was average? she thought with amusement.

Even knowing she was enjoying solitude didn't make her lowering to her haunches any less humiliating. Never in her life had she had to do something like this!

Never again would she.

To make matters worse—to complete the scenario—as she neared the completion of her task, she came to the realization that she hadn't brought any toilet paper with her.

She was gritting her teeth. "Brent, I hate you," she grumbled softly but with enough feeling so that, if he had poked his head around the trailer at that moment, she'd have tossed a rock at it.

Unless she wanted to remain in this un-flattering and completely vulnerable position all night she'd have to just go the way she was. Slowly, stiffly, she rose to a standing position, keeping her arms out at her sides as if for balance. Once erect, she pulled up her panties and then struggled with her jeans, tighter than the frown that was screwed onto her face.

Using Houdini-like contortions she finally got her denims up over her hips and was entering stage two of her battle, trying to fasten the button—

When the quiet of the night separated with the most rattling cry she'd ever heard. It was a sound so forceful that for the briefest of moments she thought she saw the trees before her part.

"*Brent!*"

And the glow of two moon-yellow eyes reached her from the darkness.

Brent too had heard the frightful cry, and was halfway out of his sleeping bag when he heard Marilyn call out for him. This caught him unawares, and he was not able to follow the trail of her voice. He shouted for her, hoping for a response that would lead him to the proper direction.

"Marilyn!"

No answer.

Not a sound.

Brent wasted no time rushing over to the trailer, scrambling inside and reaching into the rectangular compartment under the bed for his rifle. He found himself approaching a state of panic. He knew that something had happened to Marilyn; she just wasn't the type of girl for a practical joke.

He emerged from the trailer carrying not only his gun, but a flashlight as well. He clicked it on and played the beam all along the bushes on either side of the clearing.

"Marilyn!" he called again.

This time he heard a movement. From behind the trailer.

Without hesitation he rounded the side and entered into a blackness so severe that his light cut an exact path through it. Now the only movement he was aware of was his own.

About four feet beyond the rear of the trailer his beam picked up the supine form of Marilyn stretched out on the muddy ground. Her eyes were open, their sightless gaze shooting straight up into the night. A horrific, unnatural grin ripped apart her mouth.

Not a mark on her; Brent discovered this as he tentatively moved in for a closer examination. Neither had her clothes been tampered with. Yet she surely had been . . . *assaulted*.

"Marilyn?" There was no strength behind his voice.

Marilyn's head slowly turned to the side, in Brent's direction. That unnerving expression remained frozen on her face, though her eyes were rising up to him.

Drools of saliva began to slide from her mouth.

Brent didn't know what was happening, but as a series of guttural growls escaped her lips he let the flashlight drop from his hand and slowly leveled the rifle into firing position.

Marilyn was sitting up. Her moves, faintly illuminated in the off-glare of the flashlight, were slow and deliberate. Malevolent.

Brent was fighting to keep himself from falling apart. She was regarding him with the same intensity a bird of prey would a rodent. Yet beyond that there was no recognition in her eyes.

She was erect now, starting toward him with vulpine stealthiness. He was watching her over the barrel of his rifle. His finger was beginning to tug on the trigger.

He was sobbing.

Suddenly Marilyn howled—it was the same piercing cry that had only minutes before shaken the woods. Brent was so startled by this demonic sound leaving her lips that he momentarily dropped his guard. But that was all the time it took. Marilyn was upon him in a flash, knocking him to the ground. She straddled him, her face, flushed with evil, just inches from his. Brent didn't have the time to attempt even token defense, everything happened so fast. There was only the sensation of hands ripping open his shirt . . .

Steel-like fingers digging into the soft flesh of his belly.

Unconsciousness swiftly overtook him. He was spared the pain.

22

He must have been out for a while because when he woke he found himself lying in a bed that he gradually came to realize wasn't his. As his eyes regained their focus he discovered he didn't know where the hell he was. It was a bedroom, but whose?

His next sensation was of a cool pressure against the side of his face. He turned his head, carefully, and saw Sharon sitting beside him, holding an ice pack to his lower jaw.

Along with awareness came the most agonizing pain.

He groaned and rolled back his eyes.

Sharon didn't sound overly sympathetic. "You're not dead, *Clint*, though I'm surprised he didn't knock your head right off."

"I wish he had," Travis said miserably, speaking out the side of his mouth, and not without difficulty. His tongue probed along the inside of his mouth, checking for broken or missing teeth. All seemed to have withstood the blow.

He then asked, "Your place?"

"Mmmhmm."

He swallowed. "How?"

"Well, Marv carried you to the car. He's really not such a bad guy, you know."

"A prince."

Sharon finished, "I got one of my neighbors to give me a hand getting you up here. Told him you were drunk."

Travis tried to laugh, but it hurt just to break a smile.

He suddenly snapped alert. "Nicole?"

"I would have called her," Sharon was quick to explain, "but I really didn't know what to say."

Travis nodded and gave her a that-makes-two-of-us look. He then braved a touch to the left side of his face, and winced. His eyes went to Sharon for a report.

"You don't want to know, trust me."

"Oh God," he mumbled.

"Let's face it, Larry Holmes you ain't."

"Not funny, Sharon."

"Well, I'd feel sorry for you, Randall, but, heck, you were begging the guy to massacre you."

"I didn't think he'd really do it," Travis said meekly.

"I'm not surprised. You just don't push guys like that."

Travis started to lift himself from the bed, but with his first movement came a rush of dizziness that sent him dropping back to the mattress. He moaned.

"I could call Dr. MacFarlane if you want," Sharon offered.

Travis shook his head. "Gotta get home.

Think of something to tell Nicole."

"Tell her you were protecting a lady's honor," Sharon suggested.

"She'd love that." Travis tried getting up again, more carefully. "My car?" he asked.

"Out back. But maybe you shouldn't be driving. Not right away. Why don't you hang around for awhile and I'll make some coffee?"

"I'll be okay." Travis hobbled over to the door. He grabbed his Stetson from the top rack of the landing closet.

Sharon called after him: "Hey, what do we do now?"

Travis stiffly half-turned. "Huh?"

"About the Chamrais?"

"I'm going back."

"This week?"

Travis shook his head. "Too soon."

Then he was gone.

Sharon walked to the door and remained standing by it for a long while, her hand curled around the knob. Suddenly she was experiencing a loneliness that was nearly overwhelming. She actually had to fight the urge to run out after him. Admit to him *now* how much she needed him. If he could have read the thoughts that passed through her mind as she watched him lay unconscious on the bed—*her bed*—he would have known everything. Nothing would then have to be said, and maybe . . . maybe he would have been able to share with her his feelings. Oh yes, they were there. She'd known that right from the start, but recently had seen them growing. They were there in the way he talked to her. In the way he looked at her. He knew what she'd known all along: that they were so much alike. And he wanted what she wanted, every bit as much . . . only he had to be careful. It wasn't so easy for him. He had somebody else to consider. But it was all so wrong. There was no way Nicole could feel for Travis what *she* felt. They were together all day—

(But *they* were together all night.)

And Travis really liked to be with her. Share her company—

(*They* shared a bed.)

They had to be the ones who were together! They . . .

But Sharon was alone now.

Alone. The worst feeling in the world when it's a situation not made by choice.

I don't want to be alone anymore.

Sharon quickly went to the bedroom window, turning out the light so she wouldn't be noticed. She peeked out on the parking area where she'd left Travis's car. A vehicle which she believed must have been the Pontiac was just turning out of the back lane.

He was gone.

She began thinking about dying.

She trembled, but was not in control of her thoughts.

She was dead and Travis would have to live with the guilt of not staying with her tonight.

No!

That was wrong. So wrong. What would it prove? She needed Travis to care for her while she was alive, not dead.

She needed him now.

Travis was surprised to look at his watch and see that it was after ten-thirty. That meant he had to have been out for close to three hours. Although the way he felt he didn't doubt it.

He parked the car in his spot at the back of the boarding house. Then, as quietly as he could, he entered through the back way, first stopping at the kitchen to get some ice for his face. His jaw still felt like a catcher's mitt. He stepped into the hall and, mustering the courage, made himself look in the mirror. Not only was a quarter of his face as purple as a grape, it was also beginning to swell.

He grimaced. Hoped to God that Nicole was sleeping. Maybe he wouldn't look quite so grotesque in the morning.

At least he couldn't see how he could look any worse.

He heard someone step up behind him. Pressing the ice and the whole of his hand up against the bruise (too quickly, he wasn't prepared for those next seconds of excruciating pain), he turned around. Then glanced downward . . . into the dour old face of housekeeper Rosa. She was bundled in a rumpled nightgown with a sweater tied around the waist. Travis couldn't tell if she'd been sleeping or not.

"Did I wake you?" he asked in an apologetic tone.

Rosa ignored the question. "What happened to you?" she asked instead. Travis wasn't concealing his injury very well.

"Would you believe I fell into a tree?" he tried to joke.

(Don't smile, Rosa, your face will collapse.)

"Someone beat you?"

Travis sighed. "Let's just say I discovered one of the more 'tangible' hazards of my job."

"Well . . . let's see if we can do something to get that swelling down," Rosa said, and she gestured for him to follow into the kitchen.

Travis did, taken aback by Rosa's uncharacteristic thoughtfulness. He'd formed the impression that she was the type who would just walk over him if he were lying in a heap at the base of the stairs.

She sat him down at the table and then went over to the sink to wet a dish towel in cold water.

Travis asked, "Wouldn't ice be better?"

"Too harsh. Besides, with that much swelling it's better to get a more even healing."

"You're the doctor," Travis smiled.

With hands that were almost skilled in their gentleness, Rosa pressed the towel against the bruise—so lightly that Travis hardly knew it was there.

"Thanks Rosa," he said as he took hold of it, sighing at the relief it provided.

"I don't think you'll look much better for a couple of days," Rosa noted, "but at least it will keep the swelling under control."

Travis said, "Yeah. I guess there'll be no way around the questions."

Rosa smiled. Travis tried not to look surprised; it was the first time he'd seen her do so. And even though it was only a crack of a smile, he couldn't help taking note of the change it made in her appearance. He was tempted to remark on it, but why chance ruining a good thing?

"Good night," she said.

"Night."

Nicole was asleep; Travis knew that even before he entered their room. Either asleep or out somewhere (and that didn't seem likely). No light slipped out from under the closed door.

He turned the knob and gently pushed open the door. He could see Nicole's form drawn up under the covers. Her breathing told him that she was fast asleep. Good. Excellent. He slid in as tightly as he could between the door and the jamb, so as not to allow too much light to fall into the room. He crept over to the bed, not bothering to undress, and crawled under the covers with as little disturbance as was possible. He then tried to fall asleep. Although still groggy, with a face full of pain and a brain full of thoughts he knew this was going to be a long night.

23

Marv Nelson had no regrets about slugging Travis. In fact, when he woke at dawn the following day he'd forgotten it had ever happened.

He had another full day ahead of him and it was the hunt that was prominent in his thoughts. He was going to track north today, search the bush that extended about four miles unbroken until it came to a series of clearings that occasionally served as out-of-the-way camping sites.

Marv really wasn't expecting to have much luck following this direction; it wasn't likely Lloyd would move toward an area where the possibility existed that he could be spotted. Still, an experienced tracker lets no stone remain unturned.

Marv spent a few minutes polishing his knife. This had become a pre-hunt routine, and the cleaning had to be so thorough that the blade would catch the first rays of the sun just so. Maybe it was eccentric, but Marv was a man who didn't own much, and his knife was his most treasured possession.

He started on his way as soon as the sun cleared the horizon.

He prided himself on his tracking ability, knowing just what to look for in each of the beasts he stalked. With the pursuit of Lloyd Caribou he faced an additional challenge: a quarry that was as adept as the hunt as himself.

But Marv was a persistent hunter, determined to find Caribou if it took a day, a month, even a year. This had become his personal challenge.

As he moved deeper into the bush he was careful to check each area of ground that might provide a clue to Lloyd's direction. This morning there were plenty of false leads.

He was nearing a clearing. Judging by the position of the sun it had to be around eleven. Once he was out of the bush he'd take a break and have that sandwich he'd made for his lunch.

It appeared that some campers were parked in the clearing; Marv could see gear rigged up ahead. He wasn't disappointed to see this touch of civilization. If he could get them to offer a cup of coffee it would certainly go down good.

There was a station wagon and camper trailer, but apparently no one around either. A fire had recently been made, beside which were a crumpled sleeping bag and other signs of a camp. It looked as if whoever had been there had left in a hurry. There was no dampness in the stone-bordered circle where the fire had burned; it had been left to die out on its own. He peered over to the trailer.

"Hello," he called.

When nobody responded he walked over.

He tapped on the canvas enclosure.

"Anybody there?"

He waited a moment, then circled the trailer. His eyes picked up on something a few feet behind it. He moved closer.

A rifle.

Marv's puzzlement showed on his face. Why would a gun be left lying on the ground?

Checking further, he noticed a patch of discoloration on the grass. He knelt down to examine it. Just as he thought: *blood.* Blood that trailed round to the front of the trailer.

Marv slowly pulled himself up. As he went back around he thought that maybe he hadn't made the wrong decision coming this way. The signs pointed to Lloyd's having been here, all right. He may have panicked, or maybe in his desperation . . .

Marv didn't want to finish thinking what he might have done.

He prepared himself to enter the trailer. He removed and took firm hold of his knife. A cloud cover had obliterated the glare of the sun, but the blade of the knife gleamed with intensity.

Marv then unzipped and partially pulled open the door flap.

Immediately a smell so rank that it almost sent him reeling escaped through the opening. It was a smell that, as a hunter, he wasn't unfamiliar with.

The smell of death.

Marv refilled his lungs with a deep breath of good air. Then he pulled out the flap all the way. Again he was driven back, but not only by the stink.

Seated at the back of the trailer, open-legged on the bed, was a woman half-concealed by the shadows. But from what Marv could see she looked deranged in her dishevelment. She was totally naked, her stomach bloated to obscene proportion, and she was sitting in a pile of her own waste.

The inside of the trailer resembled a slaughterhouse. Blood was everywhere—smeared on the walls, the floor.

Oh God, the floor . . .

Something heavy and greasy was lying there.

An eviscerated human torso!

Recognizable only by the fact that a portion of the rib cage was visible.

Marv's widened eyes traveled back to the . . . "woman" seated on the bed. She was watching Marv, trying to move, but was so weighted down that such effort was difficult.

Marv believed he could hear her growling.

He moved farther away from the trailer.

She finally flopped forward onto the floor, landing with a slimy *thump* beside the torso. She raised her head . . . and began to slide toward the opening.

Marv held his position. He didn't know if he should run or just take the knife and plunge it into her and end this horror.

Like a pitiful slug, she continued slithering forward, entering into the light.

Marv had his knife poised for use. Looking clearly at her matted hair, wild eyes, and blood-smeared face, he knew that sanity required he drive the blade into her.

He stepped only a little closer.

She dropped out onto the ground, landing on her belly and lying still.

Marv rushed at her. He let out a yell as his

knife went for the thrust.

Just then she rolled onto her back and grabbed his arm.

She had been counting on him to make this move!

Her grip was so incredibly strong that his fingers were forced open and the knife dropped uselessly to the ground.

She began pulling him down to her.

Marv used every bit of strength he possessed to keep himself upright. But then her other hand locked around his wrist and further resistance was futile.

Her flesh-entrapped teeth gnashed in anticipation.

Marv could think of only one maneuver. He let himself be drawn a little nearer to her . . . and then, when her grasp slackened accordingly, he let loose with a heavy kick that caught her flush under the jaw and propelled her back against the trailer. Her head struck the metal base and she was momentarily dazed, though she did not lose consciousness.

Marv quickly scooped up his knife. He flipped it skillfully so that the blade landed upright in his hand.

She had grabbed onto the trailer base and was starting to pull herself up.

She didn't get far.

"Die, bitch!" Marv struck out with the weapon, embedding the blade deep in her neck.

An expression of surprise etched into her face. She slumped to the ground, gurgling as the blood bubbled up in her throat.

The body tensed, went limp.

Marv waited an additional minute or so before pulling free his knife.

That's when something unexplainable happened.

A membranaceous substance began to gel around her parted lips, spreading rapidly until it soon masked her entire face. Then it started to consume the rest of her body—more slowly, but with thoroughness.

Marv wasted no time backing away. He was horrified, at the same time fascinated. It was as though he were watching decomposition of the most radical kind.

The physical shape of the body remained, though it was now wrapped in a "living" cocoon. A pulsing, runnelled mass of gray that continued to feed on her.

Before the body could be wholly absorbed, the tissue at the base began to split. Like a wet zipper being carelessly ripped open.

Some *thing* was emerging from it.

A scream that Marv had not heard since he was a small boy suddenly erupted from the mass, piercing the woods. It was a scream that he had never forgotten, one which he remembered his grandmother warning him and the other village children about.

The cry of the Weetigo.

The Windigo!

Marv was now witness to a scene that would cause any a lesser man to lose his mind: the ancient Chamrais demon being reborn right before his eyes.

It had possessed that woman.

And had spawned in her.

Rejuvenating its evil.

The creature rose from the cocoon whole. It had the basic physical characteristics of something human, but the face that was revealed

could only have come from the darkest of night-
mares: black, stretched skin that glistened with
its "birth" fluids. Enlarged, protruding
cranium. Deep-set yellow eyes buried beneath, cold in their malignancy. Broadened nose
with no bridge and viciously flaring nostrils. A
too-wide mouth filled with saber-like teeth
opening and closing experimentally as it
apparently gave consideration to its latest incarnation.

The Windigo lived.

The Chamrais spoke not of a legend.

Although his hand was not steady, Marv
inverted the knife and prepared to pitch
it—directly into the heart of that black demon
which stood in silent, towering triumph before
him.

But then Marv remembered yet more of the
legend:

While capable of physical manifestation, the
Windigo *was* a spirit.

And a spirit can never be destroyed, though
any attempt to do so could result in a most
unpleasant death for the one whose hand holds
the weapon.

That was why, before the creature could
take good notice of Marv, the young man did
something he had never done in his life.

He turned and ran, back into the bush.

24

Then came the lecture.

But at least Nicole was considerate enough to deliver it in the privacy of their room. Not that this additional bruising was any less painful.

Still, Travis let her get it all out of her system and then responded, calmly, by admitting his beating was a result of carelessness on his part. Carelessness that he guaranteed would not be repeated. Nicole was not so easy to convince this time. She wanted him to stop his investigating until he could secure the paper's approval and assistance. He argued that he might as well give it up altogether then. That too was fine with Nicole.

No resolution or compromise was reached by the time Travis left for work. All he did promise was that that night he would be home at the usual time.

He decided to walk to the office. He needed the time to cool off as well as come up with some story to tell his co-workers. Why was that so difficult? He remembered Robbie seeing him and Sharon leaving yesterday; he wished he could get together with Sharon before work and ask her help in dreaming up something. More importantly, to ask if he could count on her corroboration. Just in case those suspicions he feared should start making the rounds at the *Clarion*.

Luck was with him this morning. He happened to glance inside the window of the Batesville Grille as he walked by and saw Sharon sitting off by herself in a far booth. He checked his watch and, realizing he did have time for a fast coffee, hurried in. Until he got to her table he walked with his hand covering his bruise, but in such a way that it looked like he was simply massaging his upper neck.

Sharon was delighted to see Travis but still couldn't resist her comment.

"The victor!" she said in a mock announcement.

Travis was then quick to slide in across from her. "Knock it off," he said quietly.

Sharon considered his injury. "Looks a lot better," she remarked.

Travis picked up his menu and, self-consciously, buried himself behind it. "Not good enough,' he mumbled.

"Can't expect miracles overnight." A sly smile then crossed Sharon's face. She said, "You know, you just missed Robbie."

Travis peered at her over the top of his menu. "Oh?" he said suspiciously.

Sharon just sat there smiling.

"Okay, what'd you tell her?" There was no humor in Travis's voice.

Sharon sniffed, said casually: "That you

look like death."

Travis slapped down his menu; his eyes remained fixed on her, his expression set.

Sharon knew that he wasn't going to let her carry on with this tease. She broke into a grin.

"Relax, Randall, I got you off the hook."

Travis was waiting for the rest.

Sharon explained, "I told her that when you were driving me home last night we almost slammed into some jerk who ran a stop sign. You stomped on the brakes so hard that your face crashed into the steering wheel."

"She believed it?" Travis asked cautiously.

"What's not to believe?" Sharon shrugged. "Of course, now she's concerned that you're all right."

Travis said thoughtfully, "I should have used that one on Nicole."

"What *did* you tell her?" And there was just a faint hint of coldness in her tone.

"The truth."

"And now she won't let you out to play?"

Sharon tensed. Wrong thing to say. *Stupid, girl, stupid!*

Travis, however, was oblivious to anything derogatory she might have meant by her crack. He took it as a joke and responded with a smile, one that he still could only half-manage.

"I don't think I can let her stop me," he then said, speaking seriously.

Sharon responded favorably to that. "I didn't think you could," she smiled.

25

Dr. MacFarlane left his office at noon that day to go over to the bus depot to pick up the package that he'd waited almost six months to receive. Shipped from Winnipeg, though at least one of the contents had come from as far as Britian.

Upon notification of that morning's delivery, MacFarlane rescheduled his afternoon appointments and informed his receptionist that she could have the rest of the day off. She knew the doctor well, and when he didn't offer an explanation, she didn't press.

MacFarlane walked the short distance to the depot, signed the necessary forms, and then hurried back to his office. Once there, he locked the door behind him and took the telephone off the hook. He didn't want any disturbances.

The package was carefully unwrapped. Contained were six hardcover books of varying thickness, books that he certainly wanted no one else to see.

A sampling of the titles: *Practices of Canni-*

balism, Cannibalism: A Clinical Evaluation.

MacFarlane slowly sorted through each of them. He chose as his first reading *Some Very Human Monsters*, subtitled: "Twenty-Five Documentations of Aberrant Behavior." A skim through its table of contents revealed a rogues'-gallery listing that ranged from Gilles de Rais to the Hillside Strangler. MacFarlane found only two cases of bonafide cannibalism within the pages: Albert Fish and Ed Gein. But neither really applied to what he was looking for.

He next flipped through the pages of *Practices of Cannibalism*. More history: the infamous Donner Trail episode of 1847; Alfred Packer, the cannibal prospector; the ordeal of the Andes plane-crash survivors, 1972. Paragraphs were also given to the atrocities committed by the Sawney Bean clan of Scotland; Adolph Leutgart, "the sausage manufacturer of Chicago"; Fritz Haarmann, the Hanover Butcher; etc. Still, there was nothing of value to MacFarlane.

He researched the origins of cannibalism contained within the volume, and the consuming of human flesh as it applied to certain cultures in the modern world. Head-hunting tribes in New Guinea, for example, practiced cannibalism, but the digestion and subsequent excretion of victims symbolized a complete conquest over their enemies. Rather than a physical or psychological need for human flesh, it was instead an "ultimate destruction." In other tribes, in place of burial, the newly dead bodies of village elders were eaten—and by the young, so that they would inherit the elders' wisdom.

MacFarlane discovered, and not with surprise, that cannibalism dated back to Neander-thal and Cro-Magnon Man, possibly even as far back as a half million years to Peking Man. Historical records noted that more "recent" tribal practices of cannibalism had occurred in such unlikely countries as Ireland and Scotland.

The author's concluding observation, that once a primitive tribe comes in contact with civilization cannibalism disappears accordingly, was not encouraging or, in the current instance, wholly accurate.

Bill Meyer was a civilized man. As were the others who had fallen victim to this outbreak. Apparently nothing in any of these books could shed light on Batesville's long-standing problem.

What they were going to do, MacFarlane still had no idea. How could he fight this . . . *disease* if there were no probable cause? Yet somewhere there had to be one, and it was this knowledge that was filling not only MacFarlane but his "partners" as well with such frustration.

God Almighty, what caused an outbreak of cannibalism in these modern times? What forces were at work? MacFarlane was a scientist, not a believer in supernatural influences, but any attempt at rational explanation still left too many questions unanswered.

Were they dealing with something beyond their comprehension? The doctor had lately begun to wonder.

26

"I've seen the Weetigo," Marv Nelson said to the old Chamrais man, one who in earlier days would have been regarded with due respect as an "elder."

Marv continued, "I'm not talkin' about having just felt the presence. I actually . . . *saw it.*"

The old man sat across from Marv, rubbing his chin and nodding as he listened.

"Y'know, I never forgot the legend," Marv said. "But not until I heard that scream did I really remember." He leaned across the table. "I asked you here tonight for a reason. I—I have to know all you can tell me about the spirit."

"For what purpose?"

Marv hesitated, then: "I gotta know if there's some way to destroy it."

The old man's expression didn't change. But he shook his head. "How can one kill something that has always been?"

"It . . . shouldn't be, old man. I've seen what it can do. What powers it possesses. It just shouldn't be."

"In that you are right," the old man concurred. "The Weetigo is the most powerful of the Chamrais spirits. Its very evil gives it strength. The ability to survive. Even if there was a way to end its existence, there are too many dangers involved."

"Tell me about the dangers," Marv said with insistence. "How could one protect himself?"

"There is no protection."

"Then tell me about it powers. Its influences."

The old man laid both his sinewy hands flat on the table. Marv noticed a slight trembling.

"There are some things better not discussed," he said cautiously.

"There ain't nothin' you can tell me that would be worse than what I saw," Marv said, and there was not only determination, but honesty in his voice.

The old man's eyes met Marv's. He spoke, but his words did not come easily.

"The Weetigo is the cannibal spirit. It has the ability to enter the body of whoever or whatever it chooses, possessing it with the hunger for human flesh. As long as the body lives, so shall the Weetigo continue to inhabit it."

"And when the body dies?" Marv asked, remembering the woman at the trailer.

"Then the spirit goes in search for a new host." His next words seemed to come especially painfully. "Often the Weetigo will feed upon the corpse to give it the strength to carry out its search."

This sparked something in Marv. "Are you

sayin' that the possibility exists for the spirit—*to starve?*"

"For it to weaken," the old man corrected.

Marv considered this. A slight, enigmatic smile crossed his face as he fixed his gaze on his companion. "But if it can weaken . . ."

"I'm not speaking as one who has encountered the spirit," the old man said. "I cannot tell you beyond what I already have what force one would be up against."

"You said it's always been," Marv said, speaking with quiet intensity, "that because of that it can't be killed. But you also say there is a weakness. Don't you see? Destruction must be possible then. It only stands to reason."

All of a sudden the old man understood. "You plan to take its destruction upon yourself?"

"Yes," and there was no hesitation. "If I can find the way."

"Then you must make one further preparation."

Marv looked at him.

"For your death."

The old man was as serious as he could be, and Marv knew that. Suddenly, and Marv couldn't explain it, it was as if he were already dead in his companion's eyes. As if he were no longer sitting at the table, no longer in the shack. The old man was looking directly at him, but was seeing nothing. Because he was "alone" there was no reason for him to stay. He slowly got up from the table and was gone.

It was weird, and Marv was receptive to the flurry of chills that had accompanied the last several moments. Not that he was made any less determined to carry out his task.

He really wasn't sure why he felt so compelled to kill the Windigo. All he knew was that it had to be done, and that he had to be the one to do it. And he now was convinced that it could be destroyed. The key was its hunger.

As the old man had said, the spirit was capable of possessing man *or* beast, its hunger favoring neither. That surely explained why its existence had gone virtually undetected all through the centuries. That was also why not only the destruction, but the tracking of such a creature, would be the ultimate challenge.

27

Late September.

The sudden cracking of a branch stirred him.

There followed a rustling in the bush.

In his semi-conscious state he momentarily forgot where he was. Why he was where he was. A call out for identification almost escaped his lips.

But he came awake quickly, scrambling to his knees and pulling himself across the floor closer to the back of the mill. He listened.

There were no further sounds. Perhaps it had just been a rabbit or some other night creature scampering from the bush. *Possible*—though he wasn't convinced enough to let himself slip back into sleep.

He rose.

Then, walking as softly as he could so as not to disturb the old floorboards, he moved over to the eyehole that he had hollowed out in the wall and peered into the night.

It was much too dark for him to make out

anything clearly, but that was all right because that also meant there were no foreign lights to worry him.

Lloyd didn't immediately leave his "window," however. For the next few moments he barely breathed. No movement. No sound. He was sure no one was out there, but he hadn't remained free this long by giving in to over-confidence.

When the stillness of the night carried on unbroken, Lloyd gradually relaxed his guard, then started back over to the corner where he slept. He was as tired as he'd ever been in his life, but now that his rest had been disturbed he knew that further sleep wouldn't come to him. Because his mind would continue on alert for whatever was left of the night.

Isn't this how an animal lives? Lloyd wondered. Always with one eye open. Always on the lookout for its enemies. If he wasn't an animal already, he was as close to one as any human being could be. It was a frightening feeling, but one that he was beginning to lose control over. Lately, even his thought processes were working differently, and only in those moments of severe self-discipline did he actually realize that he was continuing more on instinct and cunning than by relying on man's gift of reason. The ability to function mentally beyond the surface basics of day-to-day survival was quickly becoming lost on Lloyd. Outside of retaining an identity, it just wasn't needed. Not living his kind of life.

He lay down on the floor and curled into his sleeping position. Both eyes remained wide open. He listened for sounds. Even the distant buzzing of a fly couldn't escape his detection.

28

Invitations were handed out personally to the *Clarion* staff. Morris Collarman was going to be hosting the retirement party for Harold Foley. To be held a week from Saturday.

"I never thought I'd see the man so social," Sharon said bemusedly to Travis as she rolled her chair over to his desk. He was typing up some Thompson amateur hockey scores and seemed engrossed in his work.

Sharon cupped her hands around her mouth. "Earth calling Travis."

Travis continued hunt-and-pecking, but a faint smile crossed his lips. "Geez, you're a pest," he said.

"Well, how's that for a switch? The boss gets social and you become a snob."

"Two more lines and I'm yours."

Tap . . . tap . . . TAP! with a flourish. He ripped out the newsprint and regarded it admiringly.

"A work of genius," Sharon said.

"Almost," Travis winked. He leaned back in

162